W9-BRV-607

WELCOME TO THE

WORLD
OF
TIERS

The blazing plants had stopped walking, but their frantically thrashing tentacles showed that they knew what was happening to them as their eyes burned, melted, ran like sap down their trunks, hissed away in the smoke.

Kickaha started trotting...Suddenly, McKay shouted, "It's falling!" They didn't need to ask what 'it' was. They sprinted as fast as they could.

THE LAVALITE WORLD

by
Philip José Farmer

SF
ace books
A Division of Charter Communications Inc.
A GROSSET & DUNLAP COMPANY
51 Madison Avenue
New York, New York 10010

THE LAVALITE WORLD

Copyright © 1977 by Philip José Farmer

All rights reserved. No part of this book may be
reproduced in any form or by any means, except
for the inclusion of brief quotations in a review,
without permission in writing from the publisher.

All characters in this book are fictitious. Any re-
semblance to actual persons, living or dead, is
purely coincidental.

An ACE Book

Cover Art by Boris

First Ace Printing: December 1977

Published simultaneously in Canada

This Printing: August 1981

Printed in the U.S.A.

For Roger Zelazny, The Golden Spinner

My thanks to J. T. Edson, author of the Dusty Fog sagas, for his kind permission to integrate the Texas Fogs with the British Foggs.

—Philip José Farmer

CHAPTER ONE

KICKAHA WAS A quicksilver Proteus.

Few could match his speed in adapting to change. But on Earth and on other planets of the pocket universes, the hills, mountains, valleys, plains, the rivers, lakes, and seas, seldom altered. Their permanence of form and location were taken for granted.

There were small local changes. Floods, earthquakes, avalanches, tidal waves reshaped the earth. But the effects were, in the time scale of an individual, in the lifetime of a nation, minute.

A mountain might walk, but the hundreds of thousands of generations living at its foot would not know it. Only God or a geologist would see its movements as the dash of a mouse for a hole.

Not here.

Even cocksure, unfazed Kickaha, who could react to change as quickly as a mirror reflects an image, was nervous. But he wasn't going to let anyone else know it. To the others he seemed insanely cool. That was because they were going mad.

CHAPTER TWO

THEY HAD GONE TO sleep during the "night." Kickaha had taken the first watch. Urthona, Orc, Anana, and McKay had made themselves as comfortable as they could on the rusty-red tough grass and soon had fallen asleep. Their camp was at the bottom of a shallow valley ringed by low hills. Grass was the only vegetation in the valley. The tops of the hills, however, were lined with the silhouettes of trees. These were about ten feet tall. Though there was little breeze, they swayed back and forth.

When he had started the watch, he had seen only a few on the hilltops. As time passed, more and more had appeared. They had ranged themselves beside the early comers until they were a solid line. There was no telling how many were on the other side of the hills. What he was sure of was that the trees were waiting until "dawn." Then, if the humans did not come to them, they would come down the hills after them.

The sky was a uniform dark red except for a few black slowly floating shapes. Clouds. The enormous reddish mass, visually six times the size of Earth's moon, had disappeared from the sky. It would be back, though he didn't know when.

He sat down and rubbed his legs. They still hurt from the accident that had taken place twelve "days" ago. The pain in his chest had almost ceased, however. He was recovering, but he was not as agile and strong as he needed to be.

That the gravity was less than Earth's helped him, though.

He lay down for a minute. No enemy, human or beast, was going to attack. They would have to get through those killer trees first. Only the elephants and the giant variety of moosoids were big enough to do that. He wished that some of these would show up. They fed upon trees. However, at this distance Kickaha couldn't determine just what type of killer plants they were. Some were so fearsomely armed that even the big beasts avoided them.

How in hell had the trees detected the little party? They had a keen olfactory sense, but he doubted that the wind was strong enough to carry the odor of the party up over the hills. The visual ability of the plants was limited. They could see shapes through the multifaceted insectine eyes ringing the upper parts of their trunks. But at this distance and in this light, they might as well be blind.

One or more of their scouts must have come up a hill and caught a molecule or two of human odor. That was, after all, nothing to be surprised about. He and the others stank. The little water they had been able to find was used for drinking only. If they didn't locate more water tomorrow, they'd have to start drinking their own urine It could be recycled twice before it became poisonous.

Also, if they didn't kill something soon, they would be too weak from hunger to walk.

He rubbed the barrel of the hand-beamer with the fingers of his left hand. Its battery had only a few full-power discharges available. Then it would be exhausted. So far, he and Anana had refrained from using any of the power. It was the only thing that allowed them to keep the upper hand over the other three. It was also their only strong defense against the big predators. But when "dawn" came, he was going to go hunting. They had to eat, and they could drink blood to quench their thirst.

First, though, they had to get through the trees. Doing that might use up the battery. It also might not be enough. There could be a thousand trees on the other side of the hills.

The clouds were thickening. Perhaps, at long last, rain would come. If it rained as hard as Urthona said it did, it might fill this cup-shaped valley. They'd have to drown or charge into the trees. Some choice.

He lay on his back for a few minutes. Now he could hear faint creaks and groans and an occasional mutter. The earth was moving under him. Heat flowed along his back and his legs. It felt almost as warm as a human body. Under the densely packed blades and the thick tangle of roots, energy was being dissipated. The earth was shifting slowly. In what direction, toward what shapes, he did not know.

He could wait. One of his virtues was an almost-animal patience. Be a leopard, a wolf. Lie still and evaluate the situation. When action was called for, he would explode. Unfortunately, his injured leg and his weakness handicapped him. Where he had once been dynamite, he was now only black gunpowder.

He sat up and looked around. The dark reddish light smoldered around him. The trees formed a waving wall on the hill tops. The others of the party lay on their sides or their backs. McKay was snoring. Anana was muttering something in her native language, a speech older than Earth itself. Urthona's eyes were open, and he was looking directly at Kickaha. Was he hoping to catch him unawares and get hold of the beamer?

No. He was sleeping, his mouth and eyes open. Kickaha, having risen and come close to him, could hear the gentle burbling from his dry lips. The eyes looked glazed.

Kickaha licked his own sandpaper lips and swallowed. He brought the wristwatch, which he'd borrowed from Anana, close to his eyes. He pressed the minute stud on its side, and four glowing figures appeared briefly on the face. They were the numerical signs of the Lords. In Earth numerals, 15:12. They did not mean anything here. There was no sun; the sky provided light and some heat. In any event, this planet had no steady rotation on any one plane, and there were no stars. The great reddish mass that had moved slowly across the sky, becoming larger every day, was no genuine moon. It was a temporary satellite, and it was falling.

There were no shadows except under one peculiar condition. There was no north, south, east, and west. Anana's watch had compass capabilities, but they were useless. This great body on which he stood had no nickel-steel core, no electromagnetic field, no north or south pole. Properly speaking, it wasn't a planet.

And the ground was rising now. He could not detect that by its motion, since that was so slow. But the hills had definitely become lower.

The watch had one useful function. It did mark the forward movement of time. It would tell him when his hour and a half of sentinel duty was over.

When it was time to rouse Anana, he walked to her. But she sat up before he was within twelve feet. She knew that it was her turn. She had told herself to wake at the proper time, and a well-developed sense, a sort of biological clock within her, had set off its alarm.

Anana was beautiful, but she was beginning to look gaunt. Her cheekbones protruded, her cheeks were beginning to sink in, her large dark-blue eyes were ringed with the shadows of fatigue. Her lips were cracked, and that once soft white skin was dirty and rough-looking. Though she had sweat much in the twelve days they'd been here, there were still traces of smoke on her neck.

"You don't look so good yourself," she said, smiling.

Normally, her voice was a rich contralto, but now it was gravelly.

She stood up. She was slim but broad-shouldered and full-breasted. She was only two inches shorter than his six feet one inch, was as strong as any man her weight, and inside fifty yards she could outrun him. Why not? She had had ten thousand years to develop her physical potentialities.

She took a comb from the back pocket of her torn bellbottom trousers and straightened out her long hair, as black as a Crow Indian's.

"There. Is that better?" she said, smiling. Her teeth were very white and perfect. Only thirty years ago, she'd had tooth buds implanted, the hundredth set in a series.

"Not bad for a starving dehydrated old woman," he said. "In fact, if I was up to it . . ."

He quit grinning, and he waved his hand to indicate the hilltops. "We've got visitors."

It was difficult in this light to see if she'd turned pale. Her voice was steady. "If they're bearing fruit, we'll eat."

He thought it better not to say that they might be eaten instead.

He handed her the beamer. It looked like a six-shooter revolver. But the cartridges were batteries, of which only one now had a charge. The barrel contained a mechanism which could be adjusted to shoot a ray that could cut through a tree or inflict a slight burn or a stunning blow.

Kickaha went back to where his bow and a quiver of arrows lay. He was an excellent archer, but so far only two of his arrows had struck game. The animals were wary, and it had been impossible, except twice, to get close enough to any to shoot. Both kills had been small gazelles, not enough to fill the bellies of five adults in twelve days. Anana had gotten a hare with a throw of her light axe, but a long-legged baboon had dashed out from behind a hill, scooped it up, and run off with it.

Kickaha picked up the bow and quiver, and they walked three hundred feet away from the sleepers. Here he lay down and went to sleep. His knife was thrust upright into the ground, ready to be snatched in case of attack. Anana had her beamer, a light throwing-axe, and a knife for defense.

They were not worried at this time about the trees. They just wanted to keep distance between them and the others. When Anana's watch was over, she would wake up McKay. Then she'd return to lie down by Kickaha. She and her mate were not overly concerned about one of the others trying to sneak up on them while they slept. Anana had told them that her wristwatch had a device which would sound an alarm if anybody with a mass large enough to be dangerous came close. She was lying, though the device was something that a Lord could have. They probably wondered if she was deceiving them. However, they did not care to test her. She had said that if anyone tried to attack them, she would kill him immediately. They knew that she would do so.

CHAPTER THREE

HE AWOKE, SWEATING from the heat, the bright light of "day" plucking at his eyes. The sky had become a fiery light red. The clouds were gone, taking their precious moisture elsewhere. But he was no longer in a valley. The hills had come down, flattened out into a plain. And the party was now on a small hill.

He was surprised. The rate of change had been greater than he'd expected. Urthona, however, had said that the reshaping occasionally accelerated. Nothing was constant or predictable here. So, he shouldn't have been surprised.

The trees still ringed them. There were several thousand, and now some scouts were advancing toward the just-born hill. They were about ten feet tall. The trunks were barrel-shaped and covered with a smooth greenish bark. Large round dark eyes circled the trunk near its top. On one side was an opening, the mouth. Inside it was soft flexible tissue and two hard ridges holding shark-like teeth. According to Urthona, the plants were half-protein, and the digestive system was much like an animal's. The anus was the terminus of the digestive system, but it was also located in the mouth.

Urthona should know. He had designed them.

"They don't have any diseases, so there's no reason why the feces shouldn't pass through the mouth," Urthona had said.

"They must have bad breath," Kickaha had

said. "But then nobody's going to kiss them, are they?"

He, Anana, and McKay had laughed. Urthona and Red Orc had looked disgusted. Their sense of humor had atrophied. Or perhaps they'd never had much.

Above the head of the tree was a growth of many slender stems rising two feet straight up. Broad green leaves, heart-shaped, covered the stems. From the trunk radiated six short branches, each three feet long, a pair on each side, in three ranks. These had short twigs supporting large round leaves. Between each ring of branches was a tentacle, about twelve feet long and as supple as an octopus's. A pair of tentacles also grew from the base.

The latter helped balance the trunk as it moved on two short kneeless legs ending in huge round barky toeless feet. When the tree temporarily changed from an ambulatory to sedentary state, the lower tentacles bored into the soil, grew roots, and sucked sustenance from the ground. The roots could be easily broken off and the tentacles withdrawn when the tree decided to move on.

Kickaha had asked Urthona why he had had such a clumsy unnatural monster made in his biolabs.

"It pleased me to do so."

Urthona probably was wishing he hadn't done so. He had wakened the others, and all were staring at the weird—and frightening—creatures.

Kickaha walked up to him. "How do they communicate?"

"Through pheromones. Various substances they emit. There are about thirty of these, and a tree smelling them receives various signals. They don't think; their brains are about the size of a dinosaur's. They react on the instinctive—or robotic—level. They have a well-developed herd instinct, though."

"Any of these pheromones stimulate fear?"

"Yes. But you have to make one of them afraid, and there's nothing in this situation to scare them."

"I was thinking," Kickaha said, "that it's too bad you don't carry around a vial of fear-pheromones."

"I used to," Urthona said.

The nearest scout had halted thirty feet away. Kickaha looked at Anana, who was sixty feet from the group. Her beamer was ready for trouble from the three men or the tree.

Kickaha walked to the scout and stopped ten feet from it. It waved its greenish tentacles. Others were coming to join it, though not on a run. He estimated that with those legs they could go perhaps a mile an hour. But then he didn't know their full potentiality. Urthona didn't remember how fast they could go.

Even as he walked down toward the tree, he could feel the earth swelling beneath him, could see the rate of its shaping increase. The air became warmer, and spaces had appeared between the blades of grass. The earth was black and greasy-looking. If the shaping stopped, and there was no change for three days, the grass would grow enough to fill in the bare spots.

The thousand or so plants were still moving but more slowly. They leaned forward on their rigid legs, their tentacles extended to support them.

Kickaha looked closely at the nearest one and saw about a dozen apple-red spheres dangling from the branches. He called to Urthona. "Is their fruit good to eat?"

"For birds, yes," Urthona said. "I don't remember. But I can't think why I should have made them poisonous for humans."

"Knowing you, I'd say you could have done it for laughs," Kickaha said.

He motioned to Angus McKay to come to him. The black came to him warily, though his caution was engendered by the tree, not Kickaha.

McKay was an inch shorter than Kickaha but about thirty pounds heavier. Not much of the additional weight was fat, though. He was dressed in black levis, socks, and boots. He'd long ago shed his shirt and the leather jacket of the motorcyclist, but he still carried his helmet. Kickaha had insisted that it be retained to catch rainwater in, if for nothing else.

McKay was a professional criminal, a product of Detroit who'd come out to Los Angeles to be one of Urthona's hired killers. Of course, he had not known then that Urthona was a Lord. He had never been sure what Urthona, whom he knew as Mr. Callister, did. But he'd been paid well, and if Mr. Callister wasn't in a business which competed with other mobs, that was all to the good. And Mr. Callister certainly seemed to know how to handle the police.

That day which seemed so long ago, he'd had a free afternoon. He'd started drinking in a tavern in Watts. After picking up a good-looking if loud-mouthed woman, he'd driven her to his apartment in Hollywood. They'd gone to bed almost at once, after which he fell asleep. The telephone woke him up. It was Callister, excited, obviously in some kind of trouble. Emergency, though he didn't say what it was. McKay was to come to him at once. He was to bring his .45 automatic with him.

That helped to sober him up. Mr. Callister must really be in trouble if he would say openly, over a phone that could be tapped, that he was to be armed. Then the first of the troubles started. The woman was gone, and with her his wallet—five hundred dollars and his credit cards—and his car keys.

When he looked out the window into the parking space behind the building, he saw that the car was gone, too. If it hadn't been that he was needed so quickly, he would have laughed. Ripped off by a hooker! A dumb one at that, since he would be tracking her down. He'd get his wallet back and its contents, if they were still around. And his car, too. He wouldn't kill the woman, but he would rough her up a bit to teach her a lesson. He was a professional, and professionals didn't kill except for money or in self-defense.

So he'd put on his bike clothes and wheeled out on it, speeding along in the night, ready to outrun the pigs if they saw him. Callister was waiting for him. The other bodyguards weren't around. He didn't ask Callister where they were, since the boss didn't like questions. But Callister volunteered, anyway. The others were in a car which had been wrecked while chasing a man and a woman. They were not dead, but they were too injured to be of any use.

Callister then had described the couple he was after, but he didn't say why he wanted them.

Callister had stood for a moment, biting his lip. He was a big handsome honky, his curly hair yellow, his eyes a strange bright green, his face something like the movie actor's, Paul Newman.

Abruptly, he went to a cabinet, pulled a little box about the size of a sugar cube from his pocket, held it over the lock, and the door swung open.

Callister removed a strange-looking device from the cabinet. McKay had never seen anything like it before, but he knew it was a weapon. It had a gunstock to which was affixed a short thick barrel, like a sawed-off shotgun.

"I've changed my mind," Callister said. "Use this, leave your .45 here. We may be where we won't want anybody to hear gunfire. Here, I'll show you how to use it."

McKay, watching him demonstrate, began to feel a little numb. It was the first step into a series of events which made him feel as if he'd been magically transformed into an actor in a science-fiction movie. If he'd had any sense, he would have taken off then. But there wasn't one man on Earth that could have foreseen that five minutes later he wouldn't even *be* on Earth.

He was still goggle-eyed when, demonstrating the "beamer", Callister had cut a chair in half. He was handed a metal vest. At least, it looked and felt like steel. But it was flexible.

Callister put one on, too, and then he said something in a foreign language. A large circular area on the wall began glowing, then the glow disappeared, and he was staring into another world.

"Step through the gate," Callister said. He was holding a hand weapon disguised as a revolver. It wasn't pointed at McKay, but McKay felt that it would be if he refused.

Callister followed him in. McKay guessed that Callister was using him as a shield, but he didn't protest. If he did, he might be sliced in half.

They went through another "gate" and were in

still another world or dimension or whatever. And then things really began to happen. While Callister was sneaking up on their quarry, McKay circled around through the trees. All of a sudden, hell broke loose. There was this big red-haired guy with, believe it or not, a bow and arrows.

He was behind a tree, and McKay sliced the branches of the tree off on one side. That was to scare the archer, since Callister had said that he wanted the guy—his name was Kickaha, crazy!—alive. But Kickaha had shot an arrow and McKay certainly knew where it had been aimed. Only a part of his body was not hidden by the tree behind which he was concealed. But the arrow had struck McKay on the only part showing, his shoulder.

If he hadn't been wearing that vest, he'd have been skewered. Even as it was, the shock of the arrow knocked him down. His beamer flew away from his opening hands, and, its power still on, it rolled away.

Then, the biggest wolf—a wolf!—McKay had ever seen had gotten caught in the ray, and it had died, cut into four different parts. McKay was lucky. If the beamer had fallen pointing the other way, it would have severed him. Though he was stunned, his shoulder and arm completely numb, he managed to get up and to run, crouching over, to another tree. He was cursing because Callister had made him leave his automatic behind. He sure as hell wasn't going into the clearing after the beamer. Not when Kickaha could shoot an arrow like that.

Besides, he felt that he was in over his head about fifty fathoms.

There was a hell of a lot of action after that, but

McKay didn't see much of it. He climbed up on a house-sized boulder, using the projections and holes in it, hauling himself up with one hand. Later he wondered why he'd gone up where he could be trapped. But he had been in a complete panic, and it had seemed a logical thing to do. Maybe no one would think of looking for him up there. He could lie down flat and hide until things settled down. If the boss won, he'd come down. He could claim then that he'd gone up there to get a bird's-eye view of the terrain so he could call out to Callister the location of his enemies.

Meanwhile, his beamer burned itself out, half-melting a large boulder fifty feet from it while doing so.

He saw Callister running toward the couple and another man, and he thought Callister had control of the situation. Then the red-haired Kickaha, who was lying on the ground, had said something to the woman. And she'd lifted a funny-looking trumpet to her lips and started blowing some notes. Callister had suddenly stopped, yelled something, and then he'd run like a striped-ass ape away from them.

And suddenly they were in *another* world. If things had been bad before, they were now about as bad as they could be. Well, maybe not quite as bad. At least, he was alive. But there had been times when he'd wished he wasn't.

So here he was, twelve "days" later. Much had been explained to him, mostly by Kickaha. But he still couldn't believe that Callister, whose real name was Urthona, and Red Orc and Anana were thousands of years old. Nor that they had come from another world, what Kickaha called a pocket universe. That is, an artificial continuum, what the science-fiction movies called the fourth dimension, something like that.

The Lords, as they called themselves, claimed to have made Earth. Not only that, the sun, the other planets, the stars—which weren't really stars, they just looked like they were—the whole damn universe.

In fact, they claimed to have created the ancestors of all Earth people in laboratories.

Not only that—it made his brain bob up and down, like a cork on an ocean wave—there were many artificial pocket universes. They'd been constructed to have different physical laws than those on Earth's universe.

Apparently, some ten thousand or so years ago, the Lords had split. Each had gone off to his or her own little world to rule it. And they'd become enemies, out to get each other's ass.

Which explained why Urthona and Orc, Anana's own uncles, had tried to kill her and each other.

Then there was Kickaha. He'd been born Paul Janus Finnegan in 1918 in some small town in Indiana. After World War II he'd gone to the University of Indiana as a freshman, but before a year was up he was involved with the Lords. He'd first lived on a peculiar world he called the World of Tiers. There he'd gotten the name of Kickaha from a tribe of Indians that lived on one level of the planet, which seemed to be constructed like the tower of babel or the leaning tower of Pisa. Or whatever.*

Indians? Yes, because the Lord of that world,

*See *The Maker of Universes*, Philip José Farmer, Ace Books, 1977.

Jadawin, had populated various levels with people he'd abducted from Earth.

It was very confusing. Jadawin hadn't always lived on the home planet of the Lords or in his own private cosmos. For a while he'd been a citizen of Earth, and he hadn't even known it because of amnesia. Then...to hell with it. It made McKay's head ache to think about it. But some day, when there was time enough, if he lived long enough, he'd get it all straightened out. If he wasn't completely nuts before then.

CHAPTER FOUR

KICKAHA SAID, "I'm a Hoosier appleknocker, Angus. So I'm going to get us some fresh fruit. But I need your help. We can't get close because of those tentacles. However, the tree has one weak point in its defense. Like a lot of people, it can't keep its mouth shut.

"So, I'm going to shoot an arrow into its mouth. It may not kill it, but it's going to hurt it. Hopefully, the impact will knock it over. This bow packs a hell of a wallop. As soon as the thing's hit, you run up and throw this axe at a branch. Try to hit a cluster of apples if you can. Then I'll decoy it away from the apples on the ground."

He handed Anana's light throwing axe to McKay.

"What about those?" McKay said, pointing at three trees which were only twenty feet below their intended victim. They were coming slowly but steadily.

"Maybe we can get their apples, too. We need that fruit, Angus. We need the nourishment, and we need the water in them."

"You don't have to explain that," McKay said.

"I'm like the tree. I can't keep my mouth shut," Kickaha said, smiling.

He fitted an arrow to the string, aimed, and released it. It shot true, plunging deep into the O-shaped orifice. The plant had just raised the two tentacles to take another step upward and

then to fall slightly forward to catch itself on the
rubbery extensions. Kickaha had loosed the shaft
just as it was off balance. It fell backward, and it
lay on its hinder part. The tentacles threshed, but
it could not get up by itself. The branches extending from its side prevented its rolling over even if
it had been capable, otherwise, of doing so.

Kickaha gave a whoop and put a hand on
McKay's shoulder.

"Never mind throwing the axe. The apples are
knocked off. Hot damn!"

The three trees below it had stopped for a moment. They moved on up. There had not been a
sound from their mouths, but to the two men the
many rolling eyes seemed to indicate some sort of
communication. According to Urthona, however,
the creatures were incapable of thought. But they
did cooperate on an instinctual level, as ants did.
Now they were evidently coming to assist their
fallen mate.

Kickaha ran ahead of McKay, who had hesitated. He looked behind him. The two male Lords
were standing about sixty feet above them.
Anana, beamer in hand, was watching, her head
moving back and forth to keep all within eye-
range.

Urthona had, of course, told McKay to kill
Anana and Kickaha if he ever got a chance. But if
he hit the redhead from behind with the axe, he'd
be shot down by Anana. Besides, he was beginning to think that he had a better chance of survival
if he joined up with Anana and Kickaha. Anyway,
Kickaha was the only one who didn't treat him as if
he was a nigger. Not that the Lords had any feeling
for blacks as such. They regarded *everybody* but
Lords as some sort of nigger. And they weren't

friendly with their own kind.

McKay ran forward and stopped just out of reach of a threshing tentacle. He picked up eight apples, stuffing four in the pockets of his levis and holding two in each hand.

When he straightened up, he gasped. That crazy Kickaha had leaped onto the fallen tree and was now pulling the arrow from the hole. As he raised the shaft, its head dripping with a pale sticky fluid, he was enwrapped by a tentacle around his waist. Instead of fighting it, he rammed his right foot deep into the hole. And he twisted sideways.

The next moment he was flying backward toward McKay, flung by a convulsive motion of the tentacle, no doubt caused by intense pain.

McKay, instead of ducking, grabbed Kickaha and they both went down. The catcher suffered more punishment than the caught, but for a minute or more they both lay on the ground, Kickaha on top of McKay. Then the redhead rolled off and got to his feet.

He looked down at McKay. "You okay?"

McKay sat up and said, "I don't think I broke anything."

"Thanks. If you hadn't softened my fall, I might have broken my back. Maybe. I'm pretty agile. Man, there's real power in those tentacles."

Anana was with them by then. She cried, "Are you hurt, Kickaha?"

"No. Black Angus here, he seems okay, too."

McKay said, "Black Angus? Why, you son of a bitch!"

Kickaha laughed. "It's an inevitable pun. Especially if you've been raised on a farm. No offense, McKay."

Kickaha turned. The three advance scouts were

no closer. The swelling hill had steepened its slopes, making it even more difficult for them to maintain their balance. The horde behind them was also stalled.

"We don't have to retreat up the hill," Kickaha said. "It's withdrawing for us."

However, the slope was becoming so steep that, if its rate of change continued, it would precipitate everybody to the bottom. The forty-five degree angle to the horizontal could become ninety degrees within fifteen minutes.

"We're in a storm of matter-change," Kickaha said. "If it blows over quickly, we're all right, If not . . ."

The tree's tentacles were moving feebly. Apparently, Kickaha's foot had injured it considerably. Pale fluid oozed out of its mouth.

Kickaha picked up the axe that McKay had dropped. He went to the tree and began chopping at its branches. Two strokes per limb sufficed to sever them. He cut at the tentacles, which were tougher. Four chops each amputated these.

He dropped the axe and lifted one end of the trunk and swung it around so that it could be rolled down the slope.

Anana said, "You're wasting your energy."

Kickaha said, "Waiting to see what's going to happen burns up more energy. At this moment, anyway. There's a time for patience and a time for energy."

He placed himself at the middle of the trunk and pushed it. It began rolling slowly, picked up speed, and presently, flying off a slight hump, flew into a group of trees. These fell backward, some rolling, breaking their branches, others flying up and out as if shot out of a cannon.

The effect was incremental and geometrical. When it was done, at least five hundred of the things lay in a tangled heap in the ravine at the foot of the slope. Not one could get up by itself. It looked like the results of a combination of avalanche and flood.

"It's a log jam!" Kickaha said.

No log jam, however, on Earth featured the wavings of innumerable octopus-tentacles. Nor had any forest ever hastened to the aid of its stricken members.

"Birnam Wood on the march," Kickaha said.

Neither Anana nor McKay understood the reference, but they were too tired and anxious to ask him to explain it.

By now the humans were having a hard time keeping from falling down the slope. They clung to the grass while the three advance guards slid down on their "backs" toward the mess in the hollow at the base.

"I'm getting down," Kickaha said. He turned and began sliding down on the seat of his pants. The others followed him. When the friction became too great on their buttocks, they dug in their heels to brake. Halfway down they had to halt and turn over so their bottoms could cool off. Their trouser seats were worn away in several spots.

"Did you see that water?" Kickaha said. He pointed to his right.

Anana said, "I thought I did. But I assumed it was a mirage of some sort."

"No. Just before we started down, I saw a big body of water that way. It must be about fifteen miles away, at least. But you know how deceiving distances are here."

Directly below them, about two hundred feet

away, was the living log jam. The humans resumed their rolling but at an angle across the ever-steepening slope. McKay's helmet, Kickaha's bow and quiver, and Anana's beamer and axe, impeded their movements but they managed. They fell the last ten feet, landing on their feet or on all fours.

The trees paid them no attention. Apparently, the instinct to save their fellows was dominating the need to kill and eat. However, the plants were so closely spaced that there was no room for the five people to get through the ranks.

They looked up the hill. This side was vertical now and beginning to bulge at the top. Hot air radiated from the hill.

"The roots of the grass will keep that overhang from falling right away," Kickaha said. "But for how long? When it does come down, we'll be wiped out."

The plants moved toward the tangle, side by side, the tips of their branches touching. Those nearest the humans moved a little to their right to avoid bumping into them. But the outreaching tentacles made the humans nervous.

After five minutes, the apex of the hill was beginning to look like a mushroom top. It wouldn't be long before a huge chunk tore loose and fell upon them.

Anana said, "Like it or not, Kickaha, we have to use the beamer."

"You're thinking the same thing I am? Maybe we won't have to cut through every one between us and open ground. Maybe those things burn?"

Urthona said, "Are you crazy? We could get caught in the fire!"

"You got a better suggestion?"

"Yes. I think we should adjust the beamer to cutting and try to slice our way out."

"I don't think there's enough charge left to do that," Anana said. "We'd find ourselves in the middle of this mess. The plants might attack us then. We'd be helpless."

"Burn a couple," Kickaha said. "But not too near us."

Anana rotated the dial in the inset at the bottom of the grip. She aimed the weapon at the back of a tree five yards to her right. For a few seconds there was no result. Then the bark began smoking. Ten seconds later, it burst into flames. The plant did not seem immediately aware of what was happening. It continued waddling toward the tangle. But those just behind stopped. They must have smelled the smoke, and now their survival instinct—or program—was taking over.

Anana set three others on fire. Abruptly, the nearest ranks behind the flaming plants toppled. Those behind them kept on moving, rammed into them, and knocked a number down.

The ranks behind these were stopped, their tentacles waving. Then, as if they were a military unit obeying a soundless trumpet call to retreat, they turned. And they began going as fast as they could in the opposite direction.

The blazing plants had stopped walking, but their frantically thrashing tentacles showed that they were aware of what was happening. The flames covered their trunks, curled and browned the leaves, shot off from the leaf-covered stems projecting from the tops of the trunks. Their dozen eyes burned, melted, ran like sap down the trunk, hissed away in the smoke.

One fell and lay like a Yule log in a fireplace. A second later, the other two crashed. Their legs moved up and down, the broad round heels striking the ground.

The stink of burning wood and flesh sickened the humans.

But those ahead of the fiery plants had not known what was happening. The wind was carrying both the smoke and the pheromones of panic away from them. They continued to the jam until the press of bodies stopped them. Those in the front ranks were trying to pull up the fallen, but the lack of room prevented them.

"Burn them all!" Red Orc shouted, and he was seconded by his brother, Urthona.

"What good would that do?" Kickaha said, looking disgustedly at them. "Besides, they do feel pain, even if they don't make a sound. Isn't that right, Urthona?"

"No more than a grasshopper would," the Lord said.

"Have you ever been a grasshopper?" Anana said.

Kickaha started trotting, and the others followed him. The passage opened was about twenty feet broad, widening as the retreaters moved slowly away. Suddenly, McKay shouted, "It's falling!"

They didn't need to ask what *it* was. They sprinted as fast as they could. Kickaha, in the lead, was quickly left behind. His legs still hurt, and the pain in his chest increased. Anana took his hand and pulled him along.

A crash sounded behind them. Just in front of them a gigantic ball of greasy earth mixed with rusty grass-blades had slammed into the ground. It was a piece broken off and thrown upward by the impact. It struck so closely that they could not stop. Both plunged into it and for a moment felt the oily earth and the scratch of the blades. But the mass was soft enough to absorb the energy of their impact, to give way somewhat. It was not like running into a brick wall.

They got up and went around the fragment, which was about the size of a one-car garage. Kickaha spared a glance behind him. The main mass had struck only a few yards behind them. Sticking out of its front were a few branches, tentacles, and kicking feet.

They were safe now. He stopped, and Anana also halted.

The others were forty feet ahead of them, staring at the great pile of dirt that ringed the base of the hill. Even as they watched, more of the mushrooming top broke off and buried the previous fallen mass.

Perhaps a hundred of the trees had survived. They were still waddling away in their slow flight.

Kickaha said, "We'll snare us some of the trees in their rear ranks. Knock off some more apples. We're going to need them to sustain us until we can get to that body of water."

Though they were all shaken, they went after the trees at once. Anana threw her axe and McKay his helmet. Presently they had more fruit than they could carry. Each ate a dozen, filling their bellies with food and moisture.

Then they headed toward the water. They hoped they were going in the right direction. It was so easy to lose their bearings in a world of no sun and constantly changing landscape. A mountain used as a mark could become a valley within one day.

Anana, walking by Kickaha's side, spoke softly.

"Drop back."

He slowed down, with no reluctance at all, until the others were forty feet ahead. "What is it?"

She held up the beamer so that he could see the bottom of the grip. The dial in the inset was flashing a red light. She turned the dial, and the light ceased.

"There's just enough charge left for one cutting beam lasting three seconds at a range of sixty feet. Of course, if I just use mild burning or stun power, the charge will last longer."

"I don't think they'd try anything against us if they did know about it. They need us to survive even more than we need them. But when—if—we ever find Urthona's home, then we'd better watch our backs. What bothers me is that we may need the beamer for other things."

He paused and stared past Anana's head.

"Like them."

She turned her head.

Silhouetted on top of a ridge about two miles away was a long line of moving objects. Even at this distance and in this light, she could see that they were a mixture of large animals and human beings.

"Natives," he said.

CHAPTER FIVE

THE THREE MEN HAD stopped and were looking suspiciously at them. When the two came up to them, Red Orc greeted them.

"What the hell are you two plotting?"

Kickaha laughed. "It's sure nice traveling with you paranoiacs. We were discussing that," and he pointed toward the ridge.

McKay groaned and said, "What next?"

Anana said, "Are all the natives hostile to strangers?"

"I don't know," Urthona said. "I do know that they all have very strong tribal feelings. I used to cruise around in my flier and observe them, and I never saw two tribes meet without conflict of some kind. But they have no territorial aggressions. How could they?"

Anana smiled at Urthona. "Well, Uncle, I wonder how they'd feel if you were introduced to them as the Lord of this world. The one who made this terrible place and abducted their ancestors from Earth."

Urthona paled, but he said, "They're used to this world. They don't know any better."

"Is their lifespan a thousand years, as on Jadawin's world?"

"No. It's about a hundred years, but they don't suffer from disease."

"They must see us," Kickaha said. "Anyway, we'll just keep on going in the same direction."

They resumed their march, occasionally looking at the ridge. After two hours, the caravan disappeared over the other side. The ridge had not changed shape during that time. It was one of the areas in which topological mutation went at a slower rate.

"Night" came again. The bright red of the sky became streaked with darker bands, all horizontal, some broader than others. As the minutes passed, the bands enlarged and became even darker. When they had all merged, the sky was a uniform dull red, angry-looking, menacing.

They were on a flat plain extending as far as they could see. The mountains had disappeared, though whether because they had collapsed or because they were hidden in the darkness, they could not determine. They were not alone. Nearby, but out of reach, were thousands of animals: many types of antelopes, gazelles, a herd of the tuskless elephants in the distance, a small group of the giant moosoids.

Urthona said that there must also be big cats and wild dogs in the neighborhood. But the cats would be leaving, since they had no chance of catching prey on this treeless plain. There were smaller felines, a sort of cheetah, which could run down anything but the ostrich-like birds. None of these were in sight.

Kickaha had tried to walk very slowly up to the antelopes. He'd hoped they would not be alarmed enough to move out of arrow range. They didn't cooperate.

Then, abruptly, a wild chittering swept down from some direction, and there was a stampede. Thousands of hooves evoked thunder from the plain. There was no dust; the greasy earth just did not dry enough for that, except when an area was undergoing a very swift change and the heat drove the moisture out of the surface.

Kickaha stood still while thousands of running or bounding beasts raced by him or even over him. Then, as the ranks thinned, he shot an arrow and skewered a gazelle. Anana, who'd been standing two hundred yards away, ran toward him, her beamer in hand. A moment later he saw why she was alarmed. The chittering noise got louder, and out of the darkness came a pack of long-legged baboons. These were truly quadrupedal, their front and back limbs of the same length, their "hands" in nowise differentiated from their "feet."

They were big brutes, the largest weighing perhaps a hundred pounds. They sped by him, their mouths open, the wicked-looking canines dripping saliva. Then they were gone, a hundred or so, the babies clinging to the long hair on their mothers' backs.

Kickaha sighed with relief as he watched the last merge into the darkness. According to Urthona, they would have no hesitation in attacking humans under certain conditions. Fortunately, when they were chasing the antelopes, they were single-minded. But if they had no success, they might return to try their luck with the group.

Kickaha used his knife to cut up the gazelle. Orc said, "I'm getting sick of eating raw meat! I'm very hungry, but just thinking about that bloody mess makes my stomach boil with acid!"

Kickaha, grinning, offered him a dripping cut.

"You could become a vegetarian. Nuts to the nuts, fruits to the fruits, and a big raspberry to you."

McKay, grimacing, said, "I don't like it either. I keep feeling like the stuff's alive. It tries to crawl back up my throat."

"Try one of these kidneys," Kickaha said. "They're really delicious. Tender, too. Or you might prefer a testicle."

"You really are disgusting," Anana said. "You should see yourself, the blood dripping down your chin."

But she took the proffered testicle and cut off a piece. She chewed on it without expression.

Kickaha smiled. "Not bad, eh? Starvation makes it taste good."

They were silent for a while. Kickaha finished eating first. Belching, he rose with his knife in his hand. Anana gave him her axe, and he began the work of cutting off the horns of the antelope. These were slim straight weapons two feet high. After he had cut them off from the skull, he stuck them in his belt.

"When we find some branches, we'll make spear shafts and fix these at their tips."

Something gobbled in the darkness, causing all to get to their feet and look around. Presently the gobbling became louder. A giant figure loomed out of the dark red light. It was what Kickaha called a "moa," and it did look like the extinct New Zealand bird. It was twelve feet high and had rudimentary wings, long thick legs with two clawed toes, and a great head with a beak like a scimitar.

Kickaha threw the antelope's head and two of its legs as far as he could. The lesser gravity enabled him to hurl them much further than he could have on Earth. The huge bird had been loping along toward them. When the severed pieces flew through the air, it veered away from them. However, it stopped about forty feet away, looked at them with one eye, then trotted up to the offerings. After making sure that the humans were not moving toward it, it scooped up the legs between its beaks, and it ran off.

Kickaha picked up a foreleg and suggested that the others bring along a part, too. "We might need a midnight snack. I wouldn't recommend eating the meat after that. In this heat meat is going to spoil fast."

"Man, I wish we had some water," McKay said. "I'm still thirsty, but I'd like to wash off this blood."

"You can do that when we get to the lake," Kickaha said. "Fortunately, the flies are bedding down for the night. But if morning comes before we get to the water, we're going to be covered with clouds of insects."

They pushed on. They thought they'd covered about ten miles from the hill. Another two hours should bring them to the lake, if they'd estimated its distance correctly. But three hours later, by Anana's watch, they still saw no sign of water.

"It must be further than we thought," Kickaha said. "Or we've not been going in a straight line."

The plain had begun sinking in along their direction of travel. After the first hour, they were in a shallow depression four feet deep, almost a mile wide, and extending ahead and behind as far as they could see. By the end of the second hour, the edges of the depression were just above their heads. When they stopped to rest, they were at the bottom of a trough twelve feet high but now only half a mile wide.

Its walls were steep though not so much they were unclimbable. Not yet, anyway.

What Kickaha found ominous was that all the animal life, and most of the vegetable life, had gotten out of the depression.

"I think we'd better get our tails up onto the plain," he said. "I have a funny feeling about staying here."

Urthona said, "That means walking just that much farther. I'm so tired I can hardly take another step."

"Stay here then," the redhead said. He stood up. "Come on, Anana."

At that moment he felt wetness cover his feet. The others, exclaiming, scrambled up and stared around. Water, looking black in the light, was flowing over the bottom. In the short time after they'd become aware of it, it had risen to their ankles.

"Oh, oh!" Kickaha said. "There's an opening to the lake now! Run like hell, everybody!"

The nearest bank was an eighth of a mile, six hundred and sixty feet away. Kickaha left the antelope leg behind him. The quiver and bow slung over his shoulder, the strap of the instrument case over the other, he ran for the bank. The others passed him, but Anana, once more, grabbed his hand to help him. By the time they had gotten halfway to safety, the stream was up to their knees. This slowed them down, but they slogged through. And then Kickaha, glancing to his left, saw a wall of water racing toward them, its blackish front twice as high as he.

Urthona was the first to reach the top of the bank. He got down on his knees and grabbed one of McKay's hands and pulled him on up. Red Orc grabbed at the black's ankle but missed. He slid back down the slope, then scrambled back up. McKay started to reach down to help, but Urthona spoke to him, and he withdrew his hand.

Nevertheless, Orc climbed over the edge by himself. The water was now up to the waists of

Kickaha and Anana. They got to the bank, where
she let go of his hand. He slipped and fell back but
was up at once. By now he could feel the ground
trembling under his feet, sonic forerunners of the
vast oncoming mass of water.

He grabbed Anana's legs, boosted her on up,
and then began climbing after her. She grabbed his
left wrist and pulled. His other hand clutched the
grass on the lip of the bank, and he came on up.
The other three were standing near her, watching
them keenly. He cursed them because they'd not
tried to help.

Orc shrugged. Urthona grinned. Suddenly, Urthona ran at Orc and pushed him. Orc screamed
and fell sideways. McKay deftly pulled the beamer
from Anana's belt. At the same time, he pushed
with the flat of his hand against her back. Shriek-
ing, she, too, went into the stream.

Urthona whirled and said, "The Horn of Shambarimen! Give it to me!"

Kickaha was stunned at the sudden sequence of
events. He had expected treachery, but not so
soon.

"To hell with you!" he said. He had no time to
look for Anana, though he could hear her nearby.
She was yelling and, though he couldn't see her,
must be climbing up the bank. There wasn't a
sound from Red Orc.

He lifted the shoulder strap of the instrument
case holding the horn and slipped it down his arm.
Urthona grinned again, but he stopped when Kickaha held the case over the water.

"Get Anana up here! Quickly! Or I drop this!"

"Shoot him, McKay!" Urthona yelled.

"Hell, man, you didn't tell me how to operate
this thing!" McKay said.

"You utter imbecile!"

Urthona leaped to grab the weapon from the black man. Kickaha swung the instrument case with his left hand behind him and dropped it. Hopefully, Anana would catch it. He dived toward McKay, who, though he didn't know how to fire the beamer, was quick enough to use it as a club. Its barrel struck Kickaha on the top of his head, and his face smacked into the ground.

Half-stunned, he lay for a few seconds, trying to get his legs and arms to moving. Even in his condition, he felt the earth shaking under him. A roaring surged around him, though he did not know if that was the flood or the result of the blow.

It didn't matter. Something hit his jaw as he began to get up. The next he knew, he was in the water.

The coldness brought him somewhat out of his daze. But he was lifted up, then down, totally immersed, fighting for breath, trying to swim. Something smashed into him—the bottom of the channel, he realized dimly—and then he was raised again. Tumbling over and over, not knowing which way was up or down, and incapable of doing anything about it if he had known, he was carried along. Once more he was brought hard against the bottom. This time he was rolled along. When he thought that he could no longer hold his breath— his head roared, his lungs ached for air, his mouth desperately wanted to open—he was shot upward.

For a moment his head cleared the surface, and he sucked in air. Then he was plunged downward and something struck his head.

CHAPTER SIX

KICKAHA AWOKE ON his back. The sky was beginning to take on horizontal bands of alternating dark-red and fiery-red. It was "dawn."

He was lying in water which rose halfway up his body. He rolled over and got to all-fours. His head hurt abominably, and his ribs felt as if he'd gone twelve rounds in a boxing match. He stood up, weaving somewhat, and looked around. He was on shore, of course. The roaring wave had carried him up and over the end of the channel and then retreated, leaving him here with other bodies. These were a dozen or so animals that had not gotten out of the channel in time.

Nearby was a boulder, a round-shaped granite rock the size of a house. It reminded him of the one in the clearing in Anana's world. In this world there were no rock strata such as on Earth. But here were any number of small stones and occasionally boulders, courtesy of the Lord of the lavalite planet, Urthona.

He remembered Anana's speculation that some of these could conceal "gates." With the proper verbal or tactile code, these might be opened to give entrance into Urthona's castle somewhere on this world. Or to other pocket universes. Urthona, of course, would neither verify nor deny this speculation.

If he had the Horn of Shambarimen, he could sound the sequence of seven notes to determine if the rock did contain a gate. He didn't have it. It was either lost in the flood or Anana had gotten up the bank with it. If the latter had happened, Urthona now had the Horn.

A mile beyond the boulder was a mountain. It was conical, the side nearest him lower than the other, revealing a hollow. It would not be a volcano, since these did not exist here. At the moment, it did not seem to be changing shape.

There were tall hills in the distance, all lining the channel. Most of the plain was gone, which meant that the mutations had taken place at an accelerating speed.

His bow and quiver were gone, torn from him while he was being scraped against the channel bottom. He still had his belt and hunting knife, however.

His shirt was missing. The undershirt was only a rag. His trousers had holes and rips, and his shoes had departed.

Woozily, he went to the edge of the water and searched for other bodies. He found none. That was good, since it gave him hope, however slight, that Anana had survived. It wasn't likely, but if he could survive, she might.

Though he felt better, he was in no mood to whistle while he worked. He cut a leg off an antelope and skinned it. Hordes of large black green-headed flies settled on the carcass and him and began working. The bite of one fly was endurable, but a hundred at once made him feel as if he were being sandpapered all over. However, as long as he kept moving he wasn't covered by them. Every time he moved an arm or turned his head or shifted his position, he was relieved of their attack. But they zoomed back at once and began crawling, buzzing, and biting.

Finally, he was able to walk off with the antelope leg over one shoulder. Half of the flies stayed behind to nibble on the carcass. The others decided after a while that the leg he carried was more edible and also not as active. Still, he had to bat at his face to keep them from crawling over his eyes or up his nose.

Kickaha vented some of his irritation by cursing the Lord of this world. When he'd made this world and decreed its ecosystems, did he have to include flies?

It was a question that had occurred more than once to the people of Earth.

Despite feeling that he'd had enough water to last him a lifetime, he soon got thirsty. He knelt down on the channelbank and scooped up the liquid. It was fresh. According to Urthona, even the oceans here were drinkable. He ate some meat, wishing that he could get hold of fruit or vegetables to balance his diet.

The next day, some mobile plants came along. These were about six feet high. Their trunks bore spiral red-and-white-and-blue stripes, and some orange fruit dangled from their branches. Unlike the plants he'd encountered the day before, these had legs with knees. They lacked tentacles, but they might have another method of defense.

Fortunately, he was cautious about approaching them. Each plant had a large hole on each side, situated halfway down the length. He neared one that was separated from the others, and as he did so, it turned to present one of the holes. The thing had no eyes, but it must have had keen hearing. Or, for all he knew, it had a sonic transceiver, perhaps on the order of a bat's.

Whatever its biological mechanisms, it turned as he circled it. He took a few more steps toward it, then stopped. Something dark appeared in the hole, something pulsed, then a black-red mass of flesh extruded. In the center was a hole, from which, in a few seconds, protruded a short pipe of cartilage or bony material.

It looked too much like a gun to him. He threw himself down on the ground, though it hurt his ribs and head when he did so. There was a popping sound, and something shot over his head. He rolled to one side, got up, and ran after the missile. It was a dart made of bone, feathered at one end, and sharp enough to pierce flesh at the other. Something green and sticky coated the point.

The plants were carnivorous, unless the compressed-air propelled dart was used only for self-defense. This didn't seem likely.

Staying out of range, Kickaha moved around the plants. The one who'd shot at him was taking in air with loud gulping sounds. The others turned as he circled.

They had neither eyes nor tentacles. But they could "see" him, and they must have some way of getting the meat of their prey into their bodies for digestion. He'd wait and find out.

It didn't take long. The plants moved up to the now-rotting carcasses of the antelopes and gazelles. The first to get there straddled the bodies and then sat down on them. He watched for a while before he understood just how they ate. A pair of flexible lips protruded from the bottom of the trunks and tore at the meat. Evidently, the lips were lined with tiny but sharp teeth.

Urthona had not mentioned this type of flesh-eating tree. Maybe he hadn't done so because he was hoping that Kickaha and Anana would venture within range of the poison-tipped darts.

Kickaha decided to move on. He had recovered enough to walk at a fairly fast pace. But first he needed some more weapons.

It wasn't difficult to collect them. He would walk to just within range of a plant, run toward it a few steps, and then duck down. The maneuvers caused him some pain, but they were worth it. After collecting a dozen darts, he cut off a piece of his trousers with his knife, and wrapped the missiles in it. He stuck the package in his rear pocket, and, waving a jaunty thanks to the plants, started along the channel.

By now the area was beginning to fill up with animals. They'd scented the water, come running, and were drinking their fill. He went around a herd of thirty elephants which were sucking up the water into their trunks, then squirting it into their mouths. Some of the babies were swimming around and playing with each other. The leader, a big mother, eyed him warily but made no short threatening charges.

These tuskless pachyderms were as tall as African elephants but longer-legged and less massively bodied.

A half an hour later, he came across a herd attacking a "grove" of the missile-shooting plants. These spat the tiny darts into the thick hides of the elephants, which ignored them. Apparently the poison did not affect them. The adults rammed into the plants, knocked them over, and then began stripping the short branches with their trunks. After that the plants were lifted by the trunks and stuck crosswise into the great mouths. The munching began, the giant molars crushing the barky bodies until they were severed. The elephant then picked up one of the sections and masticated this. Everything, the vegetable and the protein parts, went down the great throats.

The young weaned beasts seized the fallen parts and ate these.

Some of the plants waddled away unpursued by the elephants. These became victims to a family of the giant moosoids, which also seemed impervious to the darts' poison. Their attackers, which looked like blue-haired, antlerless Canadian moose, tore the fallen plants apart with their teeth.

Kickaha, who was able to get closer to them than to the pachyderms, noted that the moosoids were careful about one thing. When they came to an organ which he supposed contained the darts, they pushed it aside. Everything else, including the fleshy-looking legs, went into their gullets.

Kickaha waited until he could grab one of the sacs. He cut it open and found a dozen darts inside it, each inside a tubule. He put these into the cloth, and went on his way.

Several times families of lion-sized rusty-colored sabertooth cats crossed his path. He discreetly waited until they had gone by. They saw him but were not, for the moment at least, interested in him. They also ignored the hoofed beasts. Evidently, their most immediate concern was water.

A pack of wild dogs trotted near him, their red tongues hanging out, their emerald eyes glowing. They were about two and a half feet tall, built like cheetahs, spotted like leopards.

Once he encountered a family of kangaroo-like beasts as tall as he. Their heads, however, looked like those of giant rabbits and their teeth were rodentine. The females bore fleshy hair-covered pouches on their abdomens; the heads of the young "rabaroos" stuck out of the pouches.

He was interested in the animal life, of course. But he also scanned the waterway. Once he thought he saw a human body floating in the middle of the channel, and his heart seemed to turn over. A closer look showed that it was some kind of hairless water animal. It suddenly disappeared, its bilobed tail resembling a pair of human legs held close together. A moment later, it emerged, a wriggling fish between long-whiskered jaws. The prey had four short thick legs, the head of a fish, and the vertical tail-fins of a fish. It uttered a gargling sound.

Urthona had said that all fish were amphibians, except for some that inhabited the stable sea-lands.

All life here, except for the grass, was mobile. It had to be to survive.

An hour later, one of the causes for the locomotive character of life on this world rose above the horizon. The reddish temporary moon moved slowly but when fully in view filled half of the sky. It was not directly overhead, being far enough away for Kickaha to see it edge-on. Its shape was that of two convex lenses placed back to back. A very extended oval. It rotated on its longitudinal axis so slowly that it had not traversed more than two degrees in a horizontal circle within two hours.

Finally, Kickaha quit watching it.

Urthona had said that it was one of the very small splitoffs. These occurred after every twelve major splitoffs. Though it looked huge, it was actually very small, not more than a hundred kilometers long. It seemed so big because it was so close to the surface.

Kickaha's knowledge of physics and celestial objects was limited to what he'd learned in high school, plus some reading of his own. He knew, however, that no object of that mass could go slowly in an orbit so near the planet without falling at once. Not in Earth's universe.

But his ideas of what was possible had been greatly extended when he had been gated into Jadawin's world many years ago. And now that he was in Urthona's world he was getting an even broader education. Different arrangements of space-matter, even of matter-energy conversion, were not only possible, they'd been realized by the Lords.

Some day, Terrestrials, if they survived long enough, would discover this. Then their scientists would make pocket universes in bubbles in space-matter outside of yet paradoxically within Earth's universe. But that would come after the shock of discovering that their extra-solar system astronomy was completely wrong.

How long would it be before the secondary returned to the primary? Urthona hadn't known; he'd forgotten. But he had said that the fact that they'd seen it every other day meant that they must be near the planet's north pole. Or perhaps the south pole. In any event, the splitoff was making a spiral orbit which would carry it southward or northward, as the case might be.

That vast thing cruising through the skies made Kickaha uneasy. It would soon fall to the main mass. Perhaps its orbit would end in one more passage around the planet. When it came down, it would do swiftly. Urthona has said that he did remember that, once it came within twelve thousand feet of the surface, it decended at about a foot every two seconds. A counterrepulsive force slowed its fall so that its impact would not turn it and the area beneath and around it into a fiery mass. Indeed, the final moment before collision could be termed an "easing" rather than a crash.

But there would be a release of energy. Hot air would roar out from the fallen body, air hot enough to fry any living thing fifty miles away. And there would be major earthquakes.

There would be animals and birds and fish and plants on the moon, life forms trapped on it when the splitoff occurred. Those on the underside would be ground into bits and the bits burned. Those on the upper surface would have a fifty-fifty chance of surviving, if they weren't near the edges.

Urthona had said, however, that the splitoff masses never fell in the neighborhood of the oceans. These were in a relatively stable area; the changes in the land surrounding them were slower.

Kickaha hoped that he was near one of the five oceans.

Of all the manifestations of life, the aerial was the most noticeable. He had passed at least a million birds and winged mammals, and the sky was often blackened by flocks that must have numbered hundreds of thousands. These included many birds that had surely been brought in from Earth. There were some, also, that looked just like those he'd known in Jadawin's world. And many were so strange, often grotesque, that he supposed their ancestors had been made in Urthona's biolabs.

Wherever they came from, they were a noisy bunch—as on Earth. Their cawings, croakings, screams, pipings, warblings, whistlings, chatterings filled the air. Some were fish-eaters, either diving into the water from a height or surface swimmers who plunged after fish or frog-like creatures. Others settled down on the elephants and moosoids and pecked at parasites. Others picked food from the teeth of enormous crocodiloids. Many settled down on the branches of various plants and ate the fruit or seeds. The trees did not object to this. But sometimes the weight of the birds was so heavy that a plant would fall over, and the birds, squawking and screaming, would soar up from the fallen like smoke from a burning log.

The tentacled plants would hasten to lift their helpless fellows upright again. The untentacled were left to their fate. More often than not this was being devoured by the pachyderms and moosoids.

Three hours passed, and the menacing mass above him became tiny. It was the only thing on this world that threw a shadow, and even that was pale compared to the shades of Earth. Physically pale, that is. The emotional shadow it cast, the anxiety and near-panic, was seldom matched by anything in Kickaha's native world. A smoking volcano, a violent earthquake, a roaring hurricane were the only comparable events.

However, he had carefully observed the reactions of the birds and animals while it was overhead. They didn't seem to be disturbed by it. This meant to him they somehow "knew" that it posed no threat. Not, at least, this time.

Had Urthona given them the instinctive mechanism to enable them to predict the area in which the splitoff would fall? If he had, then that meant that there was a pattern to the splitting off and the merging of the bodies. However, what about those creatures not made in his biolabs: those which had been brought in from other universes? They hadn't been here long enough for evolution to develop any such instinctive knowledge.

Maybe the importees observed the natives and took their cue from these.

He would ask Urthona about that when he found him. If he found him. Shortly before he killed him.

Kickaha cut off some slices of the antelope leg, and, brushing away the flies, ate the meat. It was getting strong, so he threw the rest of the limb away after his belly was satisfied. A number of scarlet crows settled down on it at once. These had gotten no more than a few pieces when two large purple green-winged eagles with yellow legs drove them off.

Watching them made him wonder where birds lay their eggs. In this world, no nest would be safe. A cranny in a mountain side could be closed up or on a plain in a few days.

He had plenty of time to observe, to get the answers to his questions about the zoology of this world. If he lived long enough.

"Day" passed while he walked steadily along the edge of the channel. Near "dusk" it had begun widening. He drove off some birds from some fruit fallen from a plant and ate the half-devoured "papayas." In the middle of the "night" some smaller varieties of the rabaroos hopped by him, two long-legged baboons after them. He threw his knife into the neck of a rabaroo male as it went by. The creature fell over, causing the baboons to return for this easier prey. Kickaha pulled the knife out and threatened the primates. They barked and showed their wicked-looking canines. One tried to get behind him while the other made short charges at him.

Kickaha didn't want to tangle with them if he could help it. He cut off the legs of the rabaroo and walked away, leaving the rest to the baboons. They were satisfied with the arrangement.

Finding a safe place to sleep was almost impossible. Not only was the night alive with prowling predators, the spreading water was a menace. Twice he awoke inches deep in it and had to retreat several hundred feet to keep from drowning. Finally, he walked to the base of the nearest mountain, which had been only a hill when he had first sighted it. There were several large boulders on its slope. He lay down just above one. When the slope got too steep, the boulder would roll. The movement would awake him—he hoped. Also, most of the action seemed to be taking place in the valley. The big cats, dogs, and baboons were out, trying to sneak up on or run down the hoofed and hopping beasts.

Kickaha awoke frequently as roars, barks, growls, and screams came up from the valley. None of them seemed to be near, though. Nor was he sure that he hadn't dreamed some of the noises.

Shortly before "dawn" he sat up, gasping, his heart thudding. There was a rumbling noise. Earthquake? No, the ground was not trembling. Then he saw that the boulder had rolled away. It wasn't the only one. About half a dozen were hurtling down the slope, which was even steeper now, shooting off swellings, thumping as they hit the surface again, gathering speed, headed toward the valley floor.

That floor, however, was now all water. The

only beasts there were a few big cats, up to their bellies in water, staying only to eat as much of their kills as possible before they were forced to take off. There were millions of birds, though, among them an estimated two hundred thousand long-legged flamingoes, green instead of pink like their Terrestrial counterparts. They were eating voraciously in the boiling water. Boiling not with heat but with life. Fish by the millions.

It was time to get up even if he had not had enough rest. The slope was tilting so that he would soon be sent rolling down it.

He scrambled down and went into the water up to his knees and then got down and drank from it. It was still fresh, though muddied by all the activity. One of the flamingoes came scooting through the water, following a trail of something fleeing under the surface. It stopped when Kickaha rose, and it screamed angrily. He ignored it and plunged his knife down. Its point went into the thing the flamingo had been chasing. He brought up a skewered thing which looked like a mud puppy. It did not taste like mud puppy, however. It had a flavor of trout.

Apparently, the water level was not going to rise higher. Not for a while, anyway. After filling his belly and washing his body, he slogged through knee-deep water along the base of the mountain. In an hour he'd gotten by that and was walking on a plain. About "noon" the plain was tilting to one side, about ten degrees to the horizontal, and the water was running down it. Three hours later, it was beginning to tilt the other way. He ate the rest of the mud puppy and threw the bones, with much meat attached, on the ground. Scarlet crows settled down on it to dispute about the tidbits.

The splitoff had not appeared again. He hoped that when it did fall, it would be far far away from him. It would form an enormous pile, a suddenly born mountain range of super-Himalayan proportions, on the surface. Then, according to Urthona, within several months it would have merged with the larger mass, itself changing shape during the process.

Some months later, another splitoff would occur somewhere else. But this would be a major one. Its volume would be about one-sixteenth of that of the planet.

God help those caught on it at liftoff. God help those on it when it returned to the mother planet.

One-sixteenth of this world's mass! A wedge-shaped mass the thin edge of which would rip out of the planet's center. Roughly, over 67,700,000,000 cubic kilometers.

He shuddered. Imagine the cataclysms, the earthquakes, the staggeringly colossal hole. Imagine the healing process as the walls of the hole slid down to fill it and the rest of the planet moved to compensate. It was unimaginable.

It was a wonder that any life at all remained. Yet there was plenty.

Just before "dusk" he came through a pass between two monolithic mountains that had not changed shape for a day. The channel lay in its center, the surface of the water a few inches below the tops of the banks. There was room on both sides of the channel for ten men abreast. He walked along the channel looking now and then at the towering wall of the mountain on the right.

Its base curved slowly, the channel also curving with it. He didn't want to settle down for the night, since there was little room to avoid any of the big predators. Or, for that matter, to keep from being trampled if a herd of the hoofed beasts was stampeded.

He pushed on, slowing now and then to get as near the mountain as possible when big cats or wild dogs came along. Fortunately, they paid him no attention. It could be that they had run into human beings before and so dreaded them. Which said much for the dangerousness of Homo sapiens here. Probably, though, they found him to be a strange thing and so were wary.

In any event, they might not be able to resist the temptation to attack him if they found him sleeping on the ground. He pushed on. By dawn he was staggering with weariness. His legs hurt. His belly told him it needed more food.

Finally, the mountain ceased. The channel ran almost straight for as far as he could see. He had a great plain to cross before reaching a row of conical mountains in the far distance. There were many plants here, few of them now moving, and herds of animals and the ubiquitous birds. At the moment all seemed peaceful. If there were predators, they were quiet.

The channel ran straight for as far as he could see. He wondered how long it was from its beginning to its end. He'd assumed that the flood had carried him for perhaps ten miles. But now it was apparent that he could have been borne for fifty miles. Or more.

The earth had suddenly split on a straight line as if the edge of an axe of a colossus bigger than a mountain had smashed into the ground. Water had poured from the sea into the trench, and he'd been carried on its front to the end of the channel and deposited there. He was very lucky not to have been ground into bits on the bottom or drowned.

No, he hadn't experienced great luck. He'd experienced a miracle.

He left the mountain pass and started across the plain. But he stopped after a hundred yards. He turned toward the hoofbeats that had suddenly alerted him.

Around the corner of the mountain to his right, concealed until then by a bulge of the mountain-wall, came a score of moosoids. Men were mounted on them, men who carried long spears.

Aware that he now saw them, they whooped and urged their beasts into a gallop.

For him to run was useless. They also serve who only stand and wait. However, this wasn't a tennis match.

CHAPTER SEVEN

THE MOOSOIDS WERE of the smaller variety, a
trifle larger than a thoroughbred horse. Like their
wild cousins, they were of different colors, roan,
black, blue, chestnut, and piebald. They were
fitted with reins, and their riders were on leather
saddles with stirrups.

The men were naked from the waist up, wearing
leather trousers which kept their legs from chafing.
Some of them had feathers affixed to their long
hair, but they were not Amerindians. Their skins
were too light, and they were heavily bearded. As
they got close enough, he saw that their faces bore
tribal scars.

Some of the spears were poles the ends of which
had been sharpened and fire-hardened. Others
were tipped with flint or chert or antelope horns or
lion teeth. There were no bows, but some carried
stone axes, and heavy war boomerangs in the belts
at their waists. There were also round leather-
covered shields, but these hung from leather
strings tied to the saddle. Evidently they thought
they didn't need them against Kickaha. They were
right.

The first to arrive halted their beasts. The others
spread out and around him.

Their chief, a gray-haired stocky man, urged his
animal closer to Kickaha. The moosoid obeyed,
but his wide rolling eyes showed he didn't like the
idea.

By then the main body of the tribe was beginning

to come from around the bend of the mountain.
They consisted of armed outriders and a caravan
of women, children, dogs, and moosoids drawing
travois on which were piled heaps of skins,
gourds, wood poles, and other materials.

The chief spoke to Kickaha in an unknown language. Of course. Not expecting them to understand him, Kickaha used test phrases in twenty
different languages, Lord, English, French, German, Tishquetmoac, Hrowakas, the degraded
High German of Dracheland, several Half-Horse
Lakota dialects, a Mycenaean dialect, and some
phrases of Latin, Greek, Italian, and Spanish he
knew.

The chief didn't understand any of them. That
was to be expected, though Kickaha had hoped
that if their ancestors came from Earth they might
speak a tongue that he at least could identify.

One good thing had happened. They hadn't
killed him at once.

But they could intend to torture him first. Knowing what the tribes on the Amerind level of Jadawin's world did to their captives, he wasn't very
optimistic.

The chief waved his feathered spear and said
something to two men. These got down off their
beasts and approached him warily. Kickaha
smiled and held out his hands, palms up.

The two didn't smile back. Their spears ready
for thrusting, they moved toward him slowly.

If Kickaha had been in his usual excellent physical condition, he would have tried to make a run
for the nearest moosoid with an empty saddle.
Even then, he would have had only one chance in
twenty of fighting his way through the ring. The
odds had been heavier against him in past situa-

tions, but then he had felt capable of anything. Not now. He was too stiff and too tired.

Both men were shorter than he, one being about five feet six inches tall and the other about an inch higher. The bigger man held his spear in one hand while the other reached out. Kickaha thought that he wanted him to hand his knife to him.

Shrugging, Kickaha slowly obeyed. There was a second when he thought of throwing the knife into the man's throat. He could grab the spear, snatch the knife out, run for . . . No, forget it.

The man took the knife and backed away. It was evident from his expression, and those of the others, that he had never seen metal before.

The chief said something. The man ran to him and gave him the knife. The gray-headed graybeard turned it over, gingerly felt its edge with his palm, and then tried it on a leather string holding his warshield.

All exclaimed when the string fell apart so easily.

The chief asked Kickaha something. Probably, he wanted to know where his captive had gotten it.

Kickaha wasn't backward about lying if it would save his life. He pointed at the mountains toward which he had been traveling.

The chief looked as if he were straining his mind. Then he spoke again, and the two dismounted men tied Kickaha's hands in front of him with a leather cord. The chief spoke again, and the scouts moved on ahead. The chief and the two aides got down off their beasts and waited. In about fifteen minutes, the front of the caravan caught up with them.

The chief seemed to be explaining the situation to his people, making frequent gestures with his spear toward the direction indicated by his captive. There was a babel of excited talk then. Finally, the chief told them to shut up. During this Kickaha had been counting the tribe. Including the scouts, there were about ninety. Thirty men, forty women, and twenty children.

The latter ranged from several babes in arms to preadolescents. The women, like the men were black- or brown-haired. The general eye color was a light brown. Some had hazel; a few, blue eyes. Some of the women weren't bad-looking. They wore only short kilts of tanned leather. The children were naked and, like their elders, dirty. All stank as if they'd been bathless for a month or so.

Some of the beasts of burden, however, carried big water skins of water. A woman milked a cow during the brief stop.

The travois, in addition to the piles of skins, weapons, carried a form of pemmican. There were no tents, which meant that when it rained the tribe just endured it.

While several men pointed spears at him, he was stripped by others. The chief was given the ragged levis and worn boots. From his expression and the tones of his voice, he had never seen anything like them before. When he tried to put on the levis, he found that his wide buttocks and bulging paunch would not accommodate them. He solved this problem by slitting them with the knife around the waist. The boots were too large for his feet, but he wore them anyway.

Finding the package of poison darts in the rear pocket of the levis, he passed them out to men whose spears lacked flint or chert tips. These tied the darts on the ends with rawhide cords and then had a good time play-jabbing at each other, laughing as they leaped away.

The only possessions left to Kickaha were his holey and dirty jockey shorts.

A big female moosoid was pulled out from the herd, fitted with reins and a saddle, and Kickaha was urged to mount it. He did so, holding the reins in his hands. The chief then said something, and a man tied the ends of a long thong under the beast's belly to Kickaha's ankles. The caravan started up then, an old woman—the only old person he saw—blowing a strange tune on a flute made from a long bone. Probably it was the legbone of a moa.

The ride lasted about an hour. Then the tribe camped—if you call such a simple quick procedure camping—by the channel. While Kickaha sat on the animal, ignored by everybody except a single guard, the people took their turn bathing.

Kickaha wondered if they meant to keep him on the moosoid until they moved on. After half an hour, during which time he was savagely bitten by a horde of blue flies, his guard decided to untie the leg thongs. Kickaha got down stiffly and waited. The guard leaned on his spear waiting until he was relieved to take a bath.

Kickaha gestured that he would like a drink of water. The guard, a slim youth, nodded. Kickaha went to the edge of the channel and got down on his knees to scoop up water with his hands. The next moment, he was in the water, propelled by a kick on his buttocks.

He came up to find everybody laughing at this splendid joke.

Kickaha swam forward until his feet touched the bottom. He turned around and cast one longing glance at the other side. It lay about three hundred feet away. He could get over to the opposite shore even with his hands tied before him. His pursuers could swim or ride across on swimming beasts. But he could beat them. If only there had been a wood nearby or a mountain, he would have tried for escape. However, there was a plain about two miles broad there. His captors would ride him down before he got to it.

Reluctantly, he hauled himself onto the bank. He stood up, looking expressionlessly at the youth. That one laughed and said something to the others, and they broke into uproarious laughter. Whatever it was he said, it wasn't complimentary to the prisoner.

Kickaha decided he might as well start his language lessons now. He pointed at the spear and asked its name. At first the youth didn't understand him. When he caught on, he said, "*Gabol*."

Gabol, as it turned out, was not a generic term. It meant a spear with a fire-hardened tip. A spear with a stone tip was a *baros*; with an antelope-horn tip, a *yava*; with a lion-tooth tip, a *grados*.

He learned later that there was no word for humankind. The tribe called itself by a word which meant, simply, The People. Other human beings were The Enemy. Children, whatever their sex, were summed under one word which meant "unformed." Adult males were distinguished by three terms: one for a warrior who had slain an enemy tribesman, one for a youth who had not yet been blooded, and a third for a sterile man. It made no difference if the sterile man had killed his enemy. He was still a *tairu*. If, however, he managed to steal a child from another tribe, then he was a full *wiru*, a blooded warrior.

Women were in three classes. If she had borne a child, she was in the top class. If she was sterile but had killed two enemy, male or female, she was in the second rank. If sterile and unblooded, she was a *shonka,* a name which originally was that of some kind of low animal.

Two days and nights passed while the tribe traveled leisurely along the channel. This was, except for the great conical mountains far ahead of them, the only permanent feature of the landscape. Sometimes it broadened and shallowed, sometimes narrowed and deepened. But it continued to run straight as an Indian chief's back for as far as the eye could see in either direction.

Hunting parties went out while the rest of the tribe either camped or moved at the rate of a mile an hour. Sometimes the younger women went with the men. Unlike the primitives who lived on the World of Tiers, the women of this tribe were not engaged from dawn to dusk in making artifacts, growing food, preparing meals, and raising children. They tended herd and shared the childraising, and sometimes they fashioned wooden poles into spears or carved boomerangs. Otherwise, they had little to do. The stronger of the young women went hunting and, sometimes, on the raiding parties.

The hunters returned with antelope, gazelle, ostrich, and moa meat. Once, a party killed a young elephant which had been separated from its herd. Then the tribe traveled two miles across the plain to the carcass. There they stripped it to the bone, gorging on the raw meat until their bellies looked like balloons.

The cutting of the meat was done with flint or chert knives. Kickaha would find out that these rare stones came from nodules which occasionally appeared when the earth opened up to deliver them. Except for the boulders, these were the only solid mineral known.

The diet included fruit and nuts from various trees. These were usually knocked off by the boomerangs as the hunters rode out of range of tentacle or dart.

Kickaha, though an enthusiastic and quick-learning linguist, took more than a week to master the rudiments of the tribe's speech. Though the tribe had a technology that an Ice Age caveman would have ranked as low, they spoke a complex language. The vocabulary was not great, but the shades of meaning, mostly indicated by subtle internal vowel changes, baffled his ear at first. It also had a feature he'd never encountered before. The final consonant of a word could alter the initial consonant of the succeeding word in a phrase. There was a rule to learn about this, but, as in all living languages, the rule had many exceptions.

Besides, the possible combinations were many.

Kickaha thought he remembered reading something about a similar consonant change in the Celtic languages. How similar, he didn't know.

Sometimes he wondered if the Thana, as the tribe called itself, could be descended from ancient Celts. If they were, however, no modern Celt would have understood them. In the course of many thousand years, the speech must have changed considerably. A male moosoid, used for riding, for instance, was called a *hikwu*. Could that possibly be related to the ancient Latin *equus*? If he remembered his reading, done so many years ago, *equus* was related to a similar word in Celtic and also to the Greek *hippos*.

He didn't know. It didn't really matter, except

as an item of curiosity. Anyway, why would the
original tribe brought in here have named a moose
after a horse? That could be because the *hikwu*
functioned more like a horse than any animal the
tribe had encountered.

During the day Kickaha either rode, his hands
bound, on a *merk*, a female riding-moosoid, or he
lazed around camp. When he was in the saddle, he
kept an eye out for signs of Anana. So far, he didn't
know the language well enough to ask anybody if
they had seen pale strangers like himself or a black
man.

The tenth day, they came through a mountain
pass which seemed to be a permanent feature. And
there, beyond a long slope, beyond a broad plain,
was the ocean.

The mountains on this side and the flat land were
covered with permanently rooted trees. Kickaha
almost cried when he saw them. They were over a
hundred feet tall, of a score of genuses, plants like
pines, oaks, cottonwoods, many fruit and nut-
bearing.

The first question occurring to him was: if this
land was unchanging, why didn't the Thana put
down their roots here? Why did they roam the
evermutating country outside the ocean-ringing
peaks?

On the way down, clouds formed, and before
they were halfway down the slope, thunder bellowed. The Thana halted, and the chief,
Wergenget, conferred with the council. Then he
gave the order to turn about and pass beyond the
mountains.

Kickaha spoke to Lukyo, a young woman
whose personality, not to mention her figure, had
attracted him.

"Why are we going back?"

Lukyo looked pale and her eyes rolled like a frightened horse's. "We're too early. The Lord's wrath hasn't cooled off yet."

At that moment the first of the lightning struck. A tree two hundred feet away split down the middle, one side falling, one remaining upright.

The chief shouted orders to hurry up, but his urging wasn't needed. The retreat almost became a stampede. The moosoids bolted, riders frantically trying to pull them up, the travois bumping up and down, dislodging their burdens. Kickaha and Lukyo were left standing alone. Not quite. A six-year old child was crying under a tree. Apparently, she had wondered off for a minute, and her parents, who were mounted, were being carried off against their will.

Kickaha managed to pick up the little girl despite the handicap of his bound wrists. He walked as fast as he could with the burden while Lukyo ran ahead of him. More thunder, more strokes of lightning. A bolt crashed behind him, dazzling him. The child threw her arms around his neck and buried her face against his shoulder.

Kickaha swore. This was the worst lightning storm he had ever been in. Yet, despite the danger of the bolts, he would have fled into it. It was his first good chance to escape. But he couldn't abandon the child.

The rain came then, striking with great force. He increased his pace, his head low while water poured over him as if he were taking a shower. The frequent bolts showed that Lukyo, propelled by fear, was drawing ahead of him. Even unburdened and in good physical condition, he might have had trouble keeping up with her. She ran like an Olympic champion.

Then she slipped and fell and slid face down on the wet grass for a few feet uphill. She was up again. But not for long. A crash deafened him; whiteness blinded him. Darkness for a few seconds. A score or more of blasts, all fortunately not as near as the last bolt. He saw Lukyo down again. She was not moving.

When he got near her, he could smell the burned flesh. He put the child down, though she fought against leaving him. Lukyo's body was burned black.

He picked up the little girl and began running as fast as he could. Then, out of the flickering checkerboard of day-turned-night he saw a ghostly figure. He stopped. What the hell? All of a sudden he was in a nightmare. No wonder the whole tribe had fled in panic, forgetting even the child.

But the figure came closer, and now he saw that it was two beings. Wergenget on his *hikwu*. The chief had managed to get control of the beast, and he had come back for them. It must not have been easy for him to conquer his fear. It certainly was difficult for him to keep the moosoid from running away. The poor animal must have thought his master was mad to venture into that bellowing death-filled valley after having escaped from it.

Now Kickaha understood why Wergenget was the chief.

The graybeard stopped his beast, which trembled violently, its upper lip drawn back, its eyes rotating. Kickaha shouted at him and pointed at the corpse. Wergenget nodded that he understood. He lifted up the girl and placed her on the saddle before him. Kickaha fully expected him to take off then. Why shoud he risk his life and the child's for a stranger?

But Wergenget controlled the *hikwu* until Kickaha could get up behind the chief. Then he turned it and let it go, and the beast was not at all reluctant. Though burdened with the three, it made speed. Presently, they were in the pass. Here there was no rain; the thunder and the lightning boomed and exploded but at a safe distance away.

CHAPTER EIGHT

WERGENGET HANDED THE child to its weeping, wailing mother. The father kissed his daughter, too, but his expression was hangdog. He was ashamed because he had allowed his fear to overcome him.

"We stay here until the Lord is through rampaging," the chief said.

Kickaha slid off the animal. Wergenget followed him. For a moment Kickaha thought about snatching the knife from the chief's belt. With it he could flee into a storm where no man dared venture. And he could lose himself in the forest. If he escaped being struck by lightning, he would be so far away the tribe would never find him.

But there was more to his decision not to run for it just now.

The truth was that he didn't want to be alone.

Much of his life, he'd been a loner. Yet he was neither asocial nor antisocial. He'd had no trouble mixing with his playmates, the neighboring farmers' children, when he was a child nor with his peers at the country schoolhouse and community high school.

Because of his intense curiosity, athletic abilities, and linguistic ability, he'd been both popular and a leader. But he was a voracious reader, and, quite often, when he had a choice between recreation with others or reading, he decided on the latter. His time was limited because a farmer's son was kept very busy. Also, he studied hard to get good grades in school. Even at a young age he'd decided he didn't want to be a farmer. He had dreams of traveling to exotic places, of becoming a zoologist or curator of a natural history museum and going to those fabulous places, deepest Africa or South America or Malaya. But that required a Ph.D. and to get that he'd have to have high grades through high school and college. Besides, he liked to learn.

So he read everything he could get his hands on.

His schoolmates had kidded him about "always having his nose stuck in a book." Not nastily and not too jeeringly, since they respected his quick temper and quicker fists. But they did not comprehend his lust for learning.

An outsider, observing him from the ages of seventeen through twenty-two, would not have known that he was often with his peers but not of them. They would have seen a star athlete and superior student who palled around with the roughest, raced around the country roads on a motorcycle, tumbled many girls in the hay, literally, got disgustingly drunk, and once was jailed for running a police roadblock. His parents had been mortified, his mother weeping, his father raging. That he had escaped from jail just to show how easy it was and then voluntarily returned to it had upset them even more.

His male peers thought this was admirable and amusing, his female peers found it fascinating though scarey, and his teachers thought it alarming. The judge, who found him reading Gibbon's *Decline and Fall of the Roman Empire* in his cell, decided that he was just a high-spirited youth with much potentiality who'd fallen among evil companions. The charges were dropped, but Paul was put on unofficial probation by the judge. The young man gave his word that he would behave as a decent respectable citizen should—during the probation period, anyway—and he had kept his word.

Paul seldom left the farm during the probation period. He didn't want to be tempted into evil by those companions whose evil had mostly come from their willingness to follow him into it. Besides, his parents had been hurt enough. He worked, studied, and sometimes hunted in the woods. He didn't mind being alone for long periods. He threw himself into solitariness with the same zest he threw himself into companionship.

And then Mr. and Mrs. Finnegan, perhaps in an effort to straighten him out even more, perhaps in an unconscious desire to hurt him as he'd hurt them, revealed something that shocked him.

He was an adopted child.

Paul was stunned. Like most children, he had gone through a phase when he believed that he was adopted. But he had not kept to the fantasy, which children conceive during periods when they think their parents don't love them. But it was true, and he didn't want to believe it.

According to his step-parents, his real mother was an Englishwoman with the quaint name of Philea Jane Fogg-Fog. Under other circumstances, he would have thought this hilarious. Not now.

Philea Jane's parents were of the English landed gentry, though his great-grandfather had married a Parsi woman. The Parsis, he knew, were Persians who had fled to India and settled there when the Moslems invaded their homeland. So . . . he was actually one-eighth Indian. But it wasn't American

Indian, among whom his step-mother counted ancestors. It was Asiatic Indian, though only in naturalization. The Parsis usually did not marry their Hindu neighbors.

His mother's mother, Roxana Fogg, was the one who'd picked up the hyphenated name of Fogg-Fog. She'd married a distant relative, an American named Fog. A branch of the Foggs had emigrated to the colony of Virginia in the 1600's. In the early 1800's some of their descendants had moved to the then-Mexican territory of Texas. By then the extra "g" had been dropped from the family name. Paul's maternal grandfather, Hardin Blaze Fog, was born on a ranch in the sovereign state, the Republic of Texas.

Roxana Fogg had married an Englishman at the age of twenty. He died when she was thirty-eight, leaving two children. Two years later she went with her son to Texas to look over some of the extensive ranch property he would inherit when he came of age. She also met some of the relatives there, including the famous Confederate war hero and Western gunfighter, Dustine "Dusty" Edward Marsden Fog. She was introduced to Hardin Blaze Fog, several years younger than herself. They fell in love, and he accompanied her back to England. She got the family's approval, despite his barbarian origins, since she announced she was going to marry him anyway and he was a wealthy shipping magnate. Blaze settled down in London to run the British office. When Roxana was forty-three years old, she surprised everybody, including herself, by conceiving. The baby was named Philea Jane.

Philea Jane Fogg-Fog was born in 1880. In 1900 she married an English physician, Doctor Reginald Syn. He died in 1910 under mysterious circumstances, leaving no children. Philea did not remarry until 1916. She had met in London a handsome well-to-do man from Indiana, Park Joseph Finnegan. The Foggs didn't like him because, one, he was of Irish descent, two, he was not an Episcopalian, and three, he had been seen with various ladies of the evening in gambling halls before he'd asked Philea to marry him. She married him anyway and went to Terre Haute, which her relatives thought was still subject to raids by the redskins.

Park Joseph Finnegan made Philea happy for the first six months, despite her difficulty in adjusting to a small Hoosier town. At least, she lived in a big house, and she suffered for no lack of material things.

Then life became hell. Finnegan resumed his spending of his fortune on women, booze, and poker games. Within a short time he'd lost his fortune, and when he found out his thirty-eight year old wife was pregnant, he deserted her. He announced he was going West to make another fortune, but she never heard from him again.

Too proud and too ashamed to return to England, Philea had gone to work as a housekeeper for a relative of her husband's. It was a terrible comedown for her, but she labored without complaint and kept a British stiff upper lip.

Paul was six months old when the gasoline-burning apparatus used to heat an iron exploded in his mother's face. The house burned down, and the infant would have perished with his mother if a young man had not dashed in through the flames and rescued him.

The relative whose house had burned died of a heart attack shortly after. Paul was scheduled to go to an orphanage. But Ralph Finnegan, a cousin of Park's, a Kentucky farmer, and his wife decided to adopt Paul. His fostermother gave him her maiden family name, Janus, as his middle name.

The revelation had shaken Paul terribly. It was after this that he began to suffer from a sense of loneliness. Or perhaps a sense of having been abandoned. Once he'd learned all the details he wanted to know about his true parents, he never spoke of them again. When he mentioned his parents to others, he spoke only of the man and woman who'd reared him.

Two years after Kickaha learned about his true parents, Mr. Finnegan fell ill with cancer and died in six months. That was grief enough, but three months after the burial, his mother had also fallen victim to the same disease. She took a longer time dying, and now Paul had no time to do anything except farm, attend school, and help take care of her. Finally, after much pain, she had died, the day before he was to graduate from high school.

Mingled with his grief was guilt. In some mysterious fashion, he thought, the shame they'd felt when he'd been arrested had caused the cancer. Considered rationally, the idea did not seem plausible. But guilt often had irrational origins. In fact, there were even times when he wondered if he hadn't somehow been responsible for his real father's having deserted his real mother and for her death.

His plans to go to college and major in zoology or in anthropology—he couldn't make up his mind—had been deferred. The farm had been mortgaged to pay for the heavy medical expenses of his parents, and Paul had to work the farm and take a part-time job in Terre Haute as a car mechanic. Nevertheless, despite the long hours of work, the lack of money, he had some time to express his innate exuberance. He would drop in occasionally at Fisher's Tavern, where some of the old gang still hung out. They'd go roaring off into the night on their motorcycles, their girls riding behind them, and finally end up in Indian Meadow, where there'd be a continuation of the beer blast and some fighting and lovemaking.

One of the girls wanted him to marry her, but he shied away from that. He wasn't in love with her, and he couldn't see himself spending the rest of his life with a woman with no intellectual interests whatever. Then she got pregnant, though fortunately not by him, and she departed to Chicago for a new life. Shortly thereafter, the gang began to drift apart.

He became alone and lonely again. But he liked to ride a horse wildly through the meadows or his chopper over the country roads. It was a good way to blow off steam.

Meantime, he had visits from an uncle who was a knifethrower, juggler, and circus acrobat. Paul learned much from him and became proficient at knife-throwing. When he felt gloomy he would go out into the backyard and practice throwing knives at a target. He knew he was working off his depression, guilt, and resentment at the lot cast for him by the fates with this harmless form of mayhem.

Five years went by swiftly. Suddenly, he was twenty-three. The farm still wasn't paid off. He couldn't see himself as a farmer the rest of his life, so he sold the farm at a very small profit. But now it was evident that his hopes of entering college and becoming an anthropologist—he'd decided by then his choice of career—would once more have to be set aside. The United States would be getting into the war in a year or two.

Loving horses so much, he enlisted in the cavalry. To his surprise and chagrin, he soon found himself driving a tank instead. Then there was a three-months' period in officers candidate training school. Though he wasn't a college graduate, he'd taken an examination which qualified him to enter it. Pearl Harbor tilted the nation into the conflict, and eventually he was with the Eighth Army and in combat.

One day, during a brief respite in the advance of Patton's forces, Paul had looked through the ruins of a small museum in a German town he'd helped clean out. He found a curious object, a crescent of some silvery metal. It was so hard that a hammer couldn't dent it or an acetylene torch melt it. He added it to his souvenirs.

Discharged from the Army, he returned to Terre Haute, where he didn't plan to stay long. A few days later, he was called into the office of his lawyer. To his surprise, Mr. Tubb handed him a check for ten thousand dollars.

"It's from your father," the lawyer said.

"My father? He didn't have a pot to pee in. You know that," Paul had said.

"Not the man who adopted you," Mr. Tubb had said. "It's from your real father."

"Where is he?" Paul had said. "I'll kill him."

"You wouldn't want to go where he is," fat old Tubb said. "He's six feet under. Buried in a church cemetery in Oregon. He got religion years ago and became a fire-eating brimstone-drinking halle-lujah-shouting revivalist. But the old bastard must've had some conscience left. He willed all his estate to you."

For a minute, Paul thought about tearing up the check. Then he told himself that old Park Finnegan owed him. Much more than this, true. But it was enough to enable him to get his Ph.D.

"I'll take it," he said. "Will the bank cash it if there's spit on it?"

"According to the law, the bank must accept it even if you crapped on it. Have a snort of bourbon, son."

Paul had entered the University of Indiana and rented a small but comfortable apartment off-campus. Paul told a friend of his, a newspaper reporter, about the mysterious crescent he'd found in Germany. The story was in the Bloomington paper and picked up by a syndicate which printed the story nationally. The university physicists, however, didn't seem interested in it.

Three days after the story appeared, a man calling himself Mr. Vannax appeared at Paul's apartment. He spoke English fluently but with a slight foreign accent. He asked to see the crescent; Paul obliged. Vannax became very excited, and he offered ten thousand dollars for the crescent. Paul became suspicious. He pumped the sum up to one hundred thousand dollars. Though Vannax was angry, he said he'd come back in twenty-four hours. Paul knew he had something, but he didn't know what.

"Make it three hundred thousand dollars, and it's yours," Paul said. "Since that's such a big sum, I'll give you an additional twenty-four hours to round up the money.

"But first, you have to tell me what this is all about."

Vannax became so troublesome that Paul forced him to leave. About two in the morning, he caught

Vannax in his apartment. His crescent was lying on the floor, and so was another.

Vannax had placed the two so that their ends met, forming a circle. He was about to step into the circle.

Paul forced him away by firing a pistol over his head. Vannax backed away, babbling, offering Paul half a million dollars for his crescent.

Following him across the room, Paul stepped into the circle. As he did so, Vannax cried out in panic for him to stay away from the crescents. Too late. The apartment and Vannax disappeared, and Paul found himself in another world.

He was standing in a circle formed by crescents just like those he'd left. But he was in a tremendous palace, as splendid as anything out of the Arabian Nights. This was, literally, on top of the new world to which Paul had been transported. It was the castle of the Lord who'd made the universe of the world of tiers.*

Paul figured out that the crescents formed some sort of "gate," a temporary opening through what he called the "fourth dimension" for lack of a better term. Vannax, he was to discover, was a Lord who'd been stranded in Earth's universe. He'd had one crescent but needed another to make a gate so he could get into a pocket universe.

Paul soon found himself not alone. Creatures called gworls came through a gate. They'd been sent by a Lord of another world to steal the Horn of Shambarimen. This was a device made ten millenia ago, when the pocket universes were just beginning to be created. Using it as a sort of sonic skeleton key, a person could unlock any gate.

*Maker of the Universes, Ace, 1977

Paul didn't know this, of course, but while hiding he saw a gworl open a gate to one of the tiers on this planet with the Horn. Paul pushed the gworl into a pool and dived through the gate with the Horn in his hand.

In the years that passed, as he traveled from level to level, the gworl trailing him, he became well acquainted with many sectors of this planet. On the Dracheland level he took the disguise of Baron Horst von Horstmann. But it was on the Amerind level that he was Kickaha, the name he preferred to be known by. Paul Janus Finnegan was someone in his distant past. Memories of Earth grew dim. He made no effort to go back to his home universe. This was a world he loved, though its dangers were many.

Then an Earthman, Robert Wolff, retired in Phoenix, Arizona, was inspecting the basement of a house for sale when the wall opened. He looked into another world and saw Kickaha surrounded by some gworl who'd finally caught up with him. Kickaha couldn't escape through the gate, but he did throw the Horn through so that the gworl couldn't have it. Wolff might have thought he was crazy or hallucinating, but the Horn was physical evidence that he wasn't.

Wolff was unhappy; he didn't like his Earthly situation. So he blew the Horn, pressing on the buttons to make notes, and he went through the gate. He found himself on the lowest level of the planet, which looked at first like Eden. As time passed, he became rejuvenated, eventually attaining the body he had had when he was twenty-five.

He also fell in love with a woman called Chryseis. Pursued by the gworl, they fled to the next level, meeting Kickaha on the way. Finally, after many adventures, Wolff reached the palace on top of the world, and he discovered that he was Jadawin, the Lord who'd made this little universe.

Later, he and Chryseis were precipitated into a series of adventures in which he met a number of the Lords. He also had to pass through a series of pocket worlds, all of which were traps designed to catch and kill other Lords.*

Meanwhile, Kickaha was engaged in a battle with the Bellers, creatures of artificial origin which could transfer their minds to the bodies of human beings. He also met and fell in love with Anana, a female Lord.**

While chasing the last survivor of the Bellers, Kickaha and Anana were gated through to Earth. Kickaha liked Earth even less than he remembered liking it. It was getting overcrowded and polluted. Most of the changes in the twenty years since he'd left it were, in his opinion, for the worse.

Red Orc, the secret Lord of the Two Earths, found out that he and Anana were in his domain. Urthona, another Lord, stranded on Earth for some time, also became Kickaha's deadly enemy. Kickaha found out that Wolff, or Jadawin, and Chryseis were prisoners of Red Orc. But they'd escaped through a gate to the lavalite world.*** Now Jadawin and Chryseis were roaming somewhere on its everchanging surface, if they were still alive. And he, Kickaha, had lost the Horn of Shambarimen and Anana. He'd never get out of this unpleasant nerve-stretching world unless he

*See *The Gates of Creation*, Philip José Farmer, Ace Books, 1977.
**See *A Private Cosmos*, Philip José Farmer, Ace Books, 1977.
***See *Behind the Walls of Terra*, Philip José Farmer, Ace Books, 1977.

somehow found a gate. Finding it wasn't going to do him any good unless he had some open-sesame to activate the gate, though. And he couldn't leave then unless he found Anana alive or dead.

For that matter, he couldn't leave until he found Wolff and Chryseis. Kickaha was a very bad enemy but a very good friend.

He had also always been extremely independent, self-assured, and adaptable. He'd lived for over twenty years without any roots, though he had been a warrior in the tribe of Hrowakas and thought of them as his people. But they were all gone now, slaughtered by the Bellers. He was in love with the beautiful Anana, who, though a Lord, had become more humane because of his influence.

For some time now he'd been wanting to quit this wandering always-changing-identities life. He wanted to establish himself and Anana some place, among a people who'd respect and maybe even love him. There he and Anana would settle down, perhaps adopt some children. Make a home and a family.

Then he'd lost her, and the only means he had to get out of this terrible place was also lost.

It was no wonder that Kickaha, the man sufficient unto himself, the ever-adaptable, the one who could find comfort even in hell, was now lonely.

This was why he suddenly decided to adopt the miserable wretches of the Thana as his people. If they'd have him.

There was also the desire not to be killed. But it was the wish to be part of a community that most strongly drove him.

CHAPTER NINE

IN HIS STILL limited Thana, he spoke to Wergenget of this. The chief didn't look surprised. He smiled, and Kickaha saw in this a pleasure.

"You could have escaped us; you still could," Wergenget said. "I saw the intent in your face briefly, though it closed almost immediately, like a fist.

"I'll tell you, Kickaha, why you have lived so long among us. Usually, we kill an enemy at once. Or, if he or she seems to be a brave person, we honor him or her with torture. But sometimes, if the person is not of a tribe familiar to us, that is, not an old enemy, we adopt him or her. Death strikes often, and we don't have enough children to replace the enemies. Our tribe has been getting smaller for some time now. Therefore, I will decree that you be adopted. You have shown courage, and all of us are grateful that you saved one of our precious children."

Kickaha began to feel a little less lonely.

Several hours later, the storm ceased. The tribe ventured again into the valley and retrieved the body of Lukyo. She was carried into camp with much wailing by the women. The rest of the day was spent in mourning while her body, washed clean, her hair combed, lay on top of a pile of skins. At "dusk" she was carried on a litter borne on the shoulders of four men to a place a mile from the camp. Here her corpse was placed on the ground, and the shaman, Oshullain, danced around her, chanting, waving a three-tined stick in ritualistic gestures. Then, singing a sad song, the whole tribe, except for some mounted guards, walked back to the camp.

Kickaha looked back once. Vultures were gliding toward her, and a band of long-legged baboons was racing to beat them to the feast. About a quarter of a mile away a pride of the maneless lions was trotting toward the body. Doubtless, they'd try to drive the baboons away, and there would be a hell of a ruckus. When the simians were in great numbers, they would harass the big cats until they forced them to abandon the meat.

On getting back to camp, the shaman recited a short poem he'd composed. It was in honor of Lukyo, and it was designed to keep her memory fresh among the tribe. It would be on everybody's lips for a while, then they'd cease singing it. And, after a while, she would be forgotten except in the memories of her child and parents. The child would forget, too, with the passage of time, and the parents would have other more pressing things to think about.

Only those who'd done some mighty deed still had songs sung about them. The others were forgotten.

The tribe stayed outside the lake country for another day. Wergenget explained that the storm season was almost always over by now. But it had been extended by the Lord, for some reason, and the tribe had made a fatal miscalculation.

"Or, perhaps," the chief said, "we have somehow offended the Lord, and he kept the lightning from going back to the heavens for a day."

Kickaha didn't comment on this. He was usually discreet about getting into arguments about religion. There was also no sense in offending the chief when it might make him change his mind about adopting him.

Wergenget called in the whole tribe and made a speech. Kickaha understood about half of the words, but the tones and the gestures were easily interpreted. Though the Lord had taken away Lukyo with one hand, he had given them Kickaha with the other. The tribe had offended the Lord. Or perhaps it was only Lukyo who had done this. In any event, the Lord still did not hate them altogether. By slaying Lukyo, the Lord had vented his wrath. To show the tribe that it was still in his favor, he'd sent Kickaha, a warrior, to the tribe. So it was up to the tribe to take him in.

The only one who objected to this was the youth, Toini, who had kicked Kickaha when he was bending over the channel. He suggested that perhaps the Lord wanted the tribe to sacrifice Kickaha to him. This, plus Lukyo's death, would satisfy the Lord.

Kickaha didn't know why Toini had it in for him. The only explanation was reactive chemistry. Some people just took an instant and unreasonable dislike to certain people in the first minute of acquaintanceship.

Toini's speech didn't exactly cause an uproar, but it did result in considerable loud argument. The chief was silent during the squabble, but apparently Toini had given him some doubts.

Kickaha, seeing that Toini might swing public opinion to his way of thinking, asked the chief if he could speak. Wergenget shouted for silence.

Kickaha, knowing that height gave a speaker a psychological advantage, mounted a *hikwu*.

"I wasn't going to say anything about a certain matter until after I was adopted by the tribe," he said. "But now I see that I must speak about it."

He paused and looked around as if he were about to reveal something which perhaps he shouldn't.

"But since there are some doubters of the Lord here, I believe that I should tell you about this now, instead of later."

They were hanging on his words now. His grave manner and the serious tones made them think that he knew something they should know about.

"Shortly before you came upon me," Kickaha said, "I met a man. He approached me, not walking, but gliding over the earth. He was in the air above the ground at twice my height."

Many gasped, and the eyes of all but Toini widened. His became narrow.

"The man was very tall, the tallest I've ever seen in my life. His skin was very white, and his hair was very red. And there was a glow about him as if he were wrapped in lightning. I waited for him, of course, since he was not the sort of person you would run away from or attack."

"When he was close to me he stopped, and then he sank to the ground. I am a brave man, people of the Thana, but he frightened me. Also, he awed me. So I sank to my knees and waited for him to speak or to act. I knew that he was no ordinary man, since what man can float through the air?"

"He walked up to me, and he said 'Do not be afraid, Kickaha. I will not harm you. You are favored in my eyes, Kickaha. Rise, Kickaha.' "

"I did as he ordered, but I was still scared. Who could this be, this stranger who soared like a bird and who knew my name, though I had never seen him before?"

Some in the crowd moaned, and others mur-

mured prayers. They knew who this stranger was. Or at least they thought they did.

"Then the stranger said, 'I am the Lord of this world, Kickaha.' "

"And I said, 'I thought so, Lord.' "

"And he said, 'Kickaha, the tribe of the Thana will soon be taking you prisoner. If they are kind to you, then they will gain favor in my eyes, since I have in mind something great for you to do. You will be my servant, Kickaha, a tool to effect a deed which I wish to be done.' "

" 'But if they try to kill or torture you, Kickaha, then I will know they are unworthy. And I will blast them all from the face of this earth. As a matter of fact, I will kill one of them as testimony that I am keeping an eye on them to demonstrate my power. If they are not convinced by this, then I will slay one more, the man who will try to keep you from being adopted by the tribe.' "

Toini had been grinning crookedly up to this moment. It was evident that he was going to denounce the captive as a prevaricator the moment he ceased speaking. But now he turned pale and began to shiver and his teeth started chattering. The others moved away from him.

The shaman was the only one who was looking doubtful. Perhaps, like Toini, he thought that Kickaha was lying to save his neck. If so, he was waiting for more developments before he gave his opinion.

"So I said, 'I am grateful, Lord, that you are honoring me by using me as your servant and tool. May I ask what task you have in mind for me?' "

"And he said, 'I will reveal that to you in the proper time, Kickaha. In the meantime, let us see how the Thana treat you. If they act as I wish, then they will go on to great glory and will prosper and thrive as no other tribe has ever done. But if they mistreat you, then I will destroy them, men, women, children, and beasts. Not even their bones will be left for the scavengers to gnaw.' "

"And then he turned and rose into the air and moved swiftly around the side of the mountain. A few minutes later, you showed up. You know what happened after that."

The effect of his lie was such that Kickaha almost began to believe in it. The tribe surged around him, fighting to touch him as if to draw to them the power he must have absorbed just by being close to the Lord. And they begged him to consider them as his friends. When the shaman, Oshullain, pushed through the mob and seized Kickaha's foot and held on as if he were absorbing the power, Kickaha knew he'd won.

Then the chief said loudly, "Kickaha! Did the Lord say anything about you leading us?"

Wergenget was concerned about his own position.

"No, the Lord did not. I believe that he just wanted me to take a place in the tribe as a warrior. If he had wanted me to be chief, he would have said so."

Wergenget looked relieved. He said, "And what about this wretch, Toini, who said that perhaps you should be sacrificed?"

"I think he knows he was very wrong," Kickaha said. "Isn't that right, Toini?"

Toini, on his knees, sobbing, said, "Forgive me, Kickaha! I didn't know what I was doing."

"I forgive you," Kickaha said. "And now, chief, what should we do?"

Wergenget said that since it was now obvious

that the Lord was no longer angry, it was safe to go into the sea-country. Kickaha hoped that the thunderstorm season was indeed over. If another storm occurred, then the tribe would know he'd been lying. Which meant it'd probably tear him apart.

For the moment, he was safe. But if anything went wrong, if it became evident that the tribe wasn't favored by the Lord, then he'd have to think up another lie fast. And if he wasn't believed, curtains for Kickaha.

Also, what if they should run into Urthona, the real Lord of this universe?

Well, he'd deal with that situation when it happened.

Anyway, if he saw any sign of Anana, any evidence that she was in the sea-land, he'd desert the Thana. It seemed to him that if she'd survived, she would have gone to this area. She'd know that if he'd lived, he would go there too.

Also, Urthona and McKay would go to where the land was relatively stable and where there'd be plenty of water. And where they were, the Horn would be.

He wondered if Orc had been caught in the flashflood which had carried him away. Or had he only been swept a little distance, enough to take him out of reach of Urthona and McKay.

Such thoughts occupied him until the caravan reached the sea. There they drank the water and let the moosoids satisfy their thirst. Some of the women and children gathered nuts and berries from the trees and bushes. The men waded around in the waves and jabbed their spears at the elusive fish. A few were successful.

Kickaha got a small portion of the raw fish, which he examined for worms before eating.

Then the Thana formed a caravan again and began the march over the white fine sand of the beach. They had come in on the right side of the channel, so they turned right. To cross the channel where it emerged from the sea, they would have had to swim a quarter mile of deep water. They passed many trees and animals felled by the lightning. The carcasses were covered with scaly amphibians, teeth flashing or dripping blood, tails flailing to sweep their competitors away, grunting and croaking, snapping. The birds were busy, too, and at many places the uproar was almost deafening.

When the tribe came across a lightning-blasted female elephant and calf, it drove away the multitude of sea, land, and air life and carved up the bodies for itself. Kickaha took some large cuts but put off eating them. When "night" came he piled branches and twigs to make a fire and he fashioned a bow-drill to start a fire. The others gathered around to watch. He worked away until the friction of the drill generated smoke, then added twigs and presently had a small fire going.

Kickaha borrowed a flint knife and cut off some smaller portions. After cooking a piece of leg and letting it cool off, he began eating as if he'd never stop. The chief and shaman accepted his invitation to dine. Though they were suspicious of cooked meat, their fears were overcome by the savory odors.

"Did the Lord teach you how to make that great heat?" Oshullain said.

"No. Where I come from all people know how

to make this . . . fire. We call it fire. In fact, your ancestors knew how to make fire. But you have forgotten how to do it.''

''I think that your ancestors, when first brought here, must have wandered for many generations before finding a sea-land. By then the scarcity of wood had made your people forget all about fire. Still, I can't understand why you didn't re-invent fire-making when you did find the sea-land, which has plenty of trees.''

He didn't say that the most primitive of humans had had fire. Wergenget might have thought he was insulting him. Which he was.

He thought about Urthona. What a sadist he was. Why, if he had to make a world and then place humans on it, had he set up such a barebones world? The potentiality of Homo sapiens could not be realized if it had almost nothing to work with. Also, the necessity to keep on the move, the never-ending changing of the earth, the limiting of human activity to constant travel while at the same time seeking for food and water, had reduced them almost to the level of beasts.

Despite which, they were human. They had a culture, one which was probably more complex than he thought. The riches of which he would learn when he became proficient in the language and knew both the customs of the tribe and its individual members.

He said, ''Fires are also good for keeping the big beasts away at night. I'll show you how to keep the fires fed.''

The chief was silent for a while. Besides his food, he was digesting a new concept. It seemed to be causing him some mental unease. After a while he said, ''Since you are the favored of the Lord, and this tribe is to be yours, you wouldn't bring in any evil to us? Would you?"

Kickaha assured him that he wouldn't—unless the Lord told him to do so.

The chief rose from his squatting position and bellowed orders. In a short while, there were a dozen large fires around the perimeter of the camp. Sleep, however, didn't come easily to it. Some big cats and dogs, their eyes shining in the reflected light, prowled around the edges of the camp. And the Thana weren't sure that the fires wouldn't attack them after they went to sleep. However, Kickaha set an example by closing his eyes, and his simulated snores soon told everybody that he, at least, wasn't worried. After awhile the children slept, and then their elders decided that it was safe.

In the morning Kickaha showed the women how to cook the meat. Half of the tribe took to the new way of preparing food with enthusiasm . . . The other decided to stick to eating the meat raw. But Kickaha was certain that before long the entire tribe, except for some dietary diehards, would have adapted.

He wasn't too sure, though, that he should have introduced cooking. When the storm season started again, the tribe would have to go outside the great valley again. Out there, because of the scarcity of firewood, it would have to eat its meat raw again. They might become discontented, then resentful and frustrated because they could do nothing to ease their discontent.

Prometheuses weren't always beneficial.

That was their problem. He didn't plan on being around when they left the valley.

In the "morning" the caravan went on the march again. Wergenget got them to moving faster than the day before. He was nervous because other tribes would be moving in, and he didn't want his to run into one on the beach. Near the end of the day, they reached their goal. This was a high hill about a half a mile inland from the shore. Though it changed shape somewhat, like the rest of the land in the valley, it did so very slowly. And it always remained a hill, though its form might alter.

On its top was a jumble of logs. This had been the walls of a stockade the last time the tribe had seen it. The mutations of the hill had lifted the circular wall a number of times and had broken the vines which held it. The tribe set to work digging new holes with sticks and flint-tipped shovels, then reset the logs. Vines were cut and dragged in and bound to hold the logs together. By the end of the third day, the wooden fortress was restored. Within the walls were a number of leantos in which the families could take shelter from the rains and sleep in.

During the rest of the season the tribe would stay in here at night. During the day, various parties would sally out to fish and hunt and gather nuts and berries. Lookouts would watch for dangerous beasts or the even more dangerous humans.

But, before they started to rest and get fat, it was necessary to initiate Kickaha into the tribe.

This was a great honor, but it was also rough on the initiate. After a long dance and recitation of numerous chants and songs, during which drums beat and bone flutes shrilled, the chief used a flint knife to cut the identification symbols of the tribe on Kickaha's chest. He was supposed to endure this without flinching or outcry.

Then he had to run a gauntlet of men, who struck at him with long sticks. Afterward, he had to wrestle the strongest man in the tribe, Mekdillong. He'd recovered entirely from his injuries by then, and he knew a hundred tricks Mekdillong was ignorant of. But he didn't want to humiliate him, so he allowed it to appear that Mekdillong was giving him a hard time. Finally, tired of the charade, he threw Mekdillong though the air with a cross-buttock. Poor Mek, the wind knocked out of him, writhed on the ground, sucking for air.

The worst part was having to prove his potency. Impotent men were driven from the tribe to wander until they died. In Kickaha's case, since he was not of the tribe born, he would have been killed. That is, he would have been if it wasn't so evident that the Lord had sent him. But, as the chief said, if the Lord had sent him, then he wouldn't fail.

Kickaha didn't try to argue with this logic. But he thought that the custom was wrong. No man could be blamed for being nervous if he knew he'd be exiled or slain if he failed. The very nervousness would cause impotency.

At least, the Thana did not demand, as did some tribes, that he prove himself publicly. He was allowed to go into a leanto surrounded by thick branches set upright into the ground. He chose the best-looking woman in the tribe for the test, and she came out several hours later looking tired but happy and announced that he'd more than passed the test.

Kickaha had some pangs of conscience about the incident, though he had enjoyed it very much. He didn't think that Anana would get angry about this trifling infidelity, especially since the circumstances were such that he couldn't avoid it.

However, it would be best not to mention this to her.

That is, if he ever found her.

That was the end of the trials. The chief and the shaman each chanted an initiation song, and then the whole tribe feasted until their bellies swelled and they could scarcely move.

Before going to sleep Wergenget told Kickaha that he'd have to pick a wife from the eligible females. There were five nubiles, all of whom had stated that they would be happy to have him as a mate. Theoretically, a woman could reject any suitor, but in practice it didn't work that way. Social pressure insisted that a woman marry as soon as she was of childbearing age. If any woman was lucky enough to have more than one suitor, then she had a choice. Otherwise, she had to take whoever asked her.

The same pressure was on a man. Even if he didn't care for any of the women available, he had to pick one. It was absolutely necessary that the tribe maintain its population.

Two of the five candidates for matrimony were pretty and well-figured. One of these was bold and brassy and looked as if she were brimming over with the juices of passion. So, if he had to take unto himself a wife, he'd choose her. It was possible she'd turn him down, but, according to the chief, all five were panting for him.

Given his pick, he'd have wived the woman he'd proved his manhood on. But she was only borrowed for the occasion, as was the custom, and her husband would try to kill Kickaha if he followed up with a repeat performance.

As it was, the woman, Shima, could make trouble. She'd told Kickaha she'd like to get together with him again. There wasn't going to be much opportunity for that, since she couldn't disappear into the woods by herself without half the tribe knowing it.

Ah, well, he'd deal with the various situations as they came along.

Kickaha looked around. Except for the sentinel on top of a platform on top of a high pole in the middle of the fort, and another stationed near the apex of the giant tree, the tribe was snoring. He could open the gate and get away and be long gone before the guards could rouse the others. In their present stuffed condition, they could never catch him.

At the same time he wanted to get out and look for Anana, he felt a counterdesire to stay with these people, miserable and wretched as they were. His moment of weakness, of longing for a home of some sort, still had him in its grip. Some moment! It could go on for years.

Logically, it was just as likely that if he stayed here, she'd be coming along. If he set out on a search, he could go in the wrong direction and have to travel the circuit of this body of water. It could be as big as Lake Michigan or the Mediterranean for all he knew. And Anana could be going in the same direction as he but always behind him. If she were alive . . .

One of these days, he'd have to leave. Meanwhile, he'd do some scouting around. He might run across some clues in this neighborhood.

He yawned and headed for the leanto assigned him by the chief. Just as he got to it, he heard giggles. Turning, he saw Shila and Gween, his two top choices for wife. Their normally flat bellies were bulging, but they hadn't eaten so much they couldn't see straight. And they'd been pretending to be asleep.

Shila, smiling, said, "Gween and I know you're going to marry one of us."

He smiled and said, "How'd you know?"

"We're the most desirable. So, we thought maybe . . . " she giggled again . . . "we'd give you a chance to see whom you like most. There'll never be another chance to find out."

"You must be joking," he said. "I've had a long hard day. The rites, the hours with Shima, the feast . . ."

"Oh, we think you have it in you. You must be a great *wiru*. Anyway, it can't hurt to try, can it?"

"I don't see how it could," Kickaha said, and he took the hand of each. "My place is rather exposed. Where shall we go?"

He didn't know how long he'd been sleeping when he was wakened by a loud hubbub. He rose on one elbow and looked around. Both girls were still sleeping. He crawled out and removed the brush in front of the leanto and stood up. Everybody was running around shouting or sitting up and rubbing their eyes and asking what was going on. The man on top of the platform was yelling something and pointing out toward the sea. The sentinel in the tree was shouting.

Wergenget, his eyes still heavy with sleep, stumbled up to Kickaha. "What's Opwel saying?"

Kickaha said the sentinel's voice was being drowned out. Wergenget began yelling for everybody to shut up, and in a minute he'd subdued them. Opwel, able to make himself understood, relayed the message of the man in the tree.

"Two men and a woman ran by on the beach. And then, a minute later, warriors of the tribe of Thans came along after them. They seemed to be chasing the two men and the woman."

Kickaha hollered. "Did the woman have long hair as black as the wing of a crow?"

"Yes!"

"And was the hair of one man yellow and the other red?"

"Onil says one man had yellow hair. The other was black-skinned and his hair was the curliest he'd ever seen. Onil said the man was black all over."

Kickaha groaned, and said, "Anana! And Urthona and McKay!"

He ran for the gate, shouting, "Anana!"

Wergenget yelled an order, and two men seized Kickaha. The chief huffed and puffed up to him, and, panting, said, "Are you crazy! You can't go out there alone! The Thans will kill you!"

"Let me loose!" Kickaha said. "That's my woman out there! I'm going to help her!"

"Don't be stupid," Wergenget said. "You wouldn't have a chance."

"Are you just going to sit here and let her be run down?" Kickaha yelled.

Wergenget turned and shouted at Opwel. He yelled at Olin, who replied. Opwel relayed the message.

"Onil says he counted twenty."

The chief rubbed his hands and smiled. "Good. We outnumber them." He began giving orders then. The men grabbed their weapons, saddled the moosoids, and mounted. Kickaha got on his own, and the moment the gate was open he urged it out through the opening. After him came Wergenget and the rest of the warriors.

CHAPTER TEN

AFTER BEING KNOCKED back into the channel, Anana had begun scrambling back up. The water by then was to her breasts, but she clawed back up the side, grabbing the grass, pulling it out, grabbing more handfuls.

Above her were yells, and then something struck her head. It didn't hurt her much, didn't even cause her to lose her grip. She looked down to see what had hit her. The case containing the Horn of Shambarimen.

She looked toward the black wall of water rushing toward her. It would hit within ten seconds. Perhaps less. But she couldn't let the Horn be lost. Without it their chances of ever getting out of this wretched world would be slight indeed.

She let herself slide back into the water and then swam after it. It floated ahead of her, carried by the current of the stream rising ahead of the flash flood. A few strokes got her to it. Her hand closed around the handle, and she stroked with one hand to the bank. The level had risen above her head now, but she did not have to stand up. She seized a tuftful of grass, shifted the handle from hand to teeth, and then began climbing again.

By then the ground was shaking with the weight of the immense body of water racing toward her. There was no time to look at it, however. Again she pulled herself up the wet slippery bank, holding her head high so the case wouldn't interfere with her arms.

But she did catch out of the corner of her eye a falling body. By then the roar of the advancing water was too loud for her to hear the splash the body made. Who had fallen? Kickaha? That was the only one she cared about.

The next moment the rumble and the roar were upon her. She was just about to shove the case over the edge of the bank and draw herself up after it when the mass struck. Despite her furious last-second attempt to reach safety, the surface waters caught her legs. And she was carried, crying out desperately, into the flood.

But she managed to hold onto the Horn. And though she was hurled swiftly along, she was not in the forefront of the water. She went under several times but succeeded in getting back to the surface. Perhaps the bouyancy of the case enabled her to keep to the surface.

In any event, something, maybe a current hurled upward by an obstruction on the bottom, sent her sprawling onto the edge of the bank. For a minute she thought she'd slip back, but she writhed ahead and presently her legs were out of reach of the current.

She released the case and rolled over and got shakily to her feet.

About a half a mile behind her were three figures. Urthona. Orc. McKay.

Kickaha was missing. So, it would have been he that had fallen over into the stream. It also would have been he who'd dropped the Horn into it. She guessed that he must have threatened to throw it in if the others didn't allow her to get out of the channel again.

Then they'd rushed him, and he'd released it and gone into the stream after it. Either on his own volition, which didn't seem likely, or he had been pushed into it.

She could see no sign of him.

He was under the surface somewhere, either drowned or fighting.

She found it difficult to believe that he was dead. He'd come through so much, fought so hard, been so wily. He was of the stuff of survival.

Still, all men and women must die sometime.

No, she wouldn't allow herself to give up hope for him. But even if he were still struggling, he would by now have been swept out of sight.

The only thing to do was to follow the channel to its end and hope that she'd run across him somewhere along it.

Red Orc was by now running away. He was going at full speed in the opposite direction. McKay had run after him but had stopped. Evidently, he either couldn't catch him or Urthona had called him back. Whatever had happened, the two were now trotting toward her. She had the Horn, and they wanted it.

She started trotting, too. After a while she was panting, but she kept on and her second wind came. If she stayed by the channel, she couldn't lose them. They'd keep going, though they had no chance with her headstart of catching her. Not until utter fatigue forced her to sleep. If they somehow could keep on going, they'd find her.

She believed that she had as much endurance as they. They'd have to lie down and rest, too, perhaps before she did. But if they pushed themselves, rose earlier from sleep, then they might come across her while she slept.

As long as she followed the channel, she couldn't lose them, ever. But across the plains, in the mountains, she might. Then she could cut back to the channel.

There was a chance, also, that she could get lost, especially when the landmarks kept changing. She'd have to risk that.

She turned and started across the plain. Now they would angle across, reducing the lead she had. Too bad. Though she felt the urge to break into a run, she resisted it. As long as she could keep ahead, out of range of the beamer, she'd be all right.

It was difficult to estimate distances in this air, which was so clear because of the almost-total lack of dust and of this light. She thought the nearest of the mountains was about five miles away. Even with the speed with which landscape changed around here, it would still be a respectably sized mountain by the time she got there.

Between her and her goal were groves of the ambulatory trees. None were so large that she couldn't go around them. There were also herds of grazing antelopes and gazelles. A herd of elephants was about a half a mile away, trotting toward the nearest grove. To her right, in the other direction, some of the giant moosoids were nearing another group of plants. She caught a glimpse of two lions a quarter of a mile away. They were using a grove as cover while sneaking up on some antelopes.

Far in the distance was the tiny figure of a moa. It didn't seem to be chasing anything, but her line of flight would lead her near to it. She changed it, heading for the other end of the base of the mountain.

She looked to her left. The two men were running now. Evidently they hoped to put on a burst of speed and make her run until she dropped.

She stepped up her pace but she did not sprint. She could maintain this pace for quite a while. Seldom in her many thousands of years of life had she gotten out of shape. She had developed a wind and an endurance that would have surprised an Olympic marathoner. Whatever her physical potential was, she had realized it to the full. Now she'd find out what its limits were.

One mile. Two miles. She was sweating, but while she wasn't exactly breathing easy, she knew she had a lot of reserve wind. Her legs weren't leaden yet. She felt that she could reach the mountain and still have plenty of strength left. Her uncle was a strong man, but he was heavier, and he'd probably indulged himself on Earth. Any fat he'd had had been melted by their ordeal here, where food hadn't been plentiful. But she doubted that he'd kept himself in tiptop condition on Earth.

The black man was powerfully built, but he wasn't the long-distance runner type. In fact, sparing a look back, she could see that he'd dropped behind Urthona. Not that her uncle had gained any on her.

The case and its contents, however, did weigh about four pounds. Needing every advantage she could get, she decided to get rid of some of it. She slowed down while she undid the clasps, removed the Horn, and dropped the case. Now, carrying the instrument in one hand, she increased her speed. In ten minutes, Urthona had lost fifty yards. McKay was even further behind his boss now.

Another mile. Now she was wishing she could abandon the throwing axe and the knife. But that was out. She'd need both weapons when it came to a showdown. Not to mention that even if she got away from them, she had to consider the predators. A knife and an axe weren't much against a lion, but they could wound, perhaps discourage it.

Another half a mile. She looked back. Urthona was half a mile away. McKay was behind Urthona by a quarter of a mile. Both had slowed considerably. They were trotting steadily, but they didn't have a chance of catching her. However, as long as they kept her in sight, they wouldn't stop.

The lions had disappeared around the other side of the trees. These were moving slowly along, headed for the channel. The wind was blowing toward them, carrying molecules of water to their sensors. When they got to the channel they would draw up along it in a row and extend their tentacles into the water to suck it up.

The antelopes and gazelles stopped eating as she approached, watched her for a moment, their heads up, black eyes bright, then bounded away as one. But they only moved to what they considered a safe distance and resumed grazing.

Anana was in the center of antelopes, with tall straight horns which abruptly curved at the tips, when they stampeded. She stopped and then crouched as big black-and-brown-checkered bodies leaped over her or thundered by. She was sure that she hadn't caused the panic. The antelopes had regarded her as not dangerous but something it was better not to let get too close.

Then she heard a roar, and she saw a flash of brownish-yellow after a half-grown antelope.

One lion had shot out of the trees after the young beast. The other was racing along parallel with its mate. It was somewhat smaller and faster. As the male cut off to one side, the female bent its path slightly inward. The prey had turned to its left to get away from the big male, then saw the other cat angling toward it. It turned away from the new peril and so lost some ground.

The male roared and frightened the antelope into changing its direction of flight again. The female cut in toward it; the poor beast turned toward the male. Anana expected that the chase would not last long. Either the cats would get their kill in the next few seconds or their endurance would peter out and the antelope would race away. If the quarry had enough sense just to run in a straight line, it would elude its pursuers. But it didn't. It kept zigzagging, losing ground each time, and then the female was on it. There was a flurry of kicking legs, and the creature was dead, its neck broken.

The male, roaring, trotted up, his sides heaving, saliva dripping from his fangs, his eyes a bright green. The female growled at him but backed off until he had disemboweled the carcass.

Then she settled down on the other side of the body, and they began tearing off chunks of meat. The herd had stopped running by then. Indifferent to the fate of the young beast, knowing that there was no more danger for the present, they resumed their feeding.

Anana was only forty feet away from the lions, but she kept on going. The cats wouldn't be interested in her unless she got too close, and she had no intention of doing that.

The trees were a species she'd not seen before. About twelve feet high, they had bark which was covered with spiral white and red streaks like a barber pole. The branches were short and thick and sprouting broad heart-shaped green leaves.

Each plant had only four "eyes," round, unblinking, multifaceted, green as emeralds. They also had tentacles. But they must not be dangerous. The lions had walked through them unharmed.

Or was there some sort of special arrangement between the cats and the trees? Had Urthona implanted in them an instinct-mechanism which made them ignore the big cats but not people? It would be like her uncle to do this. He'd be amused at seeing the nomads decide that it was safe to venture among the trees because they'd seen other animals do so. And then, stepping inside the moving forest, suddenly find themselves attacked.

For a moment she thought about taking a chance. If she plunged into that mobile forest, she could play hide-and-seek with her hunters. But that would be too risky, and she would really gain nothing by it.

She looked behind her. The two men had gained a little on her. She stepped up the pace of her trotting. When she'd passed the last of the trees she turned to her left and went past their backs. Maybe Urthona and McKay would try to go through the trees.

No, they wouldn't. It was doubtful that her uncle would remember just what their nature was. He might think that she had taken refuge in them. So, the two would have to separate to make sure. McKay would go along one side and Urthona on the other. They'd look down the rows to make sure she wasn't there, and then would meet at the rear.

By then, keeping the trees between her and the others, moving in a straight line toward the mountain from the plants, she'd be out of their sight for a while. And they would lose more ground.

She turned and headed toward her goal.

But she slowed. A half a mile away, coming toward her, was a pack of baboons. There were twenty, the males acting as outriders, the females in the middle, some with babies clinging to their backs. Was she their prey? Or had they been attracted by the roaring of the lion and were racing to the kill?

She shifted the Horn to her left hand and pulled the axe from her belt. Her path and theirs would intersect if she kept on going. She stopped and waited. They continued on in the same direction, silently, their broad, short-digited paws striking the ground in unison as if they were trained soldiers on the march. Their long legs moved them swiftly, though they could not match the hoofed plains beasts for speed. They would pick out their prey, a young calf or an injured adult. They would spread out and form a circle. The leader would rush at the quarry, and the frenzied bounding and barking of the others would stampede the herd. The pack would dart in and out of the running leaping antelopes, under their very hooves, often forced to jump sideways to avoid being trampled. But their general direction was toward their intended kill, and the circle would draw tighter. Suddenly, the running calf or limping adult would find itself surrounded. Several of the heavy powerful male simians would leap upon it and bring it to the ground. The others, excepting the mothers carrying infants, would close in.

When within twenty feet of her, the leader barked, and the pack slowed down. Had their chief decided that she would be less trouble than running off two hungry lions?

No. They were still moving, heading toward the corner of the square formed by the marching plants.

She waited until the last of the pack was gone by, then resumed trotting.

There was a sudden commotion behind her. She slowed again and turned to one side so she could see what was going on. She didn't like what she saw. Urthona and McKay had burst out of the woods. They'd not circled the plants, as she'd expected, but had instead gone in a straight line through them. So, Urthona had remembered that these were no danger to human beings. Hoping to catch her by surprise, they'd probably run at top speed.

They'd succeeded. However, they were themselves surprised. They'd come out of the trees and run headlong into the baboons. The chief simian was hurling himself toward Urthona, and three big males were loping toward McKay.

Her uncle had no choice but to use his beamer. Its ray sliced the leader from top to bottom. The two halves, smoking, skidded to a halt several feet from him. If he'd been just a little slower reacting, he'd have found the baboon's teeth in his throat.

Too bad, thought Anana.

CHAPTER ELEVEN

NOW HER UNCLE WAS being forced to discharge even more of the precious energy. McKay would be downed within a few seconds. The black was crouched, ready to fight, but he was also screaming at Urthona to shoot. Her uncle hesitated a second or two—he hated to use the beamer because he was saving its charges for his niece—but he did not want to be left alone to continue the chase. Three males tumbled over and over until they came to rest—or their halves did—just at McKay's feet. Under his dark pigment, McKay was gray.

The other baboons halted and began jumping up and down and screaming. They were only angry and frustrated. They wouldn't attack any more.

She turned and began running again. A few minutes later, she looked back. Her pursuers were moving toward her slowly. They didn't dare run with their back to the simians. These were following them at a respectable distance, waiting for a chance to rush them. Urthona was shouting and waving the beamer at them, hoping to scare them off. Every few seconds, he would stop and turn to face them. The baboons would withdraw, snarling, barking, but they wouldn't stop trailing them.

Anana grinned. She would get a big lead on the two men.

When she reached the foot of the mountain, which rose abruptly from the plain, she stopped to rest. By then the baboons had given up. Another one of the pack lay dead, and this loss had made up their minds for them. Now some were gathered around the latest casualty and tearing him apart. The others were racing to see who could get to the remaining carcasses first. A half a mile away, a giant scimitar-beaked "moa" was speeding toward the commotion. It would attempt to scare the simians from a body. Above were vultures hoping to get a share of the meat.

The slope here was a little more than a forty-five degree angle to the horizontal. Here and there were swellings, like great gas bubbles pushing out the surface of the peak. She'd have to go around these. She began climbing, leaning forward slightly. There were no trees or bushes for her to hide among. She'd have to keep going until she got to the top. From there she might be able to spot some kind of cover. It was doubtful that she would. But if she went down the other side swiftly enough, she might be able to get around the base of another mountain. And then her chasers wouldn't know where she was.

The peak was perhaps a thousand and a half feet above the plain. By the time she got there, she was breathing very heavily. Her legs felt as if they were thickly coated with cement. She was shaking with fatigue; her lungs seemed to burn. The two men would be in the same, if not worse, condition.

When she'd started ascending, the top of the peak had been as sharply pointed as the tip of an ice cream cone. Now it had slumped and become a plateau about sixty feet in diameter. The ground felt hot, indicating an increase in rate of shape-mutation.

Urthona and McKay were almost a quarter of the way up the slope. They were sitting down, facing away from her. Just above them the surface was swelling so rapidly that they would soon be hidden from her sight. If the protuberance spread out, they'd have to go around it. Which meant they'd be slowed down even more.

Her view of the plain was considerably broader now. She looked along the channel, hoping to see a tiny figure that would be Kickaha. There was none.

Even from her height, she could not see the end of the channel. About twenty miles beyond the point at which she'd left it, young mountains had grown to cut off her view. There was no telling how far the channel extended.

Where was Red Orc? In all the excitement, she had forgotten about him.

Wherever he was, he wasn't visible to her.

She scanned the area beyond her perch. There were mountains beyond mountains. But between them were, as of now, passes, and here and there were ridges connecting them. On one of the ridges was a band of green contrasting with the rusty grass. It moved slowly but not so much that she didn't know the green was an army of migrating trees. It looked as if it were five miles away.

Scattered along the slopes and in the valleys were dark splotches. These would be composed of antelopes and other large herbivores. Though basically plains creatures, they adapted readily to the mountains. They could climb like goats when the occasion demanded.

Having attained the top, should she wait a while and see what her pursuers would do? Climbing after her was very exhausting. They might think she'd try to double back on them, come down one side of the mountain, around the corner where they couldn't see her. That wasn't a bad idea.

If the two should split up, each going around the

mountain to meet in the middle, then she'd just go
straight back down as soon as they got out of sight.

However, if they didn't take action soon, she'd
have to do so. The plateau was growing outward
and downward. Sinking rather. If she stayed here,
she might find herself on the plain again.

No. that process would take at least a day.
Perhaps two. And her uncle and his thug would be
doing something in the meantime.

She began to get hungry and thirsty. When she'd
started for the mountain, she'd hoped to find water
on its other side. From what she could see, she was
going to stay thirsty unless she went back to the
channel. Or unless those wisps of clouds became
thick black rainclouds.

She waited and watched. The edge of the
plateau on which she sat slowly extended outwards. Finally, she knew she had to get off of it.
In an hour or so it would begin crumbling along
its rim. The apex of the cone was becoming a
pancake. She'd have a hard time getting off it
without being precipitated down the slope with a
piece of it.

There was an advantage. The two men below
would have to dodge falling masses. There might
be so many they'd be forced to retreat to the plain.
If she were lucky, they might even be struck by a
hurtling bounding clump.

She went to the other side—the diameter of the
circle was now a hundred feet. After dropping the
Horn and the axe, she let herself down cautiously.
Her feet dangled for a moment, and she let loose.
That was the only way to get down, even though
she had to fall thirty feet. She struck the slope,
which was still at a forty-five-degree angle, and
slid down for a long way. The grass burned her

hands as she grabbed handholds; the friction against the seat of her pants and the legs didn't make the cloth smoke. But she was sure that if she hadn't succeeded in stopping when she did, the fabric would have been hot enough to burst into flames. At least, she felt that it would.

After retrieving the Horn and axe, she walked down the slope, leaning back now. Occasionally her shoes would slip on the grass, and she'd sit down hard and slide for a few feet before she was able to brake to a stop. Once a mass of the dark greasy earth, grass blades sticking from it, thumped by her. If it had hit her, it would have crushed her.

Near the bottom she had to hurry up her descent. More great masses were rolling down the slope. One missed her only because it struck a swelling and leaped into the air over her head.

Reaching the base, she ran across the valley until she was sure she was beyond the place where the masses would roll. By then "night" had come. She was so thirsty she thought she'd die if she didn't get water in the next half hour. She was also very tired.

There was nothing else to do but to turn back. She had to have water. Fortunately, in this light, she couldn't be seen by anybody a thousand feet from her. Maybe five hundred. So she could sneak back to the channel without being detected. It was true that the two men might have figured out she'd try it and be waiting on the other side of the mountain. But she'd force herself to take an indirect route to the channel.

She headed along the valley, skirting the foot of the mountain beyond that which she'd climbed. There were housesized masses here also, these having fallen off the second mountain, too. Passing one, she scared something out which had been hiding under an overhang. She shrieked. Then, in swift reaction, she snatched out her axe and threw it at the long low scuttler.

The axehead struck it, rolling it over and over. It got to its short bowed legs, and, hissing, ran off. The blow had hurt it, though; it didn't move as quickly as before. She ran to her axe, picked it up, set herself, and hurled it again. This time the weapon broke the thing's back.

She snatched out her knife, ran to the creature—a lizardlike reptile two feet long—and she cut its throat. While it bled to death she held it up by its tail and drank the precious fluid pouring from it. It ran over her chin and throat and breasts, but she got most of it.

She skinned it and cut off portions and ate the still quivering meat. She felt much stronger afterward. Though still thirsty, she felt she could endure it. And she was in better shape than the two men—unless they had also managed to kill something.

As she headed toward the plain, she was enshrouded in deeper darkness. Rainclouds had come swiftly with a cooling wind. Before she had gone ten paces onto the flatland, she was deluged. The only illumination was lightning, which struck again and again around her. For a moment she thought about retreating. But she was always one to take a chance if the situation demanded it. She walked steadily onward, blind between the bolts, deaf because of the thunder. Now and then she looked behind her. She could see only animals running madly, attempting to get away from the deadly strokes but with no place to hide.

By the time she'd reached the channel, she was
knee-deep in water. This increased the danger of
being electrocuted, since a bolt did not now have
to hit her directly. There was no turning back.

The side of the channel nearer her had lowered
a few inches. The stream, flooding with the tor-
rential downpour, was gushing water onto the
plain. Four-legged fish and some creatures with
tentacles—not large—were sliding down the
slope. She speared two of the smaller amphibians
with her knife and skinned and ate one. After cutting the other's head off and gutting it, she carried
it by its tail. It could provide breakfast or lunch or
both.

By then the storm was over, and within twenty
minutes the clouds had rushed off. Ankle-deep in
water, she stood on the ridge and pondered.
Should she walk toward the other end of the
channel and look for Kickaha? Or should she go
toward the sea?

For all she knew, the channel extended a
hundred miles or more. While she was searching
for her man, the channel might close up. Or it
might broaden out into a lake. Kickaha could be
dead, injured, or alive and healthy. If hurt, he
might need help. If he was dead, she might find
his bones and thus satisfy herself about his fate.

On the other hand, if she went to the mountain
pass to the sea, she could wait there, and if he
was able he'd be along after awhile.

Also, her uncle and the black man would surely
go to the sea. In which case, she might be able to
ambush them and get the beamer.

While standing in water and indecision, she had
her mind made up for her. Out of the duskiness
two figures emerged. They were too distant to be

identified, but they were human. They had to be her pursuers.

Also, they were on the wrong side if she wanted to look for Kickaha. Her only path of flight, unless she ran for the mountains again, was toward the sea.

She set out trotting, the water splashing up to her knees. Occasionally, she looked back. The vague figures were drawing no closer, but they weren't losing ground either.

Time, unmeasured except by an increasing weariness, passed. She came to the channel, which had by now risen to its former height. She dived in, swam to the other side, and climbed up the bank. Standing there, she could hear Urthona and McKay swimming towards her. It would seem that she'd never been able to get far enough ahead of them to lose herself in the darkness.

She turned and went on towards the mountains. Now she was wolf-trotting, trotting for a hundred paces, then walking a hundred. The counting of paces helped the time to go by and took her mind from her fatigue. The men behind her must be doing the same thing, unable to summon a burst of speed to catch up with her.

The plain, now drained of water, moved squishily under her. She took a passage between the two mountains and emerged into another plain. After a mile of this, she found another waterway barring her path. Perhaps, at this time, many fissures opened from the sea to the area beyond the ringing mountains to form many channels. Anyone high enough above ground might see the territory as a sort of millipus, the sea and its circling mountains as the body, the waterways as tentacles.

This channel was only about three hundred yards across, but she was too tired to swim. Floating on her back, she propelled herself backwards with an occasional hand-stroke or up-and-down movement of legs.

When she reached the opposite side, she found that the water next to the bank came only to her waist. While standing there and regaining her wind, she stared into the darkness. She could neither see nor hear her pursuers. Had she finally lost them? If she had, she'd wait a while, then return to the first channel.

An estimated five minutes later, she heard two men gasping. She slid down until the water was just below her nose. Now she could distinguish them, two darker darknesses in the night. Their voices came clearly across the water to her.

Her uncle, between wheezes, said, "Do you think we got away from them?"

"Them?" she thought.

"Not so loud," McKay said, and she could no longer hear them.

They stood on the bank for a few minutes, apparently conferring. Then a man, not one of them, shouted. Thudding noises came from somewhere, and suddenly giant figures loomed behind the two. Her uncle and McKay didn't move for a moment. In the meantime, the first of the "day" bands paled in the sky. McKay, speaking loudly, said, "Let's swim for it!"

"No!" Urthona said. "I'm tired of running. I'll use the beamer!"

The sky became quickly brighter. The two men and the figures behind them were silhouetted more clearly, but she thought that she still couldn't be seen. She crouched, half of her head sticking out of the water, one hand hanging on to the grass of the bank, the other holding the Horn. She could see that newcomers were not giants but men riding moosoids. They held long spears.

Urthona's voice, his words indistinguishable, came to her. He was shouting some sort of defiance. The riders split, some disappearing below the edge of the bank. Evidently these were going around to cut off the flight of the two. The others halted along the channel in Indian file.

Urthona aimed the beamer, and the two beasts nearest him fell to the ground, their legs cut off. One of the riders fell into the channel. The other rolled out of sight.

There were yells. The beasts and their mounts behind the stricken two disappeared down the ridge. Suddenly, two came into sight on the other side. Their spears were leveled at Urthona, and they were screaming in a tongue unknown to Anana.

One of the riders, somewhat in the lead of the others, fell off, his head bouncing into the channel, his body on the edge, blood jetting from the neck. The other's beast fell, precipitating his mount over his head. McKay slammed the edge of a hand against his neck and picked up the man's spear.

Urthona gave a yell of despair, threw the beamer down, and retrieved the spear of the be-headed warrior.

The beamer's battery was exhausted. It was two against eight now; the outcome, in no doubt.

Four riders came up onto the bank. McKay and Urthona thrust their spears into the beasts and then were knocked backward into the channel by the wounded beasts. The savages dismounted and went into the water after their victims. The remaining four rode up and shouted encouragement.

Anana had to admire the fight her uncle and his aide put up. But they were eventually slugged into unconsciousness and hauled up onto the bank. When they recovered, their hands were tied behind them and they were urged ahead of the riders with heavy blows on their backs and shoulders from spear butts.

A moment later, the first of a long caravan emerged from the darkness. Presently, the whole cavalcade was in sight. Some of the men dismounted to tie the dead beasts and dead men to moosoids. These were dragged behind the beasts while their owners walked. Evidently the carcasses were to be food. And for all she knew, so were the corpses. Urthona had said that some of the nomadic tribes were cannibals.

As her uncle and McKay were being driven past the point just opposite her, she felt something slimy grab her ankle. She repressed a cry. But, when sharp teeth ripped her ankle, she had to take action. She lowered her head below the surface, bent over, withdrew her knife, and drove it several times into a soft body. The tentacle withdrew, and the teeth quit biting. But the thing was back in a moment, attacking her other leg.

Though she didn't want to, she had to drop the Horn and the amphibian to free her other hand. She felt along the tentacle, found where it joined the body, and sawed away with the knife. Suddenly, the thing was gone, but both her legs felt as if they had been torn open. Also, she had to breathe. She came up out of the water as slowly as possible, stopping when her nose was just above the surface. A body broke the water a few feet from her, dark blood welling out.

She went under again, groped around, found the Horn, and came back up. The savages had noticed the wounded creature by then. And they saw her head emerge, of course. They began yelling and pointing. Presently, several cast their spears at her. These fell short of their mark. But they weren't going to let her escape. Four men slid down the bank and began swimming toward her.

She threw the Horn upon the bank and began clawing her way up it. Her pursuers couldn't chase her on their beasts on this side. The big creatures could never get up the bank. She could get a head start on the men. But when she rolled over on the top of the bank, she saw that her wounds were deeper than she had thought. Blood was welling out over her feet. It was impossible to run any distance with those wounds.

Still . . . she put her axe in one hand and her knife in the other. The first man to come up fell back with a split skull. The second slid back with two fingers chopped off. The others decided that it was best to retreat. They went back into the water and split into two groups, each swimming a hundred yards in opposite directions. They would come up at the same time, and she could only attack one. That one would dive back into the water while the other came at her on the ground.

By then ten others were swimming across. Some of them were several hundred yards downstream; others, the same distance upstream. She had no chance to get beyond these. Flight to the mountains a mile away on this side of the channel was her only chance. But she'd be caught because of her steady loss of blood.

She shrugged, slipped off her ragged shirt, tore it into strips, and bound them around the wounds. She hoped the tentacled things hadn't injected poison into her.

The Horn and the axe couldn't be hidden. The knife went into a pocket on the inside of the right leg of her levis. She'd sewed the pocket there shortly after she'd entered the gateway into Earth. That was a little more than a month ago, but it seemed like a year.

Then she sat, her arms folded, waiting.

CHAPTER TWELVE

HER CAPTORS WERE a short, slim, dark people who looked as if they were of Mediterranean stock. Their language, however, did not seem to her to be related to any she knew. Perhaps their ancestors had spoken one of the many tongues that had died out after the Indo-Europeans and Semites had invaded the Middle Sea area.

They numbered a hundred: thirty-two men, thirty-eight women, and twenty children. The moosoids were one hundred and twenty.

Their chief clothing was a rawhide kilt, though some of the men's were of feathers. All the warriors wore thin bones stuck through their septums, and many bore dried human hands suspended from a cord around their necks. Dried human heads adorned the saddles.

Anana was brought back to the other side of the channel and flung half-drowned upon the ground. The women attacked her at once. A few struck or kicked her, but most were trying to get her jeans and boots. Within a minute, she was left lying on the ground, bleeding, bruised, stunned, and naked.

The man whose two fingers she'd severed staggered up, holding his hand, pain twisting his face. He harangued the chief for a long while. The chief evidently told him to forget it, and the man went off.

Urthona and McKay were sitting slumped on the ground, looking even more thrubbed than she.

The chief had appropriated her axe and the Horn. The woman who'd beat off the others in order to keep the jeans had managed to get them on. So far, she hadn't paid any attention to the knife inside the leg. Anana hoped that she would not investigate the heavy lump, but there didn't seem much chance of that, human curiosity being what it was.

There was a long conference with many speeches from both men and women. Finally, the chief spoke a few words. The dead men were carried off in travois to a point a mile away. The entire tribe, except for the few guards for the prisoners, followed the dead. After a half an hour of much wailing and weeping, punctuated by the shaman's leaping-abouts, chanting, and rattling of a gourd containing pebbles or seeds, the tribe returned to the channel.

If these people were cannibals, they didn't eat their own dead.

A woman, probably a wife of one of the deceased, rushed at Anana. Her fingers were out and hooked, ready to tear into the captive's face. Anana lay on her back and kicked the woman in the stomach. The whole tribe laughed, apparently enjoying the screams and writhings of the woman. When the widow had recovered, she scrambled up to resume her attack. The chief said something to a warrior, and he dragged the woman away.

By then, "dawn" had come. Some men ate pieces of one of the moosoids killed by Urthona, drank, and then rode off across the plain. The rest cut off portions for themselves and chewed at the meat with strong teeth. The flesh was supplemented by nuts and berries carried in raw leather bags. None of the captives were offered any food. Anana didn't mind, since she'd eaten but a few hours ago, and the beating hadn't improved her appetite. Also, she was somewhat cheered. If these people did intend to eat her, it seemed likely that they would want to fatten her up. That would take time, and time was her ally.

Another thought palled that consideration. Perhaps they were saving her for lunch, in which case they wouldn't want to waste food on her.

The chief, his mouth and beard bloody, approached. His long hair was in a Psyche knot through which two long red feathers were stuck. A circle of human fingers on a leather plate hung from a neck-cord over his beard. One eye socket was empty except for a few flies. He stopped, belched, then yelled at the tribe to gather around.

Anana, watching him remove his kilt, became sick. A minute later, while the tribe yelled encouragement, and made remarks that were obviously obscene, though she didn't understand a word, he did what she had thought he was going to do. Knowing how useless it was to struggle, she lay back quietly. But she visualized six different ways of killing him and hoped she'd have a chance to carry out one of them.

After the chief, grinning, got up and donned his kilts, the shaman came up to her. He apparently had in mind emulating the chief. The latter, however, pushed him away. She was going to be the chief's property. Anana was glad for at least one favor. The shaman was even dirtier and more repulsive than the chief.

She managed to get up and walked over to Urthona. He looked disgusted. She said, "Well, uncle, you can be glad you're not a woman."

"I always have been," he said. "You could run now before they could catch you and you could drown yourself in the channel. That is the only way to cleanse yourself."

He spat "Imagine that! A *leblabbiy* defiling a Lord! It's a wonder to me you didn't die of shame."

He paused, then smiled crookedly. "But then you've been mating with a *leblabbiy* voluntarily, haven't you? You have no more pride than an ape."

Anana kicked him in the jaw with her bare foot. Two minutes passed before he recovered consciousness.

Anana felt a little better. Though she would have preferred to kick the chief (though not in his jaw), she had discharged some of her rage.

"If it weren't for you and Orc," she said, "I wouldn't be in this mess."

She turned and walked away, ignoring his curses.

Shortly thereafter, the tribe resumed its march. The meat was thrown on top of piles on travois, and a more or less orderly caravan was formed. The chief rode at the head of the procession. Since attack from their left was impossible, all the outriders were put on the right.

About three hours before dusk, the men who'd been sent across the plains returned at a gallop. Anana didn't know what they reported, but she guessed that they'd gone up one of the mountains to look for enemies. Obviously, they hadn't seen any.

Why had the tribe been on the move during the night? Anana supposed that it was because many tribes would be going to the sea-country. This people wanted to be first, but they knew that others would have the same idea. So they were on a forced march, day and night, to get through the pass before they ran into enemies.

At "noon," when the sky-illumination was brightest, the caravan stopped. Everybody, including the prisoners, ate. Then they lay down with skins over their faces to shut out the light, and they slept. About six stayed awake to be lookouts. These had slept for several hours on travois, though when they woke up they looked as if they hadn't gotten a wink of sleep.

By then the captives' hands were tied in front so they could feed themselves. When nap-time came, thongs were tied around their ankles to hobble them.

Anana had also been given a kilt to wear.

She lay down near her uncle and McKay. The latter said, "These savages must've never seen a black man before. They stare at me, and they rub my hair. Maybe they think it'll bring them luck. If I get a chance, I'll show them what kind of luck they're going to get!"

Urthona spoke out of lips puffed up by a blow from a spearshaft. "They might never have seen blacks before, but there are black tribes here. I brought in specimens of all the Earth races."

McKay said, slowly, "I wonder what they'd do to you if they knew you were responsible for their being here?"

Urthona turned pale. Anana laughed, and said, "I might tell them—when I learn how to speak their tongue."

"You wouldn't do that, would you?" Urthona said. He looked at her, then said, "Yes, you would. Well, just remember, I'm the only one who can get us into my palace."

"If we ever find it," Anana said. "And if these savages don't eat us first."

She closed her eyes and went to sleep. It seemed like a minute later that she was roused by a kick in the ribs. It was the gray-haired woman in her panties, the chief's woman, who'd taken a special dislike to Anana. Or was it so special? All the women seemed to loathe her. Perhaps, though, that was the way they treated all female captives.

Obviously, the women weren't going to teach her the language. She picked on an adolescent, a short muscular lad who was keeping an eye on her. Since he seemed to be fascinated by her, she would get him to initiate her into the tribal speech. It didn't take long to learn his name, which was Nurgo.

Nurgo was eager to teach her. He rode on a moosoid while she walked, but he told her the names of things and people she pointed out. By the end of the "day," when they stopped for another two-hour snooze, she knew fifty words, and she could construct simple questions and had memorized their answers.

Neither Urthona nor McKay were interested in linguistics. They walked side by side, talking in low tones, obviously discussing methods of escape.

When they resumed their march in the deepening twilight, the chief asked her to demonstrate the use of the Horn. She blew the sequence of notes which would open any "gate"—if there had been one around. After some initial failures, he mastered the trumpet and for a half-hour amused himself by blowing it. Then the shaman said something to him. Anana didn't know what it was. She guessed the shaman was pointing out that the sounds might attract the attention of enemies.

Sheepishly, he stuck the Horn into a saddlebag.

Amazingly, the woman with her jeans had so far not been curious about the heavy lump in the leg of the cloth. Since she had never seen this type of apparel before, she must think that all jeans were weighted in this fashion.

Near the end of the "night" the caravan stopped again. Guards were posted, and everybody went to sleep. The moosoid, however, stayed awake and chomped on tree branches. These were carried on the travois or on their backs. The supply was almost gone, which meant that men would have to forage for it. That is, find a grove or forest of walking plants, kill some, and strip off the branches.

At "noon" the following day the two mountains forming the pass to the sea seemed to be very close. But she knew that distance was deceiving here. It might take two more days before the pass was reached. Apparently the tribe knew how far away it was. The beasts wouldn't make it to the sea before they became weak with hunger.

Twenty of the men and some four adolescents rode out onto the plain. As fortune had it, the necessary food was advancing toward them. It was a square of trees which she estimated numbered about a thousand. The riders waited until it was a quarter of a mile from the channel. Then, holding lariats made of fiber, they rode out. Nearing the trees, they formed an Indian file. Like redskins circling a wagon train, they rode whooping around and around it.

The plants were about ten feet high and coniferous, shaped like Christmas trees with extraordinarily broad trunks which bulged out at the bottom. About two-thirds of the way up, eyes ringed the boles, and four very long and thin greenish tentacles extended from their centers. When the tribesmen got close, the whole unit stopped, and those on the perimeter turned on four barky legs to face outward.

Anana had noticed that a herd of wild moosoids had ignored them. There must be a reason for this. And as the men rode by, about twenty feet from the outguards, she saw why. Streams of heavy projectiles shot from holes in the trunks. Though a long way from the scene, she could hear the hissing of released air.

From much experience with these plants, the humans knew what the exact range of the darts were. They stayed just outside it, the riders upwind closer than those on the downwind side.

She deduced that they knew what the ammunition count for a tree was. They were shouting short words—undoubtedly numbers—as they rode by. Then the chief, who'd been sitting to one side and listening, yelled an order. This was passed on around the circle so that those out of hearing of his voice could be informed. The riders nearest him turned their beasts and headed toward the perimeter. Meanwhile, as if the plants were a well-trained army, those who'd discharged their missiles stepped backward into spaces afforded by the moving aside of the second rank.

It was evident that those behind them would take their places. But the riders stormed in, swung, and cast their lariats. Some of them missed. The majority caught and tightened around a branch or a tentacle. The mounts wheeled, the ropes stretched, the nooses closed, and the unlucky plants were jerked off their feet. The riders urged their beasts on until the trees had been dragged out of range of the missiles. The other end of the lariats were fastened to pegs stuck into the rear of the saddles. All but one held. This snapped, and the plant was left only ten feet from the square. No matter. It couldn't get up again.

The mounts halted, the riders jumped down and approached the fallen plants. Taking care to keep out of the way of the waving tentacles, they loosened the lariats and returned to their saddles.

Once more, the procedure was repeated. After that the riders ignored the upright trees. They took their flint or chert tools and chopped off the tentacles. Their animals, now safe from the darts—which she presumed were poisoned—attacked the helpless plants. They grabbed the tentacles between their teeth and jerked them loose. After this, while the moosoids were stripping a branch, their owners chopped away branches with flint or chert tools.

The entire tribe, men, women, children, swarmed around the victims and piled the severed branches upon travois or tied bundles of them to the backs of the beasts.

Later, when she'd learned some vocabulary, Anana asked the youth, Nurgo, if the missiles were poisoned. He nodded and grinned and said, *"Yu, messt gwonaw dendert assessampt."*

She wasn't sure whether the least word meant *deadly* or *poison*. But there was no doubt that it would be better not to be struck by the darts. After the plants had been stripped, the men carefully picked up the missiles. They were about four inches long, slim-bodied, with feathery construction of vegetable origin at one end and a needdle-point at the other. The point was smeared with a blue-greenish substance.

These were put into a rawhide bag or fixed at the ends of spearshafts.

After the work was done, the caravan resumed marching. Anana, looking back, saw half of the surviving plants ranged alongside the channel. From the bottom of each a thick greenish tube was extended into the water, which was being sucked up into these. The other half stood guard.

"You must have had a lot of fun designing those," Anana said to Urthona.

"It was more amusing designing them than watching them in action," her uncle said. "In fact, designing this world entertained me more than living on it. I got bored in less than four years and left it. But I have been back now and then during the past ten thousand years to renew my acquaintance with it."

"When was the last time?"

"Oh, about five hundred years ago, I think."

"Then you must have made another world for your headquarters. One more diversified, more beautiful, I'd imagine."

Urthona smiled. "Of course. Then I also am Lord of three more, worlds which I took over after I'd killed their owners. You remember your cousin Bromion, that bitch Ethinthus, and Antamon? They're dead now, and I, I rule their worlds!"

"Do you indeed now?" Anana said. "I wouldn't say you were sitting on any thrones now. Unless you call captivity, the immediate danger of death and torture, thrones."

Urthona snarled, and said, "I'll do you as I did them, my *leblabbiy*-loving niece! And I'll come back here and wipe out these miserable scum! In fact, I may just wipe out this whole world! Cancel it!"

CHAPTER THIRTEEN

ANANA SHOOK HER head. "Uncle, I was once like you. That is, utterly unworthy of life. But there was something in me that gave me misgivings. Let us call it a residue of compassion, of empathy. Deep under the coldness and cruelty and arrogance was a spark. And that spark fanned into a great fire, fanned by a *leblabbiy* called Kickaha. He's not a Lord, but he is a *man*. That's more than you ever were or will be. And these brutish miserable creatures who've captured you, and don't know they hold the Lord of their crazy world captive . . . they're more human than you could conceive. That is, they're retarded Lords . . ."

Urthona stared and said, "What in The Spinner's name are you talking about?"

Anana felt like hitting him. But she said, "You wouldn't ever understand. Maybe I shouldn't say *ever*. After all, I came to understand. But that was because I was forced to be among the *leblabbiy* for a long time."

"And this *leblabbiy*, Kickaha, this descendant of an artificial product, corrupted your mind. It's too bad the Council is no longer in effect. You'd be condemned and killed within ten minutes."

Anana ran her gaze up and down him several times, her expression contemptuous. "Don't forget, uncle, that you, too, may be the descendant of an artificial product. Of creatures created in a laboratory. Don't forget what Shambarimen speculated with much evidence to back his statement. That we, too, the Lords, the *Lords*, may have been made in the laboratories of beings who are as high above us as we are above the *leblabbiy*. Or I should say as high above them as we are *supposed* to be.

"After all, we made the *leblabbiy* in our image. Which means that they are neither above nor below us. They are us. But they don't know that, and they have to live in worlds which we created. Made, rather. We are not creators, any more than writers of fiction or painters are creators. They make worlds, but they are never able to make more than what they know. They can write or paint worlds based on elements of the known, put together in a different order in a way to make them seem to be creators.

"We, the so-called Lords, did no more than poets, writers, and painters and sculptors. We were not, and are not, gods. Though we've come to think of ourselves as such."

"Spare me your lectures," Urthona said. "I don't care for your attempts to justify your degeneracy."

Anana shrugged and said, "You're hopeless. But in a way you're right. The thing to talk about is how we can escape."

"Yeah," McKay said. "Just how we going to do that?"

"However we do it," she said, "we can't go without the knife and the axe and the Horn. We'd be helpless in this savage world without them. The chief has the axe and the Horn, so we have to get them away from him."

She didn't think she should say anything about the knife in the jeans. They'd noticed it was gone, but she had told them she'd lost it during her flight from them.

A man untied their hobbles, and they resumed the march with the others. Anana went back to her language lessons with Nurgo.

When the tribe got to the pass, it stopped again. She didn't need to ask why. The country beyond the two mountains was black with clouds in which lived a hell of lightning bolts. It would be committing suicide to venture into it. But when a whole day and night passed, and the storm still raged, she did question the youth.

"The Lord sends down thunder and lightning into this country. He topples trees and slays beasts and any human who is foolish enough to dare him."

"That is why we only go into the sea-country when his wrath has cooled off. Otherwise, we would live there all the time. The land changes shape very slowly and insignificantly. The water is full of fish, and the trees, which do not walk, are full of birds that are good to eat. The trees also bear nuts, and there are bushes, which also do not walk, that are heavy with berries. And the game is plentiful and easier caught than on the open plains.

"If we could live there all the time, we would get fat and our children would thrive and our tribe would become more numerous and powerful. But the Lord, in his great wisdom, has decreed that we can only live there for a little while. Then the clouds gather, and his lightning strikes, and the land is no place for anyone who knows what's good for him."

Anana did not, of course, understand everything he said. But she could supply the meaning from what phrases she had mastered.

She went to Urthona and asked him why he had made such an arrangement in the sea-country.

"Primarily, for my entertainment. I liked to send my palace into that land and watch the fury of the lightning, see the devastation. I was safe and snug in my palace, but I got a joy out of seeing the lightning blaze and crack around me. Then I truly felt like a god.

"Secondarily, if it weren't for their fear of being killed, the humans would crowd in. It'd be fun to watch them fight each other for the territory. In fact, it was fun during the stormless seasons. But if there were nothing to keep them from settling down there, they'd never go back into the shifting areas."

"There are, if I remember correctly, twelve of those areas. The seas and the surrounding land each cover about five million square miles. So in an area of 200,000,000 square miles there are 60,000,000 square miles of relatively stable topography. These are never separated from the main mass, and the splitoffs never occur near the seas."

"The lightning season was designed to drive beast and human out of the sea-country except at certain times. Otherwise, they'd get overcrowded."

He stopped to point at the plain. Anana turned and saw that it was now covered with herds of animals, elephants, moosoids, antelopes, and many small creatures. The mountains were dark with birds that had settled on them. And the skies were black with millions of flying creatures.

"They migrate from near and far," Urthona said. "They come to enjoy the sea and the wooded lands while they can. Then, when the storms start, they leave."

Anana wandered away. As long as she didn't get very far from the camp, she was free to roam around. She approached the chief, who was sitting on the ground and striking the ground with the axe. She squatted down before him.

"When will the storms cease?" she said.

His eyes widened. "You have learned our language very quickly. Good. Now I can ask you some questions."

"I asked one first," she said.

He frowned. "The Lord should have ceased being angry and gone back to his palace before now. Usually, the lightning would have stopped two light-periods ago. For some reason, the Lord is very angry and he is still raging. I hope he gets tired of it and goes home soon. The beasts and the birds are piling up. It's a dangerous situation. If a stampede should start, we could be trampled to death. We would have to jump into the water to save ourselves, and that would be bad because our *grewigg* would be lost along with our supplies."

Grewigg was the plural of *gregg*, the word for a moosoid.

Anana said, "I wondered why you weren't hunting when so many animals were close by."

The chief, Trenn, shuddered. "We're not stupid. Now, what tribe is yours? And is it near here?"

Anana wondered if he would accept the truth. After all, his tribe, the Wendow, might have a tradition of having come from another world.

"We are not natives of this . . . place." She waved a hand to indicate the universe, and the flies, alarmed, rose and whirled around buzzing. They quickly settled back, however, lighting on her body, her face, and her arms. She brushed

them away from her face. The chief endured the
insects crawling all over him and into his empty
eye-socket. Possibly, he wasn't even aware of
them.

"We came through a . . . " She paused. She
didn't know the word for *gate*. Maybe there
wasn't any. "We came through a pass between
two . . . I don't know how to say it. We came from
beyond the sky. From another place where the sky
is . . . the color of that bird there."

She pointed to a small blue bird which had
landed by the channel.

The chief's eye got even larger. "Ah, you came
from the place where our ancestors lived. The
place from which the Lord drove our forefathers
countless light-periods ago because they had
sinned. Tell me, why did the Lord drive you here,
too? What did you do to anger him?"

While she was trying to think how to answer
this, the chief bellowed for the shaman, Shakann,
to join them. The little gray-bearded man, holding
the gourd at the end of a stick to which feathers
were tied, came running. Trenn spoke too rapidly
for Anana to understand any but a few words.
Shakann squatted down by the chief.

Anana considered telling them that they'd entered this world accidentally. But she didn't know
their word for accident. In fact, she doubted there
was such. From what she'd learned from Nurgo,
these people believed that nothing happened accidentally. Events were caused by the Lord or by
witchcraft.

She got an inspiration. At least, she hoped it
was. Lying might get her into even worse trouble.
Ignorant of the tribe's theology, she might offend
some article of belief, break some tabu, say some-

thing contrary to dogma.

"The Lord was angry with us. He sent us here so that we might lead some deserving tribe, yours, for instance, out of this place. Back to the place where your ancestors lived before they were cast out."

There was a long silence. The chief looked as if he were entertaining joyful thoughts. The shaman was frowning.

Finally, the chief said, "And just how are we to do this? If the Lord wants us to return to *sembart* . . . "

"What is *sembart*?"

The chief tried to define it. Anana got the idea that *sembart* could be translated as paradise or the garden of Eden. In any event, a place much preferable to this world.

Well, Earth was no paradise, but, given her choice, she wouldn't hesitate a second in making it.

"If the Lord wants us to return to *sembart*, then why didn't he come here and take us to there?"

"Because," Anana said, "he wanted me to test you. If you were worthy, then I would lead you from this world."

Trenn spoke so rapidly to Shakann that she could comprehend only half of his speech. The gist, however, was that the tribe had made a bad mistake in not treating the captives as honored guests. Everybody had better jump to straighten out matters.

Shakann, however, cautioned him not to act so swiftly. First, he would ask some questions.

"If you are indeed the Lord's representative, why didn't you come to us in his *shelbett*?"

A *shelbett*, it turned out, was a thing that flew. In

the old days, according to legend, the Lord had traveled through the air in this.

Anana, thinking fast, said, "I only obey the Lord. I dare not ask him why he does or doesn't do this or that. No doubt, he had his reasons for not giving us a *shelbett*. One might be that if you had seen us in one, you would have known we were from him. And so you would have treated us well. But the Lord wants to know who is good and who isn't."

"But it is not bad to take captives and then kill them or adopt them into the tribe. So how could we know that we were doing a bad thing? All tribes would have treated you the same."

Anana said, "It's not how you treated us at first. How you treated us when you found out that we came from the Lord will determine whether you are found good or bad in his eyes."

Shakann said, "But any tribe that believed your story would honor you and take care of you as if you were a baby. How would you know whether a tribe was doing this because it is good or because it is pretending to be good from fear of you?"

Anana sighed. The shaman was an ignorant savage. But he was intelligent.

"The Lord has given me some powers. One of them is the ability to look into the . . ."

She paused. What was the word for heart?

"To look inside people and see if they are good or bad. To tell when people are lying."

"Very well," Shakann said. "If you can indeed tell when a person lies, tell me this. I intend to take this sharp hard thing the chief took from you and split your head open. I will do it very shortly. Am I lying or am I telling the truth?"

The chief protested, but Shakann said, "Wait!

This is a matter for me, your priest, to decide. You rule the tribe in some things, but the business of the Lord is my concern."

Anana tried to appear cool, but she could feel the sweat pouring from her.

Judging from the chief's expression, she doubted that he would let the shaman have the axe. Also, the shaman must be unsure of himself. He might be a hypocrite, a charlatan, though she did not think so. Preliterate medicine men, witches, sorcerers, whatever their title was, really believed in their religion. Hyprocisy came with civilization. His only doubt was whether or not she did indeed represent the Lord of this wretched cosmos. If she were lying and he allowed her to get away with it, then the Lord might punish him.

He was in as desperate a situation as she. At least, he thought he was.

The issue was: was he lying or did he really intend to test her by trying to kill her? He knew that if she were what she said she was, he might be blasted with a bolt from the sky.

She said, "You don't know yourself whether you're lying or telling the truth. You haven't made up your mind yet what you'll do."

The shaman smiled. She relaxed somewhat.

"That is right. But that doesn't mean that you can see what I'm thinking. A very shrewd person could guess that I felt that way. I'll ask you some more questions.

"For instance, one of the things that makes me think you might be from the Lord is that thing which cut the men and the *grewigg* in half. With it he could have killed the whole tribe. Why, then, did he throw it away after killing only a few?"

"Because the Lord told him to do so. He was to

use the deadly gift of the Lord only to show you
that he did not come from this world. But the Lord
did not want him to slay an entire tribe. How then
could we lead you out of this place to *sembart*?''

"That is well spoken. You may indeed be what
you say. Or you might just be a very clever woman. Tell me, how will you lead us to *sembart*?''

Anana said, "I didn't say I will. I said I might.
What happens depends upon you and the rest of
your tribe. First, you have to cut our bonds and
then treat us as vicars of the Lord. However, I will
say this. I will guide you to the dwelling palace of
the Lord. When we get to it, we'll enter it and then
go through a pass to *sembart*.''

The shaman raised thick woolly eyebrows.
"You know where the Lord's dwelling is?''

She nodded. "It's far away. During the journey,
you will be tested.''

The chief said, "We saw the dwelling of the
Lord once countless light periods ago. We were
frightened when we saw it moving along a plain. It
was huge and had many . . . um . . . things like great
sticks . . . rising from it. It shone with many lights
from many stones. We watched it for a while, then
fled, afraid the Lord would be offended and deal
harshly with us.''

Shakann said, "What is the purpose of the thing
that makes music?''

"That will get us into the dwelling of the Lord.
By the way, we call his dwelling a palace.''

"*Bahdahss*?''

"That's good enough. But the . . . Horn . . .
belongs to me. You have no right to it. The Lord
won't like your taking it.''

"Here!'' the chief said, thrusting it at her.

"You wronged me when you raped me. I do not

know whether the Lord will forgive you for that or not."

The chief spread his hands out in astonishment. "But, I did no wrong! It is the custom for the chief to mount all female captives. All chiefs do it."

Anana had counted on avenging herself some day. She hadn't known if she'd be satisfied with castrating him or also blinding him. However, if it was the custom . . . he really hadn't thought he was doing anything evil. And if she'd been more objective about it, she would have known that, too.

After all, aside from making her nauseated, he hadn't hurt her. She'd suffered no psychic damage, and there wasn't any venereal disease. Nor could he make her pregnant.

"Very well," she said. "I won't hold that against you."

The chief's expression said, "Why should you?" but he made no comment.

The shaman said, "What about the two men? Are they your husbands? I ask that because some tribes, when they have a shortage of women, allow the women to have more than one husband."

"No! They are under my command."

She might as well get the upper hand on the two while she had the chance. Urthona would rave, but he wouldn't try to usurp her leadership. He wouldn't want to discredit her, since her story had saved his life.

She held out her hands, and the chief used a flint knife to sever the thongs. She rose and ordered the chief's mother to be brought to her. Thikka approached haughtily, then turned pale under the dirt when her son explained the situation to her.

"I won't hurt you," Anana said. "I just want my jeans and boots back."

Thikka didn't know what *jeans or boots* meant, so Anana used sign language. When they were off, Anana ordered her to take the jeans to the channel and wash them. Then she said, "No. I'll do it. You probably wouldn't know how."

She was afraid the woman might find the knife.

The chief called the entire tribe in and explained who their captives, ex-captives, really were. There were a lot of oh's and ah's, or the Wendow equivalents, and then the women who'd beaten her fell on their knees and begged forgiveness. Anana magnanimously blessed them.

Urthona's and McKay's bonds were cut. Anana told them how she had gained their freedom. However, as it turned out, they were not as free as they wished. Though the chief gave each a moosoid, he delegated men to be their body-guards. Anana suspected that the shaman was responsible for this.

"We can try to escape any time there's an opportunity," she told her uncle. "But we'll be safer if we're with them while we're looking for your palace. Once we find it, if we find it, we can outwit them. However, I hope the search doesn't take too long. They might wonder why the emissaries of the Lord are having such a hard time locating it."

She smiled. "Oh, yes. You're my subordinates, so please act as if you are. I don't think that shaman is fully convinced about my story."

Urthona looked outraged. McKay said, "It looks like a good deal to me, Miss Anana. No more beatings, we can ride instead of walking, eat plenty, and three women already said they'd like to have babies by me. One thing about them, they ain't got no color prejudice. That's about all I can say for them, though."

CHAPTER FOURTEEN

ANOTHER DAY AND night passed. The thunder and lightning showed no signs of diminishing. Anana, watching the inferno from the pass, could not imagine how anything, plants or animals, escaped the fury. The chief told her that only about one sixteenth of the trees were laid low and new trees grew very quickly. Many small beasts, hiding now, in burrows and caves, would emerge when the storms were over.

By then the plains were thick with life and the mountains were zebra-striped with lines of just-arriving migrators. The predators, the baboons, wild dogs, moas, and big cats, were killing as they pleased. But the plain was getting so crowded that there was no room to stampede away from the hunters. Sometimes, the frightened antelopes and elephants ran toward the killers and trampled them.

The valley was a babel of animal and bird cries, screams, trumpetings, buglings, croakings, bellowings, mooings, roarings.

At this place the waterway banks were about ten feet above the surface. The ground sloped upwards from this point towards the sea-land pass where the banks reached their maximum height above the surface of the water, almost a hundred feet. The chief gave orders to abandon the moosoids and swim across the channel if a stampede headed their way. The children and women jumped into the water and swam to the opposite bank and struggled up its slope. The men stayed behind to control the nervous *grewigg*. These were bellowing, rolling their eyes, drawing their lips back to show their big teeth, and dancing around. The riders were busy trying to quiet them, but it was evident that if the storm didn't stop very soon, the plains animals would bolt and with them the moosoids. As it was, the riders were not far behind the beasts in nervousness. Though they knew that the lightning wouldn't reach out between the mountains and strike them, the "fact" that the Lord was working overtime in his rage made them uneasy.

Anana had crossed the channel with the women and children. She hadn't liked leaving her *gregg* behind. But it was better to be here if a stampede did occur. The only animals on this side were those able to get up the steep banks: baboons, goats, small antelopes, foxes. There were a million birds on this side, however, and more were flying in. The squawking and screaming made it difficult to hear anyone more than five feet away even if you shouted.

Urthona and McKay were on their beasts, since it was expected that all men would handle them. Urthona looked worried. Not because of the imminent danger but because she had the Horn. He fully expected her to run away then. There was no one who could stop her on this side of the channel. It would be impossible for anyone on the other side to run parallel along the channel with the hope of eventually cutting her off. He, or they, could never get through the herds jammed all the way from the channel to the base of the mountains.

Something was going to break at any minute. Anything could start an avalanche on a hundred thousand hooves. She decided that she'd better do something about the tribe. It wasn't that she was concerned about the men. They could be trampled into bloody rags for all she cared. Nor, only two years ago, would she have been concerned about the women and children. But now she would feel—in some irrational obscure way—that she was responsible for them. And she surely did not want to be burdened with them.

She swam back across the channel, the Horn stuck in her belt, and climbed onto the bank. Talking loudly in the chief's ear, she told him what had to be done. She did not request it, she demanded it as if she were indeed the representative of the Lord. If Trenn resented her taking over, he was discreet enough not to show it. He bellowed orders, and the men got down from the *grewigg*. While some restrained the beasts, the others slid down the bank and swam to the other side. Anana went with them and told the women what they should do.

She helped them by digging away at the edge of the bank with her knife. The chief apparently was too dignified to do manual labor even in an emergency. He loaned his axe to his wife, telling her to set to with it.

The others used their flint and chert tools or the ends of their sticks. It wasn't easy, since the grass was tough and their roots were intertwined deep under the surface. But the blades and the greasy earth finally did give away. Within half an hour a trench, forty-five degrees to the horizontal, had been cut into the bank.

Then the men and Anana swam back, and the moosoids were forced over the bank and into the water. The men swam with them, urging them to make for the trench. The *grewigg* were intelligent enough to understand what the trench was for. They entered it, one by one, and clambered, sometimes slipping, up the trench. The women at the top grabbed the reins and helped pull each beast on up, while the men shoved from behind.

Fortunately, there was very little current in the channel. The *grewigg* were not carried away past the trench.

Before all, including the moosoids, had quit panting, the stampede started. There was no way to know how it started. Of a sudden the thunder of countless hooves reached them, mixed with the same noises they had heard but louder now. It wasn't a monolithic movement in one direction. About half of the beasts headed toward the pass. The other part raced toward the mountains outside those that ringed the sealand. These had resumed their cone shape of two days ago.

First through the pass was a herd of at least a hundred elephants. Trumpeting, shoulder to shoulder, those behind jamming their trunks against the rears of those ahead, they sped by. Several on the edge of the channel were forced into the water, and these began swimming toward the pass.

Behind the pachyderms came a mass of antelopes with brownish-red bodies, black legs, red necks and heads, and long black horns. The largest were about the size of a racing horse. Their numbers greatly exceeded those of the elephants; they must have been at least a thousand. The front ranks got through and then a beast slipped, those behind fell over or on him, and within a minute at least a hundred were piled up. Many were knocked over into the channel.

Anana expected the rear ranks to turn and charge off along the base of the right-hand mountain. But they kept coming, falling, and others piled up on them. The pass on that side of the channel was blocked, but the frantic beasts leaped upon the fallen and attempted to get over their struggling, kicking, horn-tossing, bleating fellows. Then they too tripped and went down and those behind them climbed over them and fell. And they too were covered.

The water was thick with crazed antelopes which swam until bodies fell on them and then others on them and others on them.

Anana yelled at the chief. He couldn't hear her because of the terrifying bedlam, so loud it smothered the bellow of thunder and explosion of lightning beyond the pass. She ran to him and put her mouth to his ear.

"The channel's going to be filled in a minute with bodies! Then the beasts'll leap over the bodies and be here! And we'll be caught!"

Trenn nodded and turned and began bellowing and waving his arms. His people couldn't hear him, but they understood his gestures. All the moosoids were mounted, and the travois were hastily attached to the harness and the skins and goods piled on them. This wasn't easy to do, since the *grewigg* were almost uncontrollable. They reared up, and they kicked out at the people trying to hold them, and some bit any hands or faces that came close.

By then the spill into the channel was taking place as far as they could see. There were thousands of animals, not only antelopes now, but elephants, baboons, dogs, and big cats, pressed despite their struggles into the water. Anana caught a glimpse of a big bull elephant tumbling headfirst off the bank, a lion on its back, its claws digging into the skin.

Now added to the roaring and screaming was the flapping of millions of wings as the birds rose into the air. Among these were the biggest winged birds she'd seen so far, a condor-like creature with an estimated wingspan of twelve feet.

Many of the birds were heading for the mountains. But at least half were scavengers, and these settled down on the top of the piles in the water or in the pass. They began tearing away at the bodies, dead or alive, or attempting to defend their rights or displace others.

Anana had never seen such a scene and hoped she never would again. It was possible that she wouldn't. The sudden lifting of the birds had snapped the moosoids' nerves. They started off, some running toward the birds, some toward the mountains, some toward the pass. Men and women hung onto the reins until they were lifted up, then lowered, their bare feet scraping on the ground until they had to let go. Those mounted pulled back on the reins with all their might but to no avail. Skins and goods bounced off the travois, which then bounced up and down behind the frenzied beasts.

Anana watched Urthona, yelling, his face red, hauling back on the reins, being carried off toward the pass. McKay had let loose of his moosoid as soon as it bolted. He stood there, watching her. Evidently he was waiting to see what she would do. She decided to run for the mountains. She looked back once and saw the black man following her. Either he had orders from her uncle not to let her out of his sight or he trusted her to do the best thing to avoid danger and was following her example.

Possibly, he was going to try to get the Horn from her. He couldn't do that without killing her. He was bigger and stronger than she, but she had her knife. He knew how skilled she was with a knife, not to mention her mastership of the martial arts.

Besides, if he attempted murder in sight of the tribe, he'd be discrediting her story that they were sent by the Lord. He surely wouldn't be that stupid.

The nearest mountain on this side of the channel was only a mile away. It was one of the rare shapes, a monolith, four-sided, about two thousand feet high. The ground around it had sunk to three hundred feet, forming a ditch about six hundred and fifty feet broad. She stopped at the edge and turned. McKay joined her five minutes later. It took him several minutes to catch his normal breathing.

"It sure is a mess, ain't it?"

She agreed with him but didn't say so. She seldom commented on the obvious.

"Why're you sticking with me?"

"Because you got the Horn, and that's the only way to get us out of this miserable place. Also, if anybody's going to survive, you are. I stick with you, I live too."

"Does that mean you're no longer loyal to Urthona?"

He smiled. "He ain't paid me recently. And what's more, he ain't never going to pay me. He's promised a lot to me, but I know that once he's safe, he's going to get rid of me."

She was silent for a while. McKay was a hired

killer. He couldn't be trusted, but he could be used.

"I'll do my best to get you back to Earth," she said. "I can't promise it. You might have to settle for some other world. Perhaps Kickaha's."

"Any world's better than this one."

"You wouldn't say that if you'd seen some of them. I give you my word that I'll try my best. However, for the time being, you'll pretend to be in my uncle's employ."

"And tell you what he plans, including any monkey business."

"Of course."

He was probably sincere. It was possible though, that Urthona had put him up to this.

By then some of the tribe had also gotten to the base of the mountain. The others were mostly riders who hadn't so far managed to control their beasts. A few were injured or dead.

The stampede was over. Those animals still on their hooves or paws had scattered. There was more room for them on the plain now. The birds covered the piles of carcasses like flies on a dog turd.

She began walking down to the channel. The tribe followed her, some talking about the unexpected bonus of meat. They would have enough to stuff themselves silly for two days before the bodies got too rank. Or perhaps three days. She didn't know just how fastidious they were. From what she'd seen, not very.

Halfway to the channel, McKay stopped, and said, "Here comes the chief."

She looked toward the pass. Coming down the slope from it was Trenn. Though his *gregg* had bolted and taken him into the valley itself, it was now under control. She was surprised to see that the heavy black clouds over the sea-country were fading away. And the lightning had stopped.

A minute later, several other *grewigg* and riders came over the top of the rise. By the time she got to the channel, they were close enough for her to recognize them. One was her uncle. Until then, the moosoids had been trotting. Now Urthona urged his into a gallop. He pulled the sweating panting saliva-flecked beast up when he got close, and he dismounted swiftly. The animal groaned, crumpled, turned over on its side and died.

Urthona had a strange expression. His green eyes were wide, and he looked pale.

"Anana! Anana!" he cried. "I saw it! I saw it!"

"Saw what?" she said.

He was trembling.

"My palace! It was on the sea! Heading out away from the shore!"

CHAPTER FIFTEEN

OBVIOUSLY, IF HE'D been able to catch up to it, he wouldn't be here.

"How fast does it travel?" she said.

"When the drive is on automatic, one kilometer an hour."

"I don't suppose that after all this time you'd have the slightest idea what path it will take?"

He spread out his hands and shrugged his shoulders.

The situation seemed hopeless. There was no time to build a sailing boat, even if tools were available, and to try to catch up with it. But it was possible that the palace would circle around the sea and come back to this area.

"Eventually," Urthona said, "the palace will leave this country. It'll go through one of the passes. Not this one, though. It isn't wide enough."

Anana did not accept this statement as necessarily true. For all she knew, the palace contained devices which could affect the shape-changing. But if Urthona had any reason to think that the palace could come through this pass, he surely would not have told her about seeing it.

There was nothing to be done about the palace at this time. She put it out of her mind for the time being, but her uncle was a worrier. He couldn't stop talking about it, and he probably would dream about it. Just to devil him, she said, "Maybe Orc got to it when it was close to shore. He might be in the palace now. Or, more probably, he's gated through to some other world."

Urthona's fair skin became even whiter. "No! He couldn't! It would be impossible! In the first place, he wouldn't dare venture into the sea-land during the storm. In the second place, he couldn't get to it. He'd have to swim . . . I think. And in the third place, he doesn't know the entrance-code."

Anana laughed.

Urthona scowled. "You just said that to upset me."

"I did, yes. But now that I think about it, Orc could have done it if he was desperate enough to risk the lightning."

McKay, who had been listening nearby, said, "Why would he take the risk unless he knew the palace was there? And how could he know it was there unless he'd already gone into the sea-land? Which he wouldn't do unless he knew . . ."

Anana said swiftly, "But he could have seen it from the pass, and that might have been enough for him."

She didn't really believe this, but she wasn't too sure. When she walked away from her uncle, she wondered if Orc just might have done it. Her effort to bug Urthona had backfired. Now *she* was worried.

A few minutes later, the storm ceased. The thunder quit rolling; the clouds cleared as if sucked into a giant vacuum cleaner. The shaman and the chief talked together for a while, then approached Anana.

Trenn said, "Agent of the Lord, we have a question. Is the Lord no longer angry? Is it safe for us to go into the sea-land?"

She didn't dare to show any hesitation. Her role called for her to be intimate with the Lord's plans.

If she guessed wrong, she'd lose her credibility.

"The wrath of the Lord is finished," she said. "It'll be safe now."

If the clouds appeared again and lightning struck, she would have to run away as quickly as possible.

The departure did not take place immediately, however. The animals that had bolted had to be caught, the scattered goods collected, and the ceremonies for the dead gone through. About two hours later the tribe headed for the pass. Anana was delighted to be in a country where there were trees that did not walk, and where thick woods and an open sea offered two ready avenues of flight.

The Wendow went down the long slope leading to sand beaches. The chief turned left, and the others followed. According to Nurgo, their destination lay about half a day's travel away. Their stronghold was about fifteen minutes' walk inland from the beach.

"What about the other tribes that come through the pass?" she said.

"Oh, they'll be coming through during the next few light-periods. They'll go even further up the beach, toward their camps. We were lucky that there weren't other tribes waiting at the pass, since the storms lasted longer than usual."

"Do you attack them as they pass by your stronghold?"

"Not unless we outnumber them greatly."

Further questioning cleared up some of her ignorance about their pattern of war. Usually, the tribes avoided any full-scale battles if it was possible. Belligerence was confined to raids by individuals or parties of three to five people. These were conducted during the dark-period and were mainly by young unblooded males and sometimes by a young woman accompanied by a male. The youth had to kill a man and bring back his head as proof of his or her manhood or womanhood. The greatest credit, however, was not for a head but for a child. To steal a child and bring it back for adoption into the tribe was the highest feat possible.

Nurgo himself was an adopted child. He'd been snatched not long after he'd started walking. He didn't remember a thing about it, though he did sometimes have nightmares in which he was torn away from a woman without a face.

The caravan came to a place which looked just like the rest of the terrain to Anana. But the tribe recognized it with a cry of joy. Trenn led them into the wooded hills, and after a while they came to a hill higher than the others. Logs lay on its top and down its slope, the ruins of what had been a stockade.

The next few days were spent in fishing, gathering nuts and berries, eating, sleeping, and rebuilding the fort. Anana put some weight back on and began to feel rested. But once she had all her energy back, she became restless.

Urthona was equally fidgety. She observed him talking softly to McKay frequently. She had no doubts about the subject of their conversation, and McKay, reporting to her, gave her the details.

"Your uncle wants to take off at the first chance. But no way is he going to leave without the Horn."

"Is he planning on taking it from me now or when he finds his palace?" she said.

"He says that we, us two, him and me, that is, would have a better chance of surviving if you was to go with us. But he says you're so tricky you might get the upper hand on us when we sight the palace. So he can't make up his mind yet. But he's going to have to do it soon. Every minute passes, the palace is getting further away."

There was a silence. McKay looked as if he was chewing something but didn't know if he should swallow it or spit it out. After a minute, his expression changed.

"I got something to tell you."

He paused, then said, "Urthona told you and Kickaha that this Wolff, or Jadawin, and his woman—Chryseis?—had been gated to this world. Well, that's a lie. They somehow escaped. They're still on Earth!"

Anana did not reply at once. McKay didn't have to tell her this news. Why had he done so? Was it because he wanted to reassure her that he had indeed switched loyalties? Or had Urthona ordered McKay to tell her that so she would think he was betraying Urthona?

In either case, was the story true?

She sighed. All Lords, including herself, were so paranoiac that they would never be able to distinguish between reality and fantasy. Their distrust of motivation made it impossible.

She shrugged. For the moment she'd act as if she believed his story. She looked around the big tree they'd been sitting behind, and she said, "Oh, oh! Here comes my uncle, looking for us. If he sees you with me, he'll get suspicious. You'd better take off."

McKay crawled off into the bushes. When Urthona found her, she said, "Hello, uncle. Aren't you supposed to be helping the fish spearers?"

"I told them I didn't care to go fishing today. And, of course, since I'm one of the Lord's agents, I wasn't challenged. I could tell they didn't like it, though.

"I was looking for you and McKay. Where is he?"

She lifted her shoulders.

"Well, it doesn't matter."

He squatted down by her.

"I think we've wasted enough time. We should get away the moment we have a chance."

"We?" she said, raising her eyebrows. "Why should I want to go with you?"

He looked exasperated. "You surely don't want to spend the rest of your life here?"

"I don't intend to. But I mean to make sure first that Kickaha is either alive or dead."

"That *leblabbiy* really means that much to you?"

"Yes. Don't look so disgusted. If you should ever feel that much for another human being, which I doubt, then you'll know why I'm making sure about him. Meanwhile . . ."

He looked incredulous. "You can't stay here."

"Not forever. But if he's alive, he'll be along soon. I'll give him a certain time to come. After that, I'll look for his bones."

Urthona bit his lower lip.

He said, "Then you won't come with us now?"

She didn't reply. He knew the answer.

There was a silence for a few minutes. Then he stood up.

"At least, you won't tell the chief what we're planning to do?"

"I'd get no special pleasure out of that," she said. "The only thing is . . . how do I explain your French leave? How do I account for a representative of the Lord, sent on a special mission to check out the Wendow tribe, my subordinate, sneaking off?"

Her uncle chewed his lips some more. He'd been doing that for ten thousand years; she remembered when she was a child seeing him gnaw on it.

Finally, he smiled. "You could tell them McKay and I are off on a secret mission, the purpose of which you can't divulge now because it's for the Lord. Actually, it would be fine if you'd say that. We wouldn't have to sneak off. We could just walk out, and they wouldn't dare prevent us."

"I could do that," she said. "But why should I? If by some chance you did find the palace right away, you'd just bring it back here and destroy me. Or use one of your fliers. In any event, I'm sure you have all sorts of weapons in your palace."

He knew it was useless to protest that he wouldn't do that. He said, "What's the difference? I'm going, one way or the other. You can't tell the chief I am because then you'd have to explain why I am. You can't do a thing about it."

"You can do what you want to," she said. "But you can't take this with you."

She held up the Horn.

His eyes narrowed, and his lips tightened. By that she knew that he had no intention of leaving without the Horn. There were two reasons why, one of which was certain. The other might exist.

No Lord would pass up the chance to get his hands on the skeleton key to the gates of all the universes.

The Horn might also be the ticket to passage from a place on this planet to his palace. Just possibly, there were gates locked into the boulders. Not all boulders, of course. Just some. She'd tried the Horn on the four big rocks she'd encountered so far, and none had contained any. But there could be gates in others.

If there were, then he wasn't going to risk her finding one and getting into the palace before he did.

Undoubtedly, or at least probably, he would tell McKay just when he planned to catch her sleeping, kill her, and take the Horn. Would McKay warn her? She couldn't take the chance that he would.

"All right," she said. "I'll go with you. I have just as much chance finding Kickaha elsewhere. And I am tired of sitting here."

He wasn't as pleased as he should have been. He smelled a trap. Of course, even if she'd been sincere, he would have suspected she was up to something. Just as she wondered if he was telling her the truth or only part of it.

Urthona's handsome face now assumed a smile. In this millenia-long and deadly game the Lords played, artifices that wouldn't work and which both sides knew wouldn't work, were still used. The combats had been partly ritualized.

"We'll do it tonight then," Anana said.

Urthona agreed. He went off to look for McKay and found him within two minutes, since McKay was watching them and saw her signal. They talked for fifteen minutes, after which the two men went down to the beach to help in the fishing. She went out to pick berries and nuts. When she returned on her first trip with two leather bags full, she stood around for a while instead of going out again. She managed to get her hands on three leather-skin waterbags and put these in her leanto. There was little she could do now until late in the night.

The tribe feasted and danced that evening. The shaman chanted for continued prosperity. The bard sang songs of heroes of the olden days. Eventually, the belly-swollen people crawled into their leantos and fell asleep. The only ones probably awake were the sentinels, one in a treetop near the shore, one on a platform in the middle of the stockade, and two men stationed along the path to the stockade.

Urthona, Anana, and McKay had eaten sparingly. They worked inside their leantos, stuffing smoked fish and antelope and fruits and berries and nuts into provision bags. The water bags would be filled when they got to the lakeshore.

When she could hear only snores and the distant cries of birds and the coughing of a lion, she crawled out of the frail structure. She couldn't see the guard on top of the platform. She hoped he had fallen asleep, too. Certainly, he had stuffed himself enough to make him nod off, whatever his good intentions.

Urthona and McKay crawled out of their respective leantos. Anana signaled to them. She stood up and walked through the dark reddish light of "midnight" until she was far enough away from the sentinel-platform to see its occupant. He was lying down, flat on his back. Whether he was asleep or not she couldn't determine, but she suspected he was. He was supposed to stay on his feet and scan the surrounding woods until relieved.

The two men went to the corral which held the moosoids. They got their three beasts out without making too much noise and began to saddle them. Anana carried over the waterbags and a full provision bag. These were tied onto a little leather platform behind the saddle.

Anana whispered, "I have to get my axe."

Urthona grimaced, but he nodded. He and his

niece had had a short argument about that earlier. Urthona thought that it was best to forget about the axe, but she had insisted that it was vital to have it. While the two men led the animals to the gate, she walked to the chief's leanto, which was larger than the others. She pushed aside the boughs which surrounded it and crawled into the interior. It was as dark as the inside of a coal mine. The loud snores of Trenn and his wife and son, a half-grown boy, tried to make up for the absence of light with a plenitude of sound. On her hands and knees she groped around, touching first the woman. Then her hand felt his leg. She withdrew it from the flesh and felt along the grass by it. Her fingers came into contact with cold iron.

A moment later she was out of the structure, the throwing axe in one hand. For just a second she'd been tempted to kill Trenn in revenge for his violation of her. But she had resisted. He might make some noise if she did, and, anyway she had already forgiven if not forgotten. Yet . . . something murderous had seized her briefly, made her long to wipe out the injury by wiping the injurer out. Then reason had driven the irrational away.

The gate was a single piece composed of upright poles to which horizontal and tanverse bars had been tied with leather cords. Instead of hinges, it was connected to the wall by more leather cords. Several thick strips of leather served as a lock. These were untied, and the heavy gate was lifted up and then turned inward by all three of them.

So far, no one had raised an outcry. The sentinel might wake at any moment. On the other hand, he might sleep all night. He was supposed to be relieved after a two-hour watch. There was no such thing as an "hour" in the tribe's vocabulary, but

these people had a rough sense of passage of time.
When the sentinel thought that he'd stood watch
long enough, he would descend from the platform
and wake up the man delegated to succeed him.

The beasts were passed through, the gate lifted
and carried back, and the cords retied. The three
mounted and rode off slowly in the half-light, heading down the hill. The moosoids grunted now and
then, unhappy at being mounted at this ungodly
hour. When the three were about a hundred yards
from where they knew the first sentinel was
placed, they halted. Anana got off and slipped
through the brush until she saw the pale figure
sitting with its back against the bole of a tree.
Snores buzz-sawed from it.

It was an easy matter to walk up to the man and
bring down the flat of her axe on top of his head.
He fell over, his snores continuing. She ran back
and told the two it was safe to continue. Urthona
wanted to slit the man's throat, but Anana said it
wasn't necessary. The guard would be unconscious for a long while.

The second sentinel was walking back and forth
to keep himself awake. He strode down the hill for
fifty paces or so, wheeled, and climbed back up the
twenty-degree slope. He was muttering a song,
something about the heroic deeds of Sheerkun.

In this comparative stillness, it would be
difficult to make a detour around him without his
hearing them. He had to be gotten out of the way.

Anana waited until he had turned at the end of
his round, ran out behind him, and knocked him
out with the flat of her axe. She went back and told
the others the way was clear for a while.

When they could see the paleness of the white
sand shore and the darkness of the sea beyond,

they stopped. The last of the sentinels was in a giant tree near the beach. Anana said, "There's no use trying to get to him. But he can yell as loudly as he wishes. There's nobody to relay his message to the village."

They rode out boldly onto the sand. The expected outcry did not come. Either the sentinel was dozing or he did not recognize them and believed some of his tribesmen were there for a legitimate reason. Or perhaps he did recognize them but dared not question the agents of the Lord.

When they were out of his sight, the three stopped. After filling the waterbags, they resumed their flight, if a leisurely pace could be called a flight. They plodded on steadily, silent, each occupied with his or her own thoughts.

There didn't seem to be any danger from Trenn's tribe. By the time one of the stunned men woke up and gave the alarm, the escapees would have too much of a headstart to be caught. The only immediate peril, Anana thought, was from Urthona and McKay. Her uncle could try to kill her now to get the Horn in his own hands. But until they found the palace, she was a strong asset. To survive, Urthona needed her.

"Dawn" came with the first paling of the bands in the sky. As the light increased, they continued. They stopped only to excrete or to drink from the sea and to allow their beasts to quench their thirst. At dusk they went into the woods. Finding a hollow surrounded by trees, they slept in it most of the night through. They were wakened several times by the howling of dogs and roars of big cats. However, no predators came near. At "dawn" they resumed their journey. At "noon," they came to the place which would lead them up to the pass.

Here Anana reined in her moosoid. She made sure that she wasn't close to them before she spoke. Her left hand was close to the hilt of her sheathed knife—she was ambidextrous—and if she had to, she could drop the reins and snatch out her axe. The men carried flint-tipped spears and had available some heavy war-boomerangs.

"I'm going up to the pass and look over the valley from there," she said. "For Kickaha, of course."

Urthona opened his mouth as if to protest. Then he smiled, and said, "I doubt it. See." He pointed up the slope.

She didn't look at once. He might be trying to get her to turn her head and thus give him a chance to attack.

McKay's expression, however, indicated that her uncle was pointing at something worth looking at. Or had he arranged beforehand that McKay would pretend to do such if an occasion arose for it?

She turned the beast quickly and moved several yards away. Then she looked away.

From the top of the slope down to the beach was a wide avenue, carpeted by the rust-colored grass. It wasn't a manmade path; nature, or, rather, Urthona, had designed it. It gave her an unobstructed view of the tiny figures just emerging from the pass. Men on moosoids. Behind them, women and children and more beasts.

Another tribe was entering the sea-land.

CHAPTER SIXTEEN

"LET'S SPLIT!" McKay said.

Anana said, "You can if you want to. I'm going to see if Kickaha is with them. Maybe he was captured by them."

Urthona bit his lip. He looked at the black man, then at his niece. Apparently, he decided that now was no time to try to kill her. He said, "Very well. What do you intend to do? Ride up to them and ask if you can check them out?"

Anana said, "Don't be sarcastic, uncle. We'll hide in the woods and watch them."

She urged her *gregg* into the trees. The others followed her, but she made sure that they did not get too close to her back. When she got to a hill which gave a good view through the trees, she halted. Urthona directed his beast toward her, but she said, "Keep your distance, uncle!"

He smiled, and stopped his moosoid below her. All three sat on their *grewigg* for a while, then, tiring of waiting, got off.

"It'll be an hour before they get here," Urthona said. "And what if those savages turn right? We'll be between the Wendow and this tribe. Caught."

"If Kickaha isn't among them," she said. "I intend to go up the pass after they go by and look for him. I don't care what you want to do. You can go on."

McKay grinned. Urthona grunted. All three understood that as long as she had the Horn they would stay together.

The *grewigg* seized bushes and low treelimbs with their teeth, tore them off, and ground the leaves to pulp. Their empty bellies rumbled as the food passed toward their big bellies. The flies gathered above beasts and humans and settled over them. The big green insects were not as numerous here as on the plains, but there were enough to irritate the three. Since they had not as yet attained the indifference of the natives, their hands and heads and shoulders were in continuous motion, batting, jerking, shrugging.

Then they were free of the devils for a while. A dozen little birds, blue with white breasts, equipped with wide flat almost duckish beaks, swooped down. They swirled around the people and the beasts, catching the insects, gulping them down, narrowly averting aerial collisions in their circles. They came very close to the three, several times brushing them with the woods. In two minutes those flies not eaten had winged off for less dangerous parts.

"I'm glad I invented those birds," Urthona said. "But if I'd known I was going to be in this situation, I'd never have made the flies."

"Lord of the flies," Anana said. "Beezlebub is thy name."

Urthona said, "What?" Then he smiled. "Ah, yes, now I remember."

Anana would have liked to climb a tree so she could get a better view. But she didn't want her uncle to take her *gregg* and leave her stranded. Even if he didn't do that, she'd be at a disadvantage when she got down out of the tree.

After an almost unendurable wait for her, since it was possible, though not very probable, that Kickaha could be coming along, the vanguard came into sight. Soon dark men wearing feathered head-dresses rode by. They carried the same weapons and wore the same type of clothes as the Wendow. Around their necks, suspended by cords, were the bones of human fingers. A big man held aloft a pole on which was a lion skull. Since he was the only one to have such a standard, and he rode in the lead, he must be the chief.

The faces were different from the Wendow's, however, and the skins were even darker. Their features were broad, their noses somewhat bigger and even more aquiline, and the eyes had a slight Mongolian cast. They looked like, and probably were, Amerindians. The chief could have been Sitting Bull if he'd been wearing somewhat different garments and astride a horse.

The foreguard passed out of sight. The outriders and the women and children, most of whom were walking, went by. The women wore their shiny raven's-wing hair piled on top of their heads, and their sole garments were leather skirts of ankle-length. Many wore necklaces of clam shells. A few carried papooses on back packs.

Anana suddenly gave a soft cry. A man on a *gregg* had come into sight. He was tall and much paler than the others and had bright red hair.

Urthona said, "It's not Kickaha! It's Red Orc!"

Anana felt almost sick with disappointment.

Her uncle turned and smiled at her. Anana decided at that moment that she was going to kill him at the first opportunity. Anyone who got that much enjoyment out of the sufferings of others didn't deserve to live.

Her reaction was wholly emotional, of course, she told herself a minute later. She needed him to survive as much as he needed her. But the instant he was of no more use to her . . .

Urthona said, "Well, well. My brother, your uncle, is in a fine pickle, my dear. He looks absolutely downcast. What do you suppose his captors have in mind for him? Torture? It would be almost worthwhile to hang around and watch it."

"He ain't tied up," McKay said. "Maybe he's been adopted, like us."

Urthona shrugged. "Perhaps. In either case, he'll be suffering. He can spend the rest of his life here with those miserable wretches for all I care. The pain won't be so intense, but it'll be much longer lasting."

McKay said, "What're we going to do now we know Kickaha's not with them?"

"We haven't seen all of them," Anana said. "Maybe . . ."

"It isn't likely that the tribe would have caught both of them," Urthona said impatiently. "I think we should go now. By cutting at an angle across the woods, we can be on the beach far ahead of them."

"I'm waiting," she said.

Urthona snorted and then spat. "Your sick lust for that *leblabbiy* makes me sick."

She didn't bother to reply. But presently, as the rearguard passed by, she sighed.

"Now are you ready to go?" Urthona said, grinning.

She nodded, but she said, "It's possible that Orc has seen Kickaha."

"What? You surely aren't thinking of . . . ? Are you crazy?"

"I'm going to trail them and when the chance comes I'll help Orc escape."

"Just because he might know something about your *leblabbiy* lover?"

"Yes."

"Urthona's red face was twisted with rage. She knew that it was not just from frustration. Distorting it were also incomprehension, disgust, and fear. He could not understand how she could be so much in love, in love at all, with a mere creature, the descendant of beings made in laboratories. That his niece, a Lord, could be enraptured by the creature Kickaha filled him with loathing for her. The fear was not caused by her action in refusing to go with them or the danger she represented if attacked. It was—she believed it was, anyway —a fear that possibly he might someday be so perverted that he, too, would fall in love with a *leblabbiy*. He feared himself.

Or perhaps she was being too analytical—ab absurdum—in her analysis.

Whatever had seized him, it had pushed him past rationality. Snarling, face as red as skin could get without bleeding, eyes tigerish, growling, he sprang at her. Both hands, white with compression, gripped the flint-headed spear.

When he charged, he was ten paces from her. Before he had gone five, he fell back, the spear dropping from his hands, his head and back thudding into the grass. The edge of her axe was sunk into his breastbone.

Almost before the blur of the whirling axe had solidified on Urthona's chest, she had her knife out.

McKay had been caught flat-footed. Whether he would have acted to help her uncle or her would never be determined.

He looked shocked. Not at what had happened to her uncle, of course, but at the speed with which it had occurred.

Whatever his original loyalty was, it was now clear that he had to aid and to depend upon her. He could not find the palace without her or, arriving there, know how to get into it. Or, if he could somehow gain entrance to it, know what to do after he was in it.

From his expression, though, he wasn't thinking of this just now. He was wondering if she meant to kill him, too.

"We're in this together, now," she said. "All the way."

He relaxed, but it was a minute before the blue-gray beneath his pigment faded away.

She stepped forward and wrenched the axe from Urthona's chest. It hadn't gone in deeply, and blood ran out from the wound. His mouth was open; his eyes fixed; his skin was grayish. However, he still breathed.

"The end of a long and unpleasant relationship," she said, wiping the axe on the grass. "Yet . . ."

McKay muttered, "What?"

"When I was a little girl, I loved him. He wasn't then what he became later. For that matter, neither was I. Excessive longevity . . . solipsism . . . boredom . . . lust for such power as you Earthlings have never known . . ."

Her voice trailed off as if it were receding into an unimaginably distant past.

McKay made no movement to get closer to her. He said, "What're you going to do?" and he pointed at the still form.

Anana looked down. The flies were swarming over Urthona, chiefly on the wound. It wouldn't be long before the predators, attracted by the odor of blood, would be coming in. He'd be torn apart, perhaps while still living.

She couldn't help thinking of these evenings on their native planet, when he had tossed her in the air and kissed her or when he had brought gifts or when he had made his first world and come to visit before going to it. The Lord of several universes had come to this . . . lying on his back, his blood eaten by insects, the flesh soon to be ripped by fangs and claws.

"Ain't you going to put him out of his misery?" McKay said.

"He isn't dead yet, which means that he still has hope," she said. "No, I'm not going to cut his throat. I'll leave his weapons and his *gregg* here. He might make it, though I doubt it. Perhaps I'll regret not making sure of him, but I can't . . ."

"I didn't like him," McKay said, "but he's going to suffer. It don't seem right."

"How many men have you killed in cold blood for money?" she said. "How many have you tortured, again just for money?"

McKay shook his head. "That don't matter. There was a reason then. There ain't no sense to this."

"It's usually emotional sense, not intellectual, that guides us humans," she said. "Come on."

She brushed by McKay, giving him a chance to attack her if he wanted to. She didn't think he would, and he stepped back as if, for some reason, he dreaded her touch.

They mounted and headed at an angle for the beach. Anana didn't look back.

When they broke out of the woods, the only creatures on the beach were birds, dead fish—the only true fish in this world were in the sea-lands—amphibians, and some foxes. The *grewigg* were breathing hard. The long journey without enough sleep and food had tired them.

Anana let the beasts water in the sea. She said, "We'll go back into the forest. We're near enough to the path to see which way they take. Either direction, we'll follow them at a safe distance."

Presently the tribe came out onto the beach on the night side of the channel. With shouts of joy they ran into the waves, plunged beneath its surface, splashed around playfully. After a while they began to spear fish, and when enough of these had been collected, they held a big feast.

When night came they retreated into the woods on the side of the path near where the two watchers were. Anana and McKay retreated some distance. When it became apparent that the savages were going to bed down, they went even further back into the woods. Anana decided that the tribe would stay put until "dawn" at least. It wasn't likely that it would make this spot a more or less permanent camp. Its members would be afraid of other tribes coming into the area.

Even though she didn't think McKay would harm her, she still went off into the bush to find a sleeping place where he couldn't see her. If he wanted to, he would find her. But he would have to climb a tree to get her. Her bed was some boughs she'd chopped and laid across two branches.

"The "night," as all nights here, was not unbroken sleep. Cries of birds and beasts startled her, and twice her dreams woke her.

The first was of her uncle, naked, bleeding from the longitudinal gash in his chest, standing above her on the tree-nest and about to lay his hands on her. She came out of it moaning with terror.

The second was of Kickaha. She'd been wandering around the bleak and shifting landscape of this world when she came across his death-pale body lying in a shallow pool. She started crying, but when she touched him, Kickaha sat up suddenly, grinning, and he cried, "April fool!" He rose and she ran to him and they put their arms around each other and then they were riding swiftly on a horse that bounced rather than ran, like a giant kangaroo. Anana woke up with her hips emulating the up-and-down movement and her whole being joyous.

She wept a little afterward because the dream wasn't true.

McKay was still sleeping where he had laid down. The hobbled moosoids were tearing off branches about fifty meters away. She bent down and touched his shoulder, and he came up out of sleep like a trout leaping for a dragonfly.

"Don't ever do that again!" he said, scowling.

"Very well. We've got to eat breakfast and then check up on that tribe. Did you hear anything that might indicate they are up and about?"

"Nothing," he said sullenly.

But when they got to the edge of the woods, they saw no sign of the newcomers except for excrement and animal and fish bones. When they rode out onto the white sands, they caught sight, to their right, of the last of the caravan, tiny figures.

After waiting until the Amerinds were out of sight, they followed. Some time later, they came to another channel running out of the sea. This had to be the waterway they had first encountered, the opening of which had swept Kickaha away. It ran straight outwards from the great body of water between the increasingly higher banks of the slope leading up to the pass between the two mountains.

They urged their beasts into the channel and rode them as they swam across. On reaching the other side they had to slide down off, get onto the beach, and pull on the reins to help the moosoids onto the sand. The Amerinds were still not in view.

She looked up the slope. "I'm going up to the pass and take a look. Maybe he's out on the plain."

"If he was trailing them," McKay said, "he would've been here by now. And gone by now, maybe."

"I know, but I'm going up there anyway."

She urged the moosoid up the slope. Twice, she looked back. The first time, McKay was sitting on his motionless *gregg*. The next time, he was coming along slowly.

On reaching the top of the pass, she halted her beast. The plain had changed considerably. Though the channel was still surrounded by flatland for a distance of about a hundred feet on each side, the ground beyond had sunk. The channel now ran through a ridge on both sides of which were very deep and broad hollows. These were about a mile wide. Mountains of all sizes and shapes had risen along its borders, thrusting up from the edges as if carved there. Even as she watched, one of the tops of the mushroom-shaped heights began breaking off at its edges. The huge pieces slid or rotated down the steep slope, some reaching the bottom where they fell into the depressions.

There were few animals along the channel, but these began trotting or running away when the first of the great chunks broke off of the mushroom peak.

On the other side of the mountains was a downward slope cut by the channel banks. On the side on which she sat was a pile of bones, great and small, that extended down into the plain and far out.

Nowhere was any human being in sight.

Softly, she said, "Kickaha?"

It was hard to believe that he could be dead.

She turned and waved to McKay to halt. He did so, and she started her beast towards him. And then she felt the earth shaking around her. Her *gregg* stopped despite her commands to keep going, and it remained locked in position, though quivering. She got down off of it and tried to pull it by the reins, but it dug in, leaning its body back. She mounted again and waited.

The slope was changing swiftly, sinking at the rate of about a foot a minute. The channel was closing up, the sides moving toward each other, and apparently the bottom was moving up, since the water was slopping over its lips.

Heat arose from the ground.

McKay was in the same predicament. His moosoid stubbornly refused to obey despite his rider's beatings with the shaft of his spear.

She turned on the saddle to look behind her. The ridge was becoming a mountain range, a tiny range now but it was evident that if this process didn't stop, it would change into a long and giant barrow. The animals along it were running down its slopes, their destination the ever-increasing depressions along its sides.

However, the two mountains that formed the pass remained solid, immovable.

Anana sighed. There was nothing she could do except sit and wait this out unless she wanted to dismount. The *gregg*, from long experience, must know the right thing to do.

It was like being on a slow-moving elevator, one in which the temperature rose as the elevator fell. Actually, she felt as if the mountains on her side were rising instead of the ground descending.

The entire change lasted about an hour. At the end the channel had disappeared, the ridge had stopped swelling and had sunk, the hollows had been filled, and the plain had been restored to the bases of the mountains just outside the sea-land. The animals which had been desperately scrambling around to adjust to the terrain-change were now grazing upon the grass. The predators were now stalking the meat on the hoof. Business as usual.

Anana tickticked with her tongue to the *gregg*, and it trotted toward the sea. McKay waited for her to come to him. He didn't ask her if she'd seen Kickaha. He knew that if she had she would have said so. He merely shook his head and said, "Crazy country, ain't it?"

"It lost us more than hour, all things considered," she said. "I don't see any reason to push the *grewigg* though. They're not fully recovered yet. We'll just take it easy. We should find those Indians sometime after dark. They'll be camped for the night."

"Yeah, some place in the woods," he said. "We might just ride on by them and in the morning they'll be on our tails."

About three hours after the bright bands of the sky had darkened, Anana's *gregg* stopped, softly rumbling in its throat. She urged it forward with soft words until she saw, through the half-light, a vague figure. She and McKay retreated for a hundred yards and held a short conference. McKay didn't object when she decided that she would take out the guards while he stayed behind.

"I hope the guard don't make any noise when you dispose of him," he said. "What'll I do if he raises a ruckus?"

"Wait and see if anyone else hears him. If they do, then ride like hell to me, bringing my *gregg*, and we'll take off the way we came. Unless, that is, most of the Indians are in the woods. Maybe there's only a guard or two on the beach itself. But I don't plan on making a mistake.

"You're the boss," McKay said. "Good luck."

She went into the woods, moving swiftly when there was no obstruction, slowly when she had to make her way among thick bushes. At last, she was opposite the guard, close enough to see that he was a short stocky man. In the dim light she couldn't make out his features, but she could hear him muttering to himself. He carried a stone-tipped spear in one hand and a war boomerang was stuck in a belt around his waist. He paced back and forth, generally taking about twenty steps each way.

Anana looked down the beach for other guards. She couldn't see any, but she was certain there would be others stationed along the edge of the woods. For all she knew, there might be one just one of eyesight.

She waited until he had gone past her in the direction of McKay. She rose from behind the bush and walked up behind him. The soft sand made little sound. The flat of her axe came down against the back of his head. He fell forward with a grunt. After waiting for a minute to make sure no one had heard the sound of the axe against the bone, she turned the man over. She had to bend close to him to distinguish his facial features. And she swore quietly.

He was Obran, a warrior of the Wendow.

He wasn't going to regain consciousness for quite a while. She hurried back to McKay, who was sitting on his mount, holding the reins of her beast.

He said, "Man, you scared me! I didn't think you'd be coming back so quick. I thought it was one of them Indians at first."

"Bad news. Those're Trenn's people. They must have come after us after all."

"How in hell did they get by us without us seeing them? Or them Indians?"

"I don't know. Maybe they went by the Indians last night without being detected and then decided to trail them in hopes of getting a trophy or two. No, if they did that they wouldn't be sleeping here. They'd be stalking the Indian camp now.

"I don't know. It could be that they held a big powwow after we escaped and it took all day for them to get the nerve up to go after us. Somehow, they passed us while we were up in the pass without them seeing us or us seeing them. The point is, they're here, and we have to get by them. You bring the *grewigg* up to the guard and make sure he doesn't wake up. I'll go ahead and take care of the other guards."

That job lasted fifteen or so minutes. She returned and mounted her beast, and they rode slowly on the white sand, reddish in the light, past another fallen man. When they thought they were out of hearing of the Wendow sleeping in the woods, they galloped for a while. After ten minutes of this, they eased their animals into a trot.

Once more they had to detect the guard before he saw them; Anana slipped off the *gregg* and knocked out three Amerinds stationed at wide intervals near the edge of the woods.

When she came back, McKay shook his head and muttered, "Lady, you're really something."

When they had first been thrown together, he had been rather contemptuous of her. This was a reflection of his attitude toward women in general. Anana had thought it strange, since he came from a race which had endured prejudice and repression for a long time and still was in 1970. His own experience should have made him wary of prejudice toward other groups, especially women, which included black females. But he thought of all women, regardless of color, as inferior beings, useful only for exploitation.

Anana has shaken this attitude considerably, though he had rationalized that, after all, she was not an Earth female.

She didn't reply. The *grewigg* were ridden to where the last unconscious sentinel lay, and they were tied to two large bushes where they could feed. She and McKay went into the woods on their bellies and presently came on the first of the sleepers, a woman with a child. Luckily, these people had no dogs to warn them. Anana suspected that the Amerinds probably did own dogs but, judging from their leanness, the tribe had been forced to eat them during the journey to the sea-land.

They snaked through a dozen snorers, moving slowly, stopping to look at each man closely. Once, a woman sat up suddenly, and the two, only a few feet behind her, froze. After some smackings of lips, the woman lay back down and resumed sleeping. A few minutes later, they found Red Orc.

He was lying on his side within a circle of five dead-to-the-world men. His hands were tied behind him, and a cord bound his ankles together.

Anana clamped her hand over her uncle's mouth at the same time that McKay pressed his heavy body on him. Red Orc struggled, and almost succeeded in rolling over, until Anana whispered in his native language, "Quiet!"

He became still, though he trembled, and Anana said, "We're here to get you away."

She removed her hand. The black stood up. She cut the rawhide cords, and Orc rose, looked around, walked over to a sleeper and took the spear lying by his side. The three walked out of camp, though slowly, until they came to an unsaddled *gregg*. Cautiously, they got a saddle and reins and put the reins on. Orc carried the saddle while Anana led the beast away. When they got to the two *grewigg* tied to the bushes, Anana told Orc some of what had happened.

The light was a little brighter here on the beach. When she stood close to him she could see that her uncle's face and body were deeply bruised.

"They beat me after they caught me," he said. "The women did, too. That went on for the first day, but after that they only kicked me now and then when I didn't move quickly enough to suit them. I'd like to go back and cut the throats of a few."

"You can do that if you like," she said. "After you've answered a question. Did you see Kickaha or hear anything about him?"

"No, I didn't see him and if those savages said anything about him I wouldn't have known it. I wasn't with them long enough to understand more than a dozen words."

"That's because you didn't try," she said. She was disappointed, though she really hadn't expected anything.

Red Orc walked over to the still unconscious sentinel, got down on his knees, put his hands around the man's neck, and did not remove them until he had strangled the life out of him.

Breathing hard, he rose. "There. That'll show them!"

Anana did not express her disgust. She waited until Orc had saddled up his animal and mounted. Then she moved her animal out ahead, and after ten minutes of a slow walk, she urged her *gregg* into a gallop. After five minutes of this she slowed it to a trot, the others following suit.

Orc rode up beside her.

"Was that why you rescued your beloved uncle? Just so you could ask me about your *leblabbiy* lover?"

"That's the only reason, of course," she said.

"Well, I suppose I owe you for that, not to mention not killing me when you got what you wanted from me. Also, my thanks, though you weren't doing it for my benefit, for taking care of Urthona. But you should have made sure he was dead. He's a tough one."

Anana took her axe from her belt and laid its flat across the side of his face. He dropped from the *gregg* and landed heavily on the sand. McKay said, "What the. . . ?"

"I can't trust him," she said. "I just wanted to get him out of earshot of the Indians."

Orc groaned and struggled to get up. He could only sit up, leaning at an angle on one arm. The other went up to the side of his face.

"Bring his *gregg* along with you," she told Mc-

Kay, and she commanded hers to start galloping. After about five minutes of this, she made it trot again. The black came up presently, holding the reins of Orc's beast.

"How come you didn't snuff him out, too?"

"There was a time when I would have. I suppose that Kickaha has made me more humane, that is, what a human should be."

"I'd hate to see you when you felt mean," he said, and thereafter for a long time they were silent.

Anana had given up searching for Kickaha. It was useless to run around, as he would have said, "like a chicken with its head cut off." She'd go around the sea, hoping that the palace might be in sight. If she could get in, then she'd take the flying machine, what the Wendow had called the *shelbett*, and look for Kickaha from the air. Her chances of coming across the mobile palace seemed, however, to be little.

No matter. What else was there to do here but to search for it?

For a while they guided their *grewigg* through the shallow water. Then they headed across the beach into the woods, where she cut off a branch and smoothed out their traces with its leaves. For the rest of the night, they holed up on top of a hill deep in the forest.

In the morning the *grewigg* got nasty. They were tired and hungry. After she and McKay had come close to being bitten and kicked, Anana decided to let them have their way. A good part of the day, the animals ate, and their two owners took turns observing from the top of a tall tree. Anana had expected the Indians to come galloping along in hot pursuit. But the daytime period had half-passed before she saw them in the distance. It was a war party, about twenty warriors.

She called McKay and told him to have the *grewigg* ready for travel, whether the animals liked the idea or not.

Now she realized that she should have taken the animals through the water at once after leaving the camp. That way, the Indians wouldn't have known which direction to take in pursuit, and they might have given up. The precaution was too late, like so many things in life.

The warriors went on by. Not for far, though. About two hundred yards past the point where the refugees had entered the woods, the party stopped. There was what looked like a hot argument between two men, one being the man holding the lion skull on the end of the pole. Whoever wanted the party to go back won. They turned their *grewigg* around and headed back at a trot toward the camp.

No, not their camp. Now she could see the first of a caravan. It was coming at the pace of the slowest walker, and the hunters met them. The whole tribe halted while a powwow was held. Then the march resumed.

She told McKay what was happening. He swore, and said, "That means we got to stay here and give them plenty of time to go by."

"We're in no hurry," she said. "But we don't have to wait for them. We'll cut down through the woods and come out way ahead of them."

That was the theory. In practice, her plan turned out otherwise. They emerged from the woods just in time to see, and be seen by, two riders. They must have been sent on ahead as scouts or perhaps they were just young fellows racing for fun. Whatever the reason for their presence, they turned back, their big beasts galloping.

Anana couldn't see the rest of the tribe. She supposed that they were not too far away, hidden by a bend of the shore. Anyway, she and McKay should have a twenty minutes' head start, at the least.

There was nothing else to do but to force the tired animals into a gallop. They rode at full speed for a while, went into a trot for a while, then broke into a gallop again. This lasted, with a few rest periods, until nightfall. Into the woods they went, and they took turns sleeping and standing watch. In the morning, the animals were again reluctant to continue. Nevertheless, after some savage tussles and beatings, the two got the *grewigg* going. It was evident, however, that they weren't up to more than one day's steady travel, if that.

By noon the first of the hunters came into view. They drew steadily though slowly nearer as the day passed.

"The poor beasts have about one more good gallop left in them," Anana said. "And that won't be far."

"Maybe we ought to take to the woods on foot," McKay said.

She had already considered that. But if these Indians were as good trackers as their Terrestrial counterparts were supposed to be, they'd catch up with their quarry eventually.

"Are you a strong swimmer?" she said.

McKay's eyes opened. He jerked a thumb toward the water. "You mean . . . out there?"

"Yes, I doubt very much that the Indians can."

"Yeah, but you don't *know*. I can swim, and I can float, but not all day. Besides, there may be sharks, or worse things, out there."

"We'll ride until the beasts drop and then we'll take to the sea. At least, I will. Once we're out of their sight, we can get back to shore some distance down, maybe a few miles."

"Not me," McKay said. "Noways. I'm heading for the woods."

"Just as you like."

She reached into a bag and withdrew the Horn. She'd have to strap that over her shoulder beforehand, but it didn't weigh much and shouldn't be much of a drag.

After a hour the pursuers were so close that it was necessary to force the *grewigg* to full speed. This wasn't equal to the pace of the less tired animals behind them. It quickly became evident that in a few minutes the Indians would be alongside them.

"No use going on any more!" she shouted. "Get off before they fall down and you break your neck!"

She pulled on the reins. When the sobbing foam-flecked animals began trotting, she rolled off the saddle. The soft sand eased the impact; she was up on her feet immediately. McKay followed a few seconds later. He rose, and shouted, "Now what?"

The warparty was about a hundred yards away and closing the gap swiftly. They whooped as they saw their victims were on foot. Some cut into the woods, evidently assuming that the two would run for it. Anana splashed into the shallow water and, when it was up to her waist, shucked her ragged jeans and boots. McKay was close behind her.

"I thought you were going for the trees?"

"Naw. I'd be too lonely!"

They began swimming with long slow strokes. Anana, looking back, saw that their pursuers were still on the shore. They were yelling with frustration and fury, and some were throwing their spears and hurling boomerangs after them. These fell short.

"You was right about one thing," McKay said as they dogpaddled. "They can't swim. Or maybe they're afraid to. Them sharks . . ."

She started swimming again, heading out toward the horizon. But, another look behind her made her stop.

It was too distant to be sure. But if the red-headed man on the *gregg* charging the Indians by himself wasn't Kickaha, then she was insane. It couldn't be Red Orc; he wouldn't do anything so crazy.

Then she saw other riders emerging from the woods, a big party. Were they chasing Kickaha so they could aid him when they caught up with him or did they want his blood?

Perhaps Kickaha was not charging the Indians singlehandedly, as she'd first thought. He was just running away from those behind him and now it was a case of the crocodile in the water and the tiger on the bank.

Whatever the situation, she was going to help him if she could. She began swimming toward the shore.

CHAPTER SEVENTEEN

WHEN KICKAHA RODE out of the woods, he had expected the people chasing Anana to be far ahead of him. He was surprised when he saw them only a hundred yards away. Most of them were dismounted and standing on the shore or in the water, yelling and gesticulating at something out in the sea.

Neither Anana nor McKay were in sight.

The discreet thing to do was to turn the *hikwu* as quickly as possible and take off in the opposite direction. However, the only reason for the strangers—whome he instantly identified as Amerinds—halting and making such a fuss here was that their quarry had taken to the sea. He couldn't see them, but they couldn't be too far out. And his tribe, the Thana, couldn't be very far behind him.

So, repressing a warcry, he rode up and launched a boomerang at the gray-headed, red-eyed man sitting on his *hikwu*. Before the heavy wooden weapon struck the man on the side of the head and knocked him off his seat, Kickaha had transferred the spear from his left hand to his right. By then the few mounted warriors were aware of his presence. They wheeled their beasts, but one, another gray-haired man, didn't complete the turn in time to avoid Kickaha. His spear drove into the man's throat; the man fell backward; Kickaha jerked it out of the flesh, reversed it, and, using the shaft as a club, slammed it alongside the head of a warrior running to his *merk*.

Having run past all the men, he halted his beast, turned it, and charged again. This time he didn't go through the main body but skirted them, charging between them and the woods. A man threw a boomerang; Kickaha ducked; it whirred by, one tip just missing his shoulder. Crouched down, holding the shaft of the spear between his arm and body, Kickaha drove its tip into the back of a man who'd just gotten onto his animal but was having trouble controlling it. The man pitched forward and over the shoulder of his *hikwu*. Kickaha yanked the spear out as the man disappeared from his beast.

By then the first of the Thana had showed up, and the mélée started.

It should have been short work. The Amerinds were outnumbered and demoralized, caught, if not with their pants down, on foot, which was the same thing to them. But just as the last five were fighting furiously, though hopelessly, more whoops and yells were added to the din.

Kickaha looked up and swore. Here came a big body of more Amerinds, enough to outnumber the Thana. Within about eighty seconds, they'd be charging into his group.

He rose on his stirrups and looked out across the waves. At first, he couldn't see anything except a few amphibians. Then he saw a head and arms splashing the water. A few seconds later, he located a second swimmer.

He looked down the beach. A number of riderless *hikwu* had bolted when he'd burst among them, and three were standing at the edge of the forest, tearing off branches. Their first loyalty was to themselves, that is, their bellies.

Speaking of loyalties, what was his? Did he owe

the Thana anything? No, not really. It was true
that they'd initiated him, made him a sort of blood
brother. But his only choice then was to submit or
die, which wasn't a real choice. So, he didn't owe
his tribe anything.

Still standing up in the stirrups, he waved his
spear at the two heads in the waves. A white arm
came up and gestured at him. Anana's, no doubt of
that. He used the spear to indicate that she should
angle to a spot further down the beach. Immediately, she and McKay obeyed.

Good. They would come out of the water some
distance from the fight and would be able to grab
two of the browsing moosoids. But it would take
them some time to do so, and before then the
Amerinds might have won. So, it was up to him to
attempt to give Anana the needed time.

Yelling, he urged his *hikwu* into a gallop. His
spear drove deep into the neck of a redskin who
had just knocked a Thana off his saddle with a big
club. Once more, Kickaha jerked the spear loose.
He swore. The flint point had come off of the
wood. Never mind. He rammed its blunt end into
the back of the head of another Indian, stunning
him enough so that his antagonist could shove his
spear into the man's belly.

Then something struck Kickaha on the head,
and he fell half-conscious onto the sand. For a
moment he lay there while hoofs churned the sand,
stomped, missing him narrowly several times, and
a body thumped onto the ground beside him. It
was a Thana, Toini, the youth who'd given him a
hard time. Though blood streamed from his head
and his shoulder, Toini wasn't out of the battle. He
staggered up, only to be knocked down as a *hikwu*
backed into him.

Kickaha got up. For the first time he became aware that he was bleeding. Whatever had struck him on top of the head had opened the scalp. There was no time to take care of that now. He leaped for a mounted Indian who was beating at a Thana with a heavy boomerang, grabbed the man's arm, and yanked him off his saddle. Yelling, the warrior came down on Kickaha, and both fell to the sand.

Kickaha fastened his teeth on the redskin's nose and bit savagely. One groping hand felt around, closed on testicles, and squeezed.

Screaming, the man rolled off. Kickaha released his teeth, spun around on this back, raised his neck to see his enemy, and kicked his head hard with the heels of his feet. The man went limp and silent.

A hoof drove down hard, scraping the side of his upper arm. He rolled over to keep from being trampled. Blood and moosoid manure fell on him, and sand was kicked into his eyes. He got to his hands and knees. Half-blind, he crawled through the fray, was knocked over once by something or other, probably the side of a flailing *hikwu*-leg, got up, and crawled some more, stopped once when a spear drove into the sand just in front of his face, and then, finally, was in the water.

Here he opened his eyes all the way and ducked his head under the surface. It came up in time for him to see two mounted battlers coming toward him, a Thana and an Amerind striking at each other with boomerangs. The male beast of one was pushing the female of another out into the water. If he stayed where he was he was going to be pounded by the hooves. He dived away, his face and chest scraping against the bottom sand. When he came up, he was about twenty feet away. By then he recognized the Thana who was being driven from the shore. He was the chief, holding in one hand Kickaha's metal knife and in the other a boomerang. But he was outclassed by the younger man. His arms moved slowly as if they were very tired and the redskin was grinning in anticipation of his triumph.

Kickaha stood up to his waist and waded toward them. He got to the chief's side just as a blow from the young man's boomerang made the older's arm nerveless. The boomerang dropped; the chief thrust with his left but his knife missed; the enemy's wooden weapon came down on his head twice.

Wergenget dropped the knife into the water. Kickaha dived after it, skimmed the bottom, and his groping hands felt the blade. Then something, Wergenget, of course, fell on him. The shock knocked the air out of Kickaha's lungs; he gasped; water filled his throat; he came up out of the sea coughing and choking. He was down again, propelled by the redskin, who had jumped off his *hikwu*. Kickaha was at a definite disadvantage, trying to get his breath, and at the same time feeling for the knife he'd dropped.

His antagonist wasn't as big as he was, but he was certainly strong and quick. His left hand closed over Kickaha's throat, and his right hand came up with the boomerang. Kickaha, looking up through watery eyes, could see death. His right leg came up between the man's legs and his knee drove into the warrior's crotch. Since the leg had to come out of the water, its force wasn't as strong as Kickaha had hoped. Nevertheless, it was enough to cause the redskin some pain. For a moment, his hand loosed the throat, and he straightened up, his face contorted.

Kickaha was still on his back in the water, and his choking hadn't stopped. But his left hand touched something hard, the fingers opened out and closed on the blade. They moved up and gripped the hilt. The Indian reached down to grab the throat of what he thought was still a much-disadvantaged enemy. But he stood to one side so Kickaha couldn't use the crotch kick again.

Kickaha drove the end of the knife into the youth's belly just above the pubic region. It slit open the flesh to the navel; the youth dropped the boomerang, the hand reaching for the throat fell away; he looked surprised, clutched his belly, and fell face forward into the water.

Kickaha spent some time seemingly coughing his lungs out. Then he scanned the scene. The two beasts ridden by the chief and the Indian had bolted. Anana and McKay were still about four hundred feet from the shore and swimming strongly. The battle on the beach had tipped in favor of the Amerinds. But here came more of the Thana, including the women and Onil and Opwel, who had came down from their sentry perches. He doubted that the redskins could stand up under the new forces.

After removing Wergenget's belt and sheath, he wrapped it around his waist. He picked up a boomerang and waded until the water was up to his knees. He followed the line of the beach, got past the action, went ashore, and ran along the sand. When he got near some riderless moosoids, he slowed down, approached them cautiously, seized the reins, and tied them to the bushes. Another unmounted *hikwu* trotted along but slowed enough when Kickaha called to him to allow his reins to be grabbed. Kickaha tied him up and waded out into the sea to help the swimmers. They came along several minutes later. They were panting and tired. He had to support both to get them in to shore without collapsing. They threw themselves down on the sand and puffed like a blacksmith's bellows.

He said, "You've got to get up and on the *hikwu*."

"*Hikwu*?" Anana managed to say.

"The meese. Your steeds await to carry off you from peril."

He jerked a thumb at the beasts.

Anana succeeded in smiling. "Kickaha? Won't you ever quit kidding?"

He pulled her up, and she threw her arms around him and wept a little. "Oh, Kickaha, I thought I'd never see you again!"

"I've never been so happy," he said, "but I can become even happier if we get out of here now."

They ran to the animals, untied them, mounted, and galloped off. The clash and cry of battle faded away, and when they rounded another big bend they lost both sight and sound of it. They settled into a fast trot. Kickaha told her what had happened to him, though he discreetly omitted certain incidents. She then told her tale, slightly censored. Both expected to supply the missing details later, but now did not seem like a good time.

Kickaha said, "At any time, when you were up in a tree, did you see anything that could have been the palace?"

She shook her head.

"Well, I think we ought to climb one of those mountains surrounding the sea and take a look. Some are about five thousand feet high. If we could get to the top of one of those, we could see, hmm, it's been so long I can't remember. Wait a minute, I think from that height the horizon is, ah, around ninety-six statute miles.

"Well, it doesn't matter. We can see a hell of a long ways, and the palace is really big, according to Urthona. On the other hand, the horizon of this planet may not be as far away as Earth's. Anyway, it's worth a try."

Anana agreed. McKay didn't comment since the two were going to do what they wanted to do. He followed them into the woods.

It took three days to get to the top of the conical peak. The climb was difficult enough, but they had to take time out to hunt and to allow themselves and the beasts to rest. After hobbling the animals, Anana and Kickaha set out on foot, leaving McKay to make sure the *hikwu* didn't stray too far. The last hundred feet of the ascent was the hardest. The mountain ended in a harp spire that swayed back and forth due to the slightly changing shape of the main mass. The very tip, though it looked needle-sharp from below, actually was a dirt platform about the size of a large dining room table. They stood on it and swept the sea with their gaze and wished they had a pair of binoculars.

After a while, Kickaha said, "Nothing."

"I'm afraid so," Anana said. She turned around to look over the vista outside the sea-land, and she clutched his arm.

"Look!"

Kickaha's eyes sighted along the line indicated by her arm.

"I don't know," he said. "It looks like a big dark rock, or a hill, to me."

"No, it's moving! Wait a minute."

The object could easily have been hidden by one

of two mountains if it had been on the left or right
for a half a mile. It was moving just beyond a very
broad pass and going up a long gentle slope. Kickaha estimated that it was about twenty miles away
and of an enormous size.

"That *has* to be the palace!" he said. "It must
have come through a pass from the sea-land!"

The only thing damping his joy was that it was so
far away. By the time they got down off the mountain, traveled to the next pass and got through it,
the palace would be even further away. Not only
that, they could not depend upon the two mountains to guide them. By the time they got there, the
mountains could be gone or they could have split
into four or merged into one. It was so easy to lose
your bearings here, especially when there was no
east or north or south or west.

Still, the range that circled the sea-lands would
be behind them and it changed shape very little.

"Let's go!" he said, and he began to let himself
backward over the lip of the little plateau.

CHAPTER EIGHTEEN

IT WAS ELEVEN days later. The trio hoped that within a few days they would be in sight of the palace. The twin peaks between which it had gone had become one breast-shaped giant. Deep hollows had formed around it, and these were full of water from a heavy rain of the day before. It was necessary to go about ten miles around the enormous moat.

Before they rounded it, the mountain grew into a cone, the hollows pushed up, spilling the water out. They decided to climb the mountain then to get another sight of Urthona's ex-abode. Though the climb would delay them even more, they thought it worth it. The mobile structure could have headed on a straight line, turned in either direction, or even be making a great curve to come behind them. According to Anana's uncle, when it was on automatic, its travel path was random.

On top of the mountain, they looked in all directions. Plains and ranges spread out, slowly shifting shape. There was plenty of game and here and there dark masses which were groves and forests of traveling plants. Far off to the right were tiny figures, a line of tribespeople on their way to the sea-land.

All three strained their eyes and finally Kickaha saw a dot moving slowly straight ahead. Was it an army of trees or the palace?

"I don't think you could see it if it was composed of plants," Anana said. "They don't get very high, you know. At this distance that object would have to be something with considerable height."

"Let's hope so," Kickaha said.

McKay groaned. He was tired of pushing themselves and the animals to the limit.

There was nothing to do but go on. Though they traveled faster than their quarry, they had to stop to hunt, eat, drink, and sleep. It continued on at its mild pace, a kilometer an hour, like an enormous mindless untiring turtle in tepid heat looking for a mate. And it left no tracks, since it floated a half-meter above the surface.

For the next three days it rained heavily. They slogged on through, enduring the cold showers, but many broad depressions formed and filled with water, forcing them to go around them. Much mileage was lost.

The sixth day after they'd sighted the palace again, they lost Anana's beast. While they were sleeping, a lion attacked it, and though they drove the lion off, they had to put the badly mauled *hikwu* out of its misery. This provided for their meat supply for several days before it got too rotten to eat, but Anana had to take turns riding behind the two men. And this slowed them down.

The sixteenth day, they climbed another mountain for another sighting. This time they could identify it, but it wasn't much closer than the last time seen.

"We could chase it clear around this world," McKay said disgruntledly.

"If we have to, we have to," Kickaha said cheerfully. "You've been bitching a lot lately, Mac. You're beginning to get on my nerves. I know it's a very hard life, and you haven't had a woman

for many months, but you'd better grin and bear it.
Crack a few jokes, do a cakewalk now and then."

McKay looked sullen. "This ain't no minstrel
show."

"True, but Anana and I are doing our best to
make light of it. I suggest you change your attitude. You could be worse off. You could be dead.
We have a chance, a good one, to get out of here.
You might even get back to Earth, though I suppose it'd be best for the people there if you didn't.
You've stolen, tortured, killed, and raped. But
maybe, if you were in a different environment, you
might change. That's why I don't think it'd be a
good idea for you to return to Earth."

"How in hell did we get off from my bitching to
that subject," McKay said.

Kickaha grinned. "One thing leads to another.
The point I'm getting at is that you're a burden.
Anana and I could go faster if we didn't have to
carry you on our moosoid."

"Yours?" McKay blazed, sullenness becoming
open anger. "She's riding on my *gregg*!"

"Actually, it belongs to an Indian. Did, I should
say. Now its whoever has the strength to take it.
Do I make myself clear?"

"You'd desert me?"

"Rationally, we should. But Anana and I won't
as long as you help us. So," he suddenly shouted,
"quit your moaning and groaning!"

McKay grinned. "Okay. I guess you're right. I
ain't no crybaby, normally, but this . . ." He
waved a hand to indicate the whole world. "Too
much. But I promise to stop beefing. I guess I ain't
been no joy for you two."

Kickaha said, "Okay. Let's go. Now, did I ever
tell you about the time I had to hide out in a fully

stocked wine cellar in a French town when the
Krauts retook it?''

Two months later, the traveling building still had
not been caught. They were much closer now.
When they occasionally glimpsed it, it was about
ten miles away. Even at that distance, it looked
enormous, towering an estimated 2600 feet, a little
short of half a mile. Its width and length were each
about 1200 feet, and its bottom was flat.

Kickaha could see its outline but could not, of
course, make out its details. According to Urthona, it would, at close range, look like an ambulatory Arabian Nights city with hundreds of
towers, minarets, domes, and arches. From time
to time its surface changed color, and once it was
swathed in rainbows.

Now, it was halfway on the other side of an
enormous plain that had opened out while they
were coming down a mountain. The range that had
ringed it was flattening out, and the animals that
had been on the mountainsides were now great
herds on the plains.

''Ten miles away,'' Kickaha said. ''And it must
have about thirty miles more to go before it
reaches the end of the plain. I say we should try to
catch it now. Push until our *hikwu* drop and then
chase it on foot. Keep going no matter what.''

The others agreed, but they weren't enthusiastic. They'd lost weight, and their faces were
hollow-cheeked, their eyes ringed with the dark of
near-exhaustion. Nevertheless, they had to make
the effort. Once the palace reached the mountains,
it would glide easily up over them, maintaining the
same speed as it had on the plain. But its pursuers
would have to slow down.

As soon as they reached the flatland, they urged

the poor devils under them into a gallop. They responded as best they could, but they were far from being in top condition. Nevertheless, the ground was being eaten up. The herds parted before them, the antelopes and gazelles stampeding. During the panic the predators took advantage of the confusion and panic. The dogs, baboons, moas, and lions caught fleeing beasts and dragged them to the ground. Roars, barks, screams drifted by the riders as they raced toward their elusive goal.

Now Kickaha saw before them some very strange creatures. They were mobile plants— perhaps—resembling nothing he'd ever come across before. In essence, they looked like enormous logs with legs. The trunks were horizontal, pale-gray, with short stubby branches bearing six or seven diamond-shaped black-green leaves. From each end rose structures that looked like candelabra. But as he passed one he saw that eyes, enormous eyes, much like human eyes, were at the ends of the candelabra. These turned as the two moosoids galloped by.

More of these weird-looking things lay ahead of them. Each had a closed end and an open end.

Kickaha directed his *hikwu* away from them, and McKay followed suit. Kickaha shouted to Anana, who was seated behind him, "I don't like the looks of those things!"

"Neither do I!"

One of the logoids, about fifty yards to one side, suddenly began tilting up its open end, which was pointed at them. The other end rested on the ground while the forelegs began telescoping upward.

Kickaha got the uneasy impression that the

thing resembled a cannon the muzzle of which was being elevated for firing.

A moment later, the dark hole in its raised end shot out black smoke. From the smoke something black and blurred described an arc and fell about twenty feet to their right.

It struck the rusty grass, and it exploded.

The moosoid screamed and increased its gallop as if it had summoned energy from somewhat within it.

Kickaha was half-deafened for a moment. But he wasn't so stunned he didn't recognize the odor of the smoke. Black gunpowder!

Anana said, ''Kickaha, you're bleeding!''

He didn't feel anything, and now was no time to stop to find out where he'd been hit. He yelled more encouragement to his *hikwu*. But that yell was drowned the next moment when at least a dozen explosions circled him. The smoke blinded him for a moment, then he was out of it. Now he couldn't hear at all. Anana's hands were still around his waist, though, so he knew she was still with him.

He looked back over his shoulder. Here came McKay on his beast flying out of black clouds. And behind him came a projectile, a shell-shaped black object, drifting along lazily, or so it seemed. It fell behind McKay, struck, went up with a roar, a cloud of smoke in the center of which fire flashed. The black man's *hikwu* went over, hooves over hooves. McKay flew off the saddle, struck the ground, and rolled. The big body of his *hikwu* flipflopped by, narrowly missing him.

But McKay was up and running.

Kickaha pulled his *hikwu* up, stopping it.

Through the drifting smoke he could see that a

dozen of the plants had erected their front open ends and pointed them toward the humans. Out of the cannonlike muzzles of two shot more smoke, noise, and projectiles. These blew up behind McKay at a distance of forty feet. He threw himself on the ground—too late, of course to escape their effects—but he was up and running as soon as they had gone off.

Behind him were two small craters in the ground.

Miraculously, McKay's moosoid had not broken its neck or any legs. It scrambled up, its lips drawn back to reveal all its big long teeth, its eyes seemingly twice as large. It sped by McKay whose mouth opened as he shouted curses that Kickaha couldn't hear.

Anana had already grasped what had to be done. She had slipped off the saddle and was making motions to Kickaha, knowing he couldn't hear her. He kicked the sides of the beast and yelled at it, though he supposed it was as deaf as he. It responded and went after McKay's fleeing beast. The chase was a long one, however, and ended when McKay's mount stopped running. Foam spread from its mouth and dappled its front, and its sides swelled and shrank like a bellows. It crumpled, rolled over on its side, and died.

Its rear parts were covered with blood.

Kickaha rode back to where Anana and McKay stood. They were wounded, too, mainly in the back. Blood welled from a score of little objects half-buried in the skin. Now he became aware that blood was coming from just behind and above his right elbow.

He grabbed the thing stuck in his skin and pulled it out. Rubbing the blood from its surface, he looked at it. It was a six-pointed crystalline star.

"Craziest shrapnel I ever saw," he said. No one heard him.

The plants, which he had at once named cannonlabra, had observed that their shelling had failed to get the passersby. They were now heading away, traveling slowly on their hundred or so pairs of thin big-footed legs. Fifteen minutes later he was to see several lay their explosive eggs near enough to an elephant calf to kill it. Some of the things then climbed over the carcass and began tearing at it with claws which appeared from within the feet. The foremost limbs dropped pieces of meat into an aperture on the side.

Apparently McKay's dead animal was too far away to be observed.

Anana and McKay spent the next ten minutes painfully pulling the "shrapnel" from their skins. Pieces of grass were applied to the wounds to stop the bleeding.

"I'd sure like to stuff Urthona down the muzzle of one of those," Kickaha said. "It'd be a pleasure to see him riding its shell. He must have had a lot of sadistic pleasure out of designing those things."

He didn't know how the creature could covert its food into black gunpowder. It took charcoal, sodium or potassium nitrate, and sulfur to make the explosive. That was one mystery. Another was how the things "grew" shell-casings. A third was how they ignited the charge that propelled the shells.

There was no time to investigate. A half-hour had been lost in the chase, and McKay had no steed.

"Now, you two, don't argue with me," he said. He got off the *hikwu*. "Anana, you ride like hell after the palace. You can go faster if I'm not on it, and you're the lightest one so you'll be the least burden for the *hikwu*. I was thinking for a minute that maybe McKay and I could run alongside you, hanging onto the saddle. But we'd start bleeding again, so that's out.

"You take off now. If you catch up with the palace, you might be able to get inside and stop it. It's a slim chance, but it's all we got.

"We'll be moseying along."

Anana said, "That makes sense. Wish me luck."

She said, "*Heekhyu!*", the Wendow word for "Giddap!", and the moosoid trotted off. Presently, under Anana's lashings, it was galloping.

McKay and Kickaha started walking. The flies settled on their wounds. Behind them explosions sounded as the cannonlabra laid down an artillery barrage in the midst of an antelope herd.

An hour passed. They were trotting now, but their leaden legs and heavy breathing had convinced them they couldn't keep up the pace. Still, the palace was bigger. They were gaining on it. The tiny figures of Anana and her beast had merged into the rusty grass of what seemed a never-ending plain.

They stopped to drink bad-tasting water from the bag McKay had taken off of his dead *hikwu*. McKay said, "Man, if she don't catch that palace, we'll be stranded here for the rest of our life."

"Maybe it'll reverse its course," Kickaha said. He didn't sound very optimistic.

Just as he was lifting the bag to pour water into his open mouth, he felt the earth shaking. Refusing to be interrupted, he quenched his thirst. But as he put the bag down he realized that this was no ordinary tremor caused by shape-shifting. It was a genuine earthquake. The ground was lifting up and down, and he felt as if he were standing on a plate in an enormous bowl of jelly being shaken by a giant. The effect was scarey and nauseating.

McKay had thrown himself down on the earth. Kickaha decided he might as well do so, too. There was no use wasting energy trying to stand up. He faced toward the palace, however, so he could see what was happening in that direction. This was really rotten luck. While this big temblor was going on, Anana would not be able to ride after the palace.

The shaking up-and-down movement continued. The animals had fled for the mountains, the worst place for them if the quake continued. The birds were taking off, millions salt-and-peppering the sky, then coalescing to form one great cloud. They were all heading toward the direction of the palace.

Presently, he saw a dot coming toward him. In a few minutes it became a microscopic Anana and *hikwu*. Then the two separated, both rolling on the ground. Only Anana got up. She ran toward him or tried to do so, rather. The waves of grass-covered earth were like swells in the sea. They rose beneath her and propelled her forward down their slope, casting her on her face. She got up and ran some more, and, once, she disappeared behind a big roller, just like a small boat in a heavy sea.

"I'm going to get sick," McKay said. He did. Up to then Kickaha had been able to manage his own nausea, but the sound of the black man's heavings and retchings sparked off his own vomit.

Now, above the sounds he was making, he heard a noise that was as loud as if the world were cracking apart. He was more frightened then he'd ever been in his life. Nevertheless, he got to his hands and knees and stared out toward where Anana had been. He couldn't see her, but he could see just beyond where she'd been.

The earth was curling up like a scroll about to be rolled. Its edges were somewhat beyond where he'd last seen Anana. But she could have fallen into the gigantic fissure.

He got to his feet and cried, "Anana! Anana!" He tried to run toward her, but he was pitched up so violently that he rose a foot into the air. When he came down he slid on his face down the slope of a roller.

He struggled up again. For a moment he was even more confused and bewildered, his sense of unreality increasing. The mountains in the far distance seemed to be sliding downward as if the planet had opened to swallow them.

Then he realized that they were not falling down.

The ground on which he stood was rising.

He was on a mass being torn away to make a temporary satellite for the main body of the planet.

The palace was out of sight now, but he had seen that it was still on the main body. The fissure had missed by a mile or so marooning it with its pursuers.

CHAPTER NINETEEN

THE SPLITOFF NOW was one hundred miles above the primary and in a stable, if temporary, orbit. It would take about four hundred days before the lesser mass started to fall into the greater. And that descent would be a slow one.

The air seemed no less thick than that on the surface of the planet. The atmosphere had the same pressure at an altitude of 528,000 feet as it had at ground zero. Urthona had never explained the physical principles of this phenomenon. This was probably because he didn't know them. Though he had made the specifications for the pocket universe, he had left it up to a team of scientists to make his world work. The scientists were dead millenia ago, and the knowledge long lost. But their manufactures survived and apparently would until all the universes ran down.

The earthquakes had not ceased once the splitoff had torn itself away. It had started readjusting, shaping from a wedgeform into a globe. This cataclysmic process had taken twelve days, during which its marooned life had had to move around much and swiftly to keep from being buried. Much of it had not succeeded. The heat of energy released during the transformation had been terrible, but it had been alleviated by one rainstorm after another. For almost a fortnight, Kickaha and his companions had been living in a Turkish bath. All they wanted to do was to lie down and pant. But they had been forced to keep moving, sometimes vigorously.

On the other hand, because of the much weaker gravity, only one-sixteenths that of the primary, their expenditure of energy took them much more swiftly and further than it would have on the planet. And there were so many carcasses and dead plants around that they didn't have to hunt for food. Another item of nourishment was the flying seed. When the separation had started, every plant on the moon had released hundreds of seeds which were borne by the wind on tissue-thin alates or masses of threads. These rose, some drifting down towards the parent world, others falling back onto the satellite. They were small, but a score or so made a mouthful and provided a protein-high vegetable. Even the filmy wings and threads could be eaten.

"Nature's, or Urthona's, way of making sure the various species of plants survive the catastrophe," Kickaha said.

But when the mutations of terrain stopped and the carcasses became too stinking to eat, they had to begin hunting. Though the humans could run and jump faster, once they learned the new method of locomotion, the animals were proportionately just as speedy. But Kickaha fashioned a new type of bola, two or three antelope skulls connected by a rawhide cord. He would whirl this around and around and then send it skimming along the ground to entangle the legs of the quarry. McKay and Anana made their own bolas, and all three were quite adept at casting them. They even caught some of the wild moosoids with these.

Those seeds that fell back on the splitoff put down roots, and new plants grew quickly. The grass and the soil around them became bleached as the nutritional elements were sucked up. The plantling would grow a set of legs and pull up the main root or break it off and move on to rich soil. The legs would fall off but a new set, longer and stronger, would grow. After three moves, the plants stayed rooted until they had attained their full growth. Their maturation period was exceedingly swift by Terrestrial standards.

Of course, many were eaten by the elephants, moosoids, and other animals which made plants their main diet. But enough survived to provide countless groves of ambulatory trees and bushes.

The three had their usual troubles with baboons, dogs, and the feline predators. Added to those was a huge bird they'd never seen before. Its wing-spread was fifty feet, though the body was comparatively small. Its head was scarlet; the eyes, cold yellow; the green beak, long, hooked, and sharp. The wings and body were bluish, and the short thick heavily taloned legs were ochre. It swooped down from the sky just after dusk, struck, and carried its prey off. Since the gravity was comparatively weak here, it could lift a human into the air. Twice, one of them almost got Anana. Only by throwing herself on the ground when Kickaha had cried a warning had she escaped being borne away.

"I can't figure out what it does when there is no satellite," Kickaha said. "It could never lift a large body from the surface of the primary. So what does it live on between-times?"

"Maybe it just soars around, living off its fat, until the planet spits up another part of it," Anana said.

They were silent for a while then, imagining these huge aerial creatures gliding through the air fifty miles up, half-asleep most of the time, waiting for the mother planet to propel its meat on a Moon-sized dish up to it.

"Yes, but it has to land somewhere on the satellite to eat and to mate," he said. "I wonder where?"

"Why do you want to know?"

"I got an idea, but it's so crazy I don't want to talk about it yet. It came to me in a dream last night."

Anana suddenly gripped his arm and pointed upward. He and McKay looked up. There, perhaps a half a mile above them, the palace was floating by.

They stood silently watching it until it had disappeared behind some high mountains.

Kickaha sighed and said, "I guess that when it's on automatic it circles the satellite. Urthona must have set it to do that so that he could observe the moon. Damn! So near yet so far!"

The Lord must have gotten pleasure out of watching the shifts in the terrain and the adjustments of people and animals to it. But surely he hadn't lived alone in it. What had he done for companionship and sex? Abducted women from time to time, used them, then abandoned them on the surface? Or kicked them out and watched them fall one hundred miles, perhaps accompanying them during the descent to see their horror, hear their screams?

It didn't matter now. Urthona's victims and Urthona were all dead now. What was important was how they were going to survive the rejoining of primary and secondary.

Anana said that her uncle had told her that about a month prior to this event, the satellite again mutated form. It changed from a globe to a rough

rectangle of earth, went around the primary five
times, and then lowered until it became part of the
mother world again.

Only those animals that happened to be on the
upper part had a chance to live through the impact.
Those on the undersurface would be ground into
bits and their pieces burned. And those living in
the area of the primary onto which the satellite fell
would also be killed.

Urthona had, however, given some a chance to
get out and from under. He'd given them an instinctive mechanism which made them flee at their
fastest speed from any area over which the satellite came close. It had a set orbital path prior to
landing, and as it swung lower every day, the
animals "knew" that they had to leave the area.
Unfortunately, only those on the outer limits of the
impact had time to escape.

The plants were too slow to get out in time, but
their instincts made them release their floating
seeds.

All of this interested Kickaha. His chief concern, however, was to determine which side of the
moon the three would be on when the change from
a globe to a rectangle was made. That is, whether
they would be on the upper side, that opposite the
planet, or on the underside.

"There isn't any way of finding out," Anana
said. "We'll just have to trust to luck."

"I've depended on that in the past," he said.
"But I don't want to now. You only use luck when
there's nothing else left."

He did much thinking about their situation in the
days and nights that slid by. The moon rotated
slowly, taking about thirty days to complete a
single spin. The colossal body of the planet hang-

ing in the sky revealed the healing of the great
wound made by the withdrawal of the splitoff. The
only thing for which they had gratitude for being
on the secondary was that they weren't in the area
of greatest shape-change, that near the opening of
the hole, which extended to the center of the
planet. They saw, when the clouds were missing,
the sides fall in, avalanches of an unimaginable but
visible magnitude. And the mass shrank before
their eyes as adjustments were made all over the
planet. Even the sea-lands must be undergoing
shakings of terrifying strength, enough to make the
minds and souls of the inhabitants reel with the
terrain.

"Urthona must have enjoyed the spectacle
when he was riding around in his palace," Kickaha
said. "Sometimes I wish you hadn't killed him,
Anana. He'd be down there now, finding out what
a horror he'd subjected his creations to."

One morning Kickaha told his companions
about a dream he'd had. It had begun with him
enthusiastically telling them about his plan to get
them off the moon. They'd thought it was wonder-
ful, and all three had started at once on the project.
First, they'd walked to a mountain the top of
which was a sleeping place for the giant birds,
which they called rocs. They'd climbed to the top
and found that it contained a depression in which
the rocs rested during the day.

The three had slid down the slope of the hollow,
and each had sneaked up on a sleeping roc. Then
each had killed his or her bird by driving the knives
and a pointed stick through the bird's eye into its
brain. Then they'd hidden under a wing of the dead
bird until the others had awakened and flown off.
After which they'd cut off the wings and tail feath-

ers and carried them back to their camp.

"Why did we do this?" Anana said.

"So we could use the wings and tails to make gliders. We attached them to fuselages of wood, and . . ."

"Excuse me," Anana said, smiling. "You've never mentioned having any glider experience."

"That's because I haven't. But I've read about gliders, and I did take a few hours' private instruction in a Piper Cub, just enough to solo. But I had to quit because I ran out of money."

"I haven't been up in a glider for about thirty years," Anana said. "But I've built many, and I've three thousand hours flight time in them."

"Great! Then you can teach Mac and me how to glide. Anyway, in this dream we attached the wings to the fuselage and, to keep the wings from flexing, we tied wood bars to the wing bones, and we used rawhide strips instead of wires . . ."

Anana interrupted again. "How did you control this makeshift glider?"

"By shifting our weight. That's how John Montgomery and Percy Pilcher and Otto and Gustave Lilienthal did it. They hung under or between the wings, suspended in straps or on a seat, and they did all right. Uh . . . until John and Otto and Percy were killed, that is."

McKay said, "I'm glad this was just a dream."

"Yeah? Dreams are springboards into reality."

McKay groaned, and he said, "I just knew you was in earnest."

Anana, looking as if she was about to break into laughter, said, "Well, we could make gliders out of wood and antelope hide, I suppose. They wouldn't work once we got into the primary's gravity field, though, even if they would work here. So there's no use being serious about this.

"Anyway, even if we could glide down a mountain slope here and catch an updraft, we couldn't go very high. The moon's surface has no variety of terrain to make termals, no plowed fields, no paved roads, and so on."

"What's the use even talking about this?" McKay said.

"It helps pass the time," she said. "So, Kickaha, how did you plan to get the gliders high enough to get out of the moon's gravity?"

Kickaha said, "Look, if we shoot up, from our viewpoint, we're actually shooting downward from the viewpoint of people on the surface of the primary. All we have to do is get into the field of the primary's gravity, and we'll fall."

McKay, looking alarmed, said, "What do you mean—*shoot*?"

He had good reason to be disturbed. The redhead had gotten him into a number of dangerous situations because of his willingness to take chances.

"Here's how it was in the dream. We located a battery of cannonlabra, killed four of them, and carried them to our camp. We cut off their branches and eyestalks to streamline their bodies. Then . . ."

"Wait a minute," Anana said. "I think I see where you're going. You mean that you converted those cannon-creatures into rockets? And tied the gliders to them and then launched the rockets and after the rockets were high up cut the gliders loose?"

Kickaha nodded. Anana laughed loudly and long.

McKay said, "It's only a dream, ain't it?"

Kickaha, his face red, said, "Listen, I worked it all out. It could be done. What I did . . ."

"It would work in a dream," she said. "But in reality, there'd be no way to control the burning of the gunpowder. To get high enough, you'd have to stuff the barrel with powder to the muzzle. But when the fuel exploded, and it would, all of it at once, the sudden acceleration would tear the glider from the rocket, completely wreck the structure and wings of the glider, and also kill you."

"Look, Anana," Kickaha said, his face even redder, "isn't there some way we could figure out to get controlled explosions?"

"Not with the materials we have available. No, forget it. It was a nice dream, but . . . oh, hah, hah, hah!"

"I'm glad your woman's got some sense," McKay said. "How'd you ever manage to live so long?"

"I guess because I haven't followed through with all my wild ideas. I'm only half-crazy, not completely nuts. But we've got to get off of here. If we end up on the under side when it changes shape, we're done for. It's the big kissoff for us."

There was a very long silence. Finally, Anana said, "You're right. We have to do something. We must look for materials to make gliders that could operate in the primary's field. But getting free of the moon's gravity is something else. I don't see how . . ."

"A hot-air balloon!" Kickaha cried. "It could take us and the gliders up and away and out!"

Kickaha thought that, if the proper materials could be found to make a balloon and gliders, the liftoff should take place after the moon changed its shape. It would be spread out then, the attenuation of the body making the local gravity even weaker. The balloon would thus have greater lifting power.

Anana said that he had a good point there. But the dangers from the cataclysmic mutation were too high. They might not survive these. Or, if they did, their balloon might not. And they wouldn't have time after the shape-change to get more materials.

Kickaha finally agreed with her.

Another prolonged discussion was about the gliders. Anana, after some thought, said that they should make parawings instead. She explained that a parawing was a type of parachute, a semi-glider the flight of which could be controlled somewhat.

"The main trouble is still the materials," she said. "A balloon of partially cured antelope hide might lift us enough, considering the far weaker gravity. But how would the panels be held together? We don't have any adhesive, and stitching them together might not, probably will not, work. The hot air would escape through the overlaps. Still . . ."

McKay, who was standing nearby, shouted. They turned to look in the direction at which he was pointing.

Coming from around a pagoda-shaped mountain, moving slowly towards them, was a gigantic object. Urthona's palace. It floated along across the plain at a majestic pace at an estimated altitude of two hundred feet.

They waited for it, and after two hours it reached them. They had retreated to one side far enough for them to get a complete view of it from top to bottom. It seemed to be cut out of a single block of smooth stone on material which looked like stone. This changed color about every fifteen minutes, glowing brightly, running the spectrum, finishing it with a rainbow sheen of blue, white, green, and rose-red. Then the cycle started over again.

There were towers, minarets, and bartizans on the walls, thousands of them, and these had windows and doors, square, round, diamond-shaped, hexagonal, octagonal. There were also windows on the flat bottom. Kickaha counted two hundred balconies, then gave up.

Anana said, "I know we can't reach it. But I'm going to try the Horn anyway."

The seven notes floated up. As they expected, no shimmering prelude to the opening of a gate appeared on its walls.

Kickaha said, "We should've choked the codeword out of Urthona. Or cooked him over a fire."

"That wouldn't help us in this situation," she said.

"Hey!" McKay shouted. "Hey! Look!"

Staring from a window on the bottom floor was a face. A man's.

CHAPTER TWENTY

THE WINDOW WAS round and taller than the man. Even at that distance and though he was moving, they could see that he was not Urthona or Red Orc. It was impossible to tell without reference points how tall the young man was. His hair was brown and pulled tightly back as if it were tied in a pony tail. His features were handsome. He wore a suit of a cut which Kickaha had never seen before, but which Anana would tell him was of a style in fashion among the Lords a long time ago. The jacket glittered as if its threads were pulsing neon tubes. The shirt was ruffled and open at the neck.

Presently the man had passed them, but he reappeared a minute later at another window. Then they saw him racing by the windows. Finally, out of breath, he stopped and put his face to the corner window. After a while, he was out of sight.

"Did you recognize him?" Kickaha said.

"No, but that doesn't mean anything," Anana said. "There were many Lords, and even if I'd known him for a little while, I might have forgotten him after all those years."

"Not mean enough, heh?" Kickaha said. "Well then, if he isn't one of them, what's he doing in Urthona's palace? How'd he get there? And if he's interested in us, which he was from his actions, why didn't he change the controls to manual and stop the palace?"

She shrugged. "How would I know?"

"I didn't really expect you to. Maybe he doesn't know how to operate the controls. He may be trapped. I mean—he gated into the place and doesn't know how to get out."

"Or he's found the control room but is afraid to enter because he knows it'll be trapped."

McKay said, "Maybe he'll figure out a way to get in without getting caught."

"By then he won't be able to find us even if he wants to," she said.

"The palace'll be coming around again," Kickaha said. "Maybe by then . . ."

Anana shook her head. "I doubt the palace stays on the same orbit. It probably spirals around."

On the primary, the palace was only a few feet above the ground. Here, for some reason, if floated about a hundred feet from the surface. Anana speculated that Urthona might've set the automatic controls for this altitude because the palace would accompany the moon when it fell.

"He could go down with it and yet be distant enough so the palace wouldn't be disturbed by the impact."

"If that's so, then the impact must not be too terrible. If it were, the ground could easily buckle to a hundred feet or more. But what about a mountain falling over on it?"

"I don't know. But Urthona had a good reason for doing it. Unfortunately for us, it removes any chance for us to get to the palace while it's on the moon."

They did not see the palace. Evidently, it did follow a spiral path.

The days and sometimes the nights that succeeded the appearance of the building were busy.

In addition to hunting, which took much time, they had to knock over and kill trees and skin the antelopes they slew. Branches were cut from the trees and shaped with axe and knife. The skins were scraped and dehaired, though not to Anana's satisfaction. She fashioned needles from wood and sewed the skins together. Then she cut away parts of these to make them the exact shape needed. After this, she sewed the triangular form onto the wooden structure.

The result was a three-cornered kite-shape. The rawhide strips used as substitutes for wires were tied onto the glider.

Anana had hoped to use a triangular trapeze bar for control. But their efforts to make one of three wooden pieces tied at the corners failed. It just wasn't structurally sound enough. It was likely to fall apart when subjected to stress of operation.

Instead, she settled for the parallel bar arrangement. The pilot would place his armpits over the bars and grasp the uprights. Control would be effected, she hoped, through shifting of the pilot's weight.

When the bars and uprights were installed, Anana frowned.

"I don't know if it'll stand up under the stress. Well, only one way to find out."

She got into position underneath the glider. Then, instead of running, as she would have had to do on the planet, she crouched down and leaped into the wind. She rose thirty-five feet, inclined the nose upwards a little to catch the wind, and glided for a short distance. She stalled the machine just before landing and settled down.

The others had bounded after her. She said, grinning, "The first antelope-hide glider in history has just made its first successful flight."

She continued making the short glides, stopping when she had gone two miles. They walked back then, and Kickaha, after receiving instructions again—for the twentieth time—tried his skill. McKay succeeded him without mishap, and they called it a day.

"Tomorrow we'll practice on the plain again," she said. "The day after, we'll go up a mountain a little ways and try our luck there. I want you two to get some practice in handling a glider in a fairly long glide. I don't expect you to become proficient. You just need to get the feel of handling it."

On the fifth day of practice, they tried some turns. Anana had warned them to pick up plenty of speed when they did, since the lower wing in a bank lost velocity. If it slowed down too much, the glider could stall. They followed her prescription faithfully and landed safely.

"It'd be nice if we could jump off a cliff and soar," she said. "That'd really give you practice. But there are no thermals. Still, you'd be able to glide higher. Maybe we should."

The men said that they'd like to give it a go. But they had to wait until a nearby mountain would form just the right shape needed. That is, a mountain with a slope on one side up which they could walk and more or less right-angles verticality on the other side. By the time that happened, she had built her parawing. This was not to be folded for opening when the jump was made. The hide was too stiff for that. It was braced with lightweight wood to form a rigid structure.

They climbed the mountain to the top. Anana, without any hesitation, grabbed the wing, holding it above her head but with its nose pointed down to keep the wind from catching in it. She leaped off the four thousand foot high projection, released her hold, dropped, was caught in the harness, and was off. The two men retreated from the outthrust of earth just in time. With only a slight sound, the ledge gave way and fell.

They watched her descend, more swiftly than in the glider, pull the nose cords to dive faster, release them to allow the nose to lift, and then work the ropes so that she could bank somewhat.

When they saw her land, they turned and went back down the mountain.

The next day McKay jumped and the following day Kickaha went off the mountain. Both landed without accident.

Anana was pleased with their successful jumps. But she said, "The wing is too heavy to use over the primary. We have to find a lighter wood and something that'll be much lighter than the antelope hides for a wing-covering."

By then the covering was stinking badly. It was thrown away for the insects and the dogs to eat.

She did, however, make another wing, installing this time steering slots and antistall nose flaps. They took it up another mountain, the cliffside of which was only a thousand feet high. Anana jumped again and seemed to be doing well when a roc dived out of the sky and fastened its claw in the wing. It lifted then, flapping its wings, which had a breadth of fifty feet, heading for the mountain on which it roosted.

Anana threw her throwing axe upwards. Its point caught on the lower side of the bird's neck, then dropped. But the bird must have decided it had hold of a tough customer. It released the parawing, and she glided swiftly down. For a few minutes the bird followed her. If it had attacked her while she was on the ground, it could have had her in a defenseless situation. But it swooped over her, uttering a harsh cry, and then rose in search of less alien and dangerous prey.

Anana spent an hour looking for the axe, failed to find it, and ran home because a moa had appeared in the distance. The next day the three went back to search for it. After half a day McKay found it behind a boulder that had popped out of the earth while they were looking.

The next stage in the project was to make a small test balloon. First, though, they had to build a windbreak. The wind, created by the passage of the moon through the atmosphere at an estimated ten miles an hour, never stopped blowing. Which meant that they would never be able to finish the inflation of the balloon before it blew away.

The work took four weeks. They dug up the ground with the knives, the axe, and pointed sticks. When they had a semicircle of earth sixteen feet high, they added a roof supported by the trunks of dead plants of a giant species.

Then came the antelope hunting. At the end of two days' exhausting hunting and transportation of skins from widely scattered places, they had a large pile. But the hides were in varying stages of decomposition.

There was no time to rest. They scraped off the fat and partially dehaired the skins. Then they cut them, and Anana and Kickaha sewed the panels together. McKay had cut strips and made a network of them.

Dawn found them red-eyed and weary. But they started the fire on the earthen floor of the little basket. Using a gallows of wood, they hoisted the limp envelope up so that the heat from the fire would go directly into the open neck of the bag. Gradually it inflated. When it seemed on the brink of rising, they grabbed the cords hanging from the network around the bag and pulled it out from under the roof. The wind caught it, sent it scooting across the plain, the basket tilting to one side. Some of the fire was shifted off the earth, and the basket began to burn. But the balloon, the envelope steadily expanding, rose.

Pale-blue smoke curled up from the seams.

Anana shook her head. "I knew it wasn't tight enough."

Nevertheless, the aerostat continued to rise. The basket hanging from the rawhide ropes burned and presently one end swung loose, spilling what remained of the fire. The balloon rose a few more feet, then began to sink, and shortly was falling. By then it was at least five miles away horizontally and perhaps a mile high. It passed beyond the shoulder of a mountain, no doubt to startle the animals there and to provide food for the dogs and the baboons and perhaps the lions.

"I wish I'd had a camera," Kickaha said. "The only rawhide balloon in the history of mankind."

"Even if we find a material suitable for the envelope covering," Anana said, "it'll be from an animal. And it'll rot too quickly."

"The natives know how to partially cure rawhide," he said. "And they might know where we could get the wood and the covering we need. So, we'll find us some natives and interrogate them."

Four weeks later, they were about to give up looking for human beings. They decided to try for three days more. The second day, from the side of a shrinking mountain, they saw a small tribe moving across a swelling plain. Behind them, perhaps a mile away, was a tiny figure sitting in the middle of the immensity.

Several hours later, they came upon the figure. It was covered by a rawhide blanket. Kickaha walked up to it and removed the blanket. A very old woman had been sitting under it, her withered legs crossed, her arms upon her flabby breasts, one hand holding a flint scraper. Her eyes had been closed, but they opened when she felt the blanket move. They became huge. Her toothless mouth opened in horror. Then, to Kickaha's surprise, she smiled, and she closed her eyes again, and she began a high-pitched whining chant.

Anana walked around her, looking at the curved back, the prominent ribs, the bloated stomach, the scanty white locks, and especially at one foot. This had all the appearance of having been chewed on by a lion long ago. Three toes were missing, it was scarred heavily, and it was bent at an unnatural angle.

"She's too old to do any more work or to travel," Anana said.

"So they just left her to starve or be eaten by the animals," Kickaha said. "But they left her this scraper. What do you suppose that's for? So she could cut her wrists?"

Anana said, "Probably. That's why she smiled when she got over her fright. She figures we'll put her out of her misery at once."

She fingered the rawhide. "But she's wrong. She can tell us how to cure skins and maybe tell us a lot more, too. If she isn't senile."

Leaving McKay to guard the old woman, the others went off to hunt. They returned late that day, each bearing part of a gazelle carcass. They also carried a bag full of berries picked from a tree they'd cut out of a grove, though Kickaha's skin had a long red mark from a lashing tentacle. They offered water and berries to the crone, and after some hesitation she accepted. Kickaha pounded a piece of flank to make it more tender for her, and she gummed away on it. Later, he dug a hole in the ground, put water in it, heated some stones, dropped them in the water, and added tiny peices of meat. The soup wasn't hot, and it wasn't good, but it was warm and thick, and she was able to drink that.

While one stood guard that night, the others slept. In the morning, they made some more soup, adding berries for an experiment, and the old woman drank it all from the proferred gourd. Then the language lessons began. She was an eager teacher once she understood that they weren't just fattening her up so they could eat her.

The next day Kickaha set out after the people who'd abandoned her. Two days later he returned with flint spear heads, axes, hand scrapers, and several war boomerangs.

"It was easy. I sneaked in at night while they were snoring away after a feast of rotten elephant meat. I picked what I wanted and took off. Even the guards were sleeping."

Learning the old woman's language proceeded swiftly. In three weeks Shoobam was telling them jokes. And she was a storehouse of information. A treasure trove, in fact.

Primed with data, the three set to work. While one of the three guarded Shoobam, the others went out to get the materials needed. They killed the plants which she had told them were likely to contain gallotannin, or its equivalent, in certain pathological growths. Another type of tree which they caught and killed had an exceptionally light-weight wood yet was stress-resistant.

Kickaha made a crutch for Shoobam so she could become mobile, and Anana spent some time every day massaging the old woman's semiparalyzed legs. She was not only able to get around better, she began to put on some weight. Still, though she enjoyed talking to the three and felt more important than she had for a long time, she wasn't happy. She missed the tribal life and especially her grandchildren. But she had the stoic toughness of all the natives, who could make a luxury out of what was to the three the barest necessity.

Several months passed. Kickaha and company worked hard from dawn to long past dusk. Finally, they had three parawings much superior in light-ness of weight, strength, and durability to the orig-inal made by Anana. These were stiffened with wooden ribs and were not to be folded.

Told by Shoobam about a certain type of tree the bark of which contained a powerful poison, Kick-aha and Anana searched for a grove. After finding one, they pulled a dozen plants over with lariats and killed them. During the process, however, they narrowly escaped being caught and burned with the poison exuded by the tentacles. The old woman instructed them in the techniques of ex-tracting the poison.

Kickaha was very happy when he discovered that the branches of the poison-plant were similar to those of yew. He made bows with strings from goat intestines. The arrows were fitted with the flint heads he'd stolen from Shoobam's tribe, and these were dipped in the poison.

Now they were in the business of elephant hunting.

Though the pachyderms were immune to the venom on the darts propelled by certain plants, they succumbed to that deriv from the "yew" trees. At the end of another month, they had more than the supply of elephant stomach lining needed. The membranes weighed, per square yard, two-thirds less than the gazelle hides. Anana stripped the hides from the parawings and replaced them with the membranes.

"I think the wings'll be light enough now to work in the planet's field," she said. "In fact, I'm sure. I wasn't too certain about the hides."

Another plant yielded, after much hard work and some initial failures, a glue-like substance. This could seal the edges of the strips which would compose the balloon envelope. They sealed some strips of membrane together and tested them over a fire. Even after twenty hours, the glue did not deteriorate. But with thirty hours' of steady temperature, it began to decompose.

"That's fine," Anana said. "We won't be in the balloon more than an hour, I hope. Anyway, we can't carry enough wood to burn for more than an hour's flight."

It looks like we might make it after all," Kickaha said. "But what about her?"

He gestured at Shoobam.

"She's saved our necks or at least given us a fighting chance? But what're we going to do with her when we lift off? We can't just leave her. But we can't take her with us, either."

Anana said, "Don't worry about that. I've talked with her about it. She knows we'll be leaving some day. But she's grateful that she's lived this long, not to mention that we've given her more food than she's had for a long time."

"Yes? What happens when we go?"

"I've promised to slit her wrists."

Kickaha winced. "You're a better man than I am, Gunga Din. I don't think I could do it."

"You have a better idea?"

"No. If it has to be, so be it. I suppose I would do it, but I'm glad I don't have to."

CHAPTER TWENTY-ONE

ANANA DECIDED THAT it would be better to make three smaller balloons instead of one large one.

"Here's how it is. To get equal strength the material of a large balloon has to be much stronger and heavier per square inch than that of a smaller balloon. By making three smaller ones, instead of one large one, we gain in strength of material and lose in weight. So, each of us will ascend in his aerostat."

She added, "Also, since the smaller ones won't present as much area to the wind, they'll be easier to handle."

Kickaha had lost too many arguments with her to object.

McKay resented being "bossed" by a woman, but he had to admit that she was the authority.

They worked frantically to make the final preparations. Even Shoobam helped, and the knowledge of what would happen on the day of liftoff did not shadow her cheeriness. At least, if she felt sorrow or dread, she did not show it.

Finally, the time came. The three bags lay on the ground, stretched out behind the wall of the windbreak. A net of thin but tough cured membrane strips enclosed each bag. These, the suspension ropes, were attached directly to the basket. Anana would have liked to have tied them to a suspension hoop below which the basket would be hung by foot ropes. This arrangement afforded better stability.

However, it was almost impossible to carve three rings from wood. Besides, if the ring was made strong enough to stand up under the weight of the basket, its passenger, and the fuel, it would have to be rather heavy.

The ends of the suspension ropes were tied to the corners and along the sides of a rectangular car or basket made of pieces of bark glued together. In the center of the car was a thick layer of earth, on top of which were piled sticks. Wood shavings were packed at the bottom of the pile so the fire could be started easily. A layer of tinder would be ignited by sparks from a flint and a knife or the axe.

The wall of earth serving as a windbreak had been tumbled over four times because of the shape-changing of terrain. The fifth one was almost twice as high and four times as long as the one built for the test balloon. It was roofed over by branches laid on cross-logs supported by uprights.

Three gallows, primitive cranes, stood near the open end of the enclosure. A cable made of twisted cords ran from the upper sides of the horizontal arm to the top of the balloon. One end was tied around the top of the balloon.

The three people pulled the envelopes up, one by one, until all three hung limply below the gallows arms. The ends of the hoist ropes were secured to nearby uprights. McKay, who had wanted to be first to lift off, probably because it made him nervous to wait, lit the fire. Smoke began to ascend into a circular skin hanging down from the neck of the balloon.

When the bag had started to swell from the expanding hot air, Anana lit the fire in her car. Kickaha waited a few minutes and then started a flame in his basket.

The bands of the "dawn" sky began to glow. Snorts and barks and one roar came from the animals on the plains, awakening to another day of feeding and being fed upon. The wind was at an estimated minimum eight miles an hour velocity and without gusts.

McKay's envelope began to inflate. As soon it was evident that it would stand up by itself, McKay leaped up past the balloon, reached out with his axe, and severed the cable attached to the top. He fell, back, landing at the same time the cable did. After rising, he waited another minute, then pulled the balloon from beneath the gallows by the basket.

When Anana's balloon had lifted enough to support itself, she cut the cable, and Kickaha soon did the same to his.

Shoobam, who had been sitting to one side, pulled herself up on the crutch and hobbled over to Anana. She spoke in a low tone, Anana embraced her, then slashed at the wrists held out to her. Kickaha wanted to look away, but he thought that if someone else did the dirty work he could at least observe it.

The old woman sat down by Anana's basket and began wailing a death chant. She didn't seem to notice when he waved farewell.

Tears were running down Anana's cheeks, but she was busy feeding the fire.

McKay shouted, "So long! See you later! I hope!"

He pulled the balloon out until it was past the overhang. Then he climbed quickly aboard the car, threw on some more sticks, and waited. The balloon leaned a little as the edge of the wind coming over the roof struck its top. It began rising, was caught by the full force of the moving air, and rose at an angle.

Anana's craft ascended a few minutes later. Kickaha's followed at the same interval of time.

He looked up the bulge of the envelope. The parawing was still attached to the net and was undamaged. It had been tied to the upper side when the bag had been laid out on the ground. An observer at a distance might have thought it looked like a giant moth plastered against a giant light bulb.

He was thrilled with his flight in an aerostat. There had been no sensation of moving; he could just as well have been on a flying carpet. Except that there was no wind against his face. The balloon moved at the same speed as the air.

Above and beyond him the other two balloons floated. Anana waved once, and he waved back. Then he tended the fire.

Once he looked back at the windbreak. Shoobam was a dim tiny figure who whisked out of sight as the roof intervened.

The area of vision expanded; the horizon rushed outwards. Vistas of mountains and plains and here and there large bodies of water where rain had collected in temporary depressions spread out for him.

Above them hung the vast body of the primary. The great wound made by the splitoff had healed. The mother planet was waiting to receive the baby, waiting for another cataclysm.

Flocks of birds and small winged mammals passed him. They were headed for the planet, which meant that the moon's shape-change wasn't far off. The three had left just in time.

Briefly, his craft went through a layer of winged

and threaded seeds, soaring, whirling.

The flames ate up the wood, and the supply began to look rather short to Kickaha. The only consolation was that as the fuel burned, it relieved the balloon of more weight. Hence, the aerostat was lighter and ascended even more swiftly.

At an estimated fifteen miles altitude, Kickaha guessed that he had enough to go another five miles.

McKay's balloon was drifting away from the others. Anana's was about a half a mile from Kickaha's, but it seemed to have stopped moving away from it.

At twenty miles—estimated, of course—Kickaha threw the last stick of wood onto the fire. When it had burned, he scraped the hot ashes over the side, leewards, and then pushed the earth after it. After which he closed the funnel of rawhide which had acted as a deflector. This would help keep the hot air from cooling off so fast.

His work done for the moment, he leaned against the side of the basket. The balloon would quickly begin to fall. If it did, he would have to use the parawing to glide back to the moon. The only chance of survival then would be his good luck in being on the upper side after the shape-change.

Suddenly, he was surrounded by warm air. Grinning, he waved at Anana, though he didn't expect her to see him. The rapid change in the air temperature must mean that the balloon had reached what Urthona called the gravity interface. Here the energy of the counterrepulsive force dissipated or "leaked" somewhat. And the rising current of air would keep the aerostats aloft for a while. He hoped that they would be bouyed long enough.

As the heat became stronger, he untied the funnel, and he cut it away with his knife. The situation was uncertain. Actually, the balloon was falling, but the hot air was pushing it upwards faster than it descended. A certain amount was entering the neck opening as the hotter air within the bag slowly cooled. But the bag was beginning to collapse. It would probably not completely deflate. Nevertheless, it would fall.

Since the balloon was not moving at the speed of the wind now, Kickaha felt it. When the descent became rapid enough, he would hear the wind whistling through the suspension ropes. He didn't want to hear that.

The floor of the car began to tilt slowly. He glanced at Anana's balloon. Yes, her car was swinging slowly upwards, and the gasbag was also beginning to revolve.

They had reached the zone of turnover. He'd have to act swiftly, no hesitations, no fumbles.

Some birds, looking confused but determined, flapped by.

He scrambled up the ropes and onto the net, and as he did so the air became even hotter. It seemed to him that it had risen from a estimated 100° Fahrenheit to 130° within sixty seconds. Sweat ran into his eyes as he reached the parawing and began cutting the cords that bound it to the net. The envelope was hot but not enough to singe his hands and feet. He brushed the sweat away and severed the cords binding the harness and began working his way into it. It wasn't easy to do this, since he had to keep one foot and hand at all times on the net ropes. Several times his foot slipped, but he managed to get it back between the rope and skin of the envelope.

He looked around. While he'd been working, the turnover had been completed. The great curve of the planet was directly below him; the smaller curve of the moon, above.

McKay's balloon was lost in the red sky. Anana wasn't in sight, which meant that she too was on the side of the balloon and trying to get into the harness.

Suddenly, the air was cooler. And he was even more aware of the wind. The balloon, its bag shrinking with heart-stopping speed, was headed for the ground.

The harness tied, the straps between his legs, he cut the cord which held the nose of the wing to the net. There was one more to sever. This held the back end, that pointing downward, to the net. Anana had cautioned him many times to be sure to cut the connection at the top before he cut that at the bottom. Otherwise, the uprushing air would catch the wing on its undersurface. And the wing would rise, though still attached at its nose to the balloon. He'd be swung out at the end of the shrouds and be left dangling. The wing would flatten its upper surface against the bag, pushed by the increasingly powerful wind.

He might find it impossible to get back to the ropes and climb up to the wing and make the final cut.

"Of course," Anana had said, "you do have a long time. It'll be eighty miles to the ground, and you might work wonders during that lengthy trip. But I wouldn't bet on it."

Kickaha climbed down the ropes to the rear end of the wing, grabbed the knot which connected the end to the net, and cut with the knife in his other hand. Immediately, with a quickness which took his breath away, he was yanked upwards. The envelope shot by him, and he was swinging at the end of the shrouds. The straps cut into his thighs.

He pulled on the control cords to depress the nose of the wing. And he was descending in a fast glide. Or, to put it another way, he was falling relatively slowly.

Where was Anana? For a minute or so, she seemed to be lost in the reddish sky. Then he located a minute object, but he couldn't be sure whether it was she or a lone bird. It was below him to his left. He banked, and he glided towards her or it. An immeasurable time passed. Then the dot became larger and after a while it shaped itself into the top of a parawing.

Using the control shrouds to slip air out of the wing, he fell faster and presently was at the same level as Anana. When she saw him she banked. After some jockeying around, they were within twenty feet of each other.

He yelled, "You O.K.?"

She shouted, "Yes!"

"Did you see McKay?"

She shook her head.

Two hours later, he spotted a large bird-shaped object at an estimated two thousand feet below him. Either it was McKay or a roc. But a long squinting at it convinced him that it must be a bird. In any event, it was descending rapidly, and if it continued its angle, it would reach the ground far away from them.

If it was McKay, he would just have to take care of himself. Neither he, Kickaha, nor Anana owed him anything.

A few seconds later he forgot about McKay. The first of a mass migration from the moon passed him. These were large geese-type birds which must have numbered in the millions. After a while they became mixed with other birds, large and small. The air around him was dark with bodies, and the beat of wings, honks, caws, trills, and whistles was clamorous.

Their wings shot through a craggle of cranes which split, one body flapping to the right, one to the left. Kickaha supposed that they'd been frightened by the machines, but a moment later he wasn't sure. Perhaps it was the appearance of an armada of rocs which had scared them.

These airplane-sized avians now accompanied them as if they were a flying escort. The nearest to Anana veered over and glared at her with one cold yellow eye. When it got too close, she screamed at it and gestured with her knife. Whether or not she had frightened it, it pulled away. Kickaha sighed with relief. If one of those giants attacked, its victim would be helpless.

However, the huge birds must have had other things on their minds. They maintained the same altitude while the parawings continued descending. After a while the birds were only specks far above and ahead.

Anana had told him that this would not be the longest trip he'd ever taken, but it would be the most painful. And it would seem to be the longest. She'd detailed what would happen to them and what they must do. He'd listened, and he'd not liked what he heard. But his imagination fallen short of the reality by a mile.

When used as a glider, the parawing had a sinking speed of an estimated four feet a second. Which meant that, if they glided, it would take them twenty hours to reach the ground. By then, or before that, gangrene would have set into their legs.

But if the wing was used as a parachute, it would sink at twenty feet per second. The descent would be cut to a mere six hours, roughly estimated.

Thus, after locating each other, the two had pulled out some panels, and from then on they were travelling a la parachute. Kickaha worked his legs and arms to increase the circulation, and sometimes he would spill a little air out of the side of the wing to fall even faster. This procedure could only be done at short intervals, however. To go down too fast might jerk the shrouds loose when the wing slowed down again.

By the time they were at an estimated ten thousand feet from the earth, he felt as if his arms and legs had gone off flying back to the moon. He hung like a dummy except when he turned his head to see Anana. She would have been above him because, being lighter, she would not have fallen so fast. That is, she would not have if she had not arranged for her rip-panels to be somewhat larger than his. She, too, hung like a piece of dead meat.

One of the things that had worried him was that they might encounter a strong updraft which would delay their landing even more. But they had continued to fall at an even pace.

Below them were mountains and some small plains. But by the time they'd reached four thousand feet, they were approaching a large body of water. It was one of the many great hollows temporarily filled with rainwater. At the moment the bottom of the depression was tilting. The water was draining out of one end through a pass between two mountains. The animals on land near

the lower end were running to avoid being over-
taken by the rising water. What seemed like a
million amphibians were scrambling ashore or
waddling as fast as they could go towards higher
ground.

Kickaha wondered why the amphibians were in
such a hurry to leave the lake. Then he saw several
hundred or so immense animals, crocodilian in
shape, thrashing through the water. They were
scooping up the fleeting prey.

He yelled at Anana and pointed at the monsters.
She shouted back that they should slip out some
air from the wings. They didn't want to land any-
where near those beasts.

With a great effort, he pulled on the shrouds. He
fell ten seconds later into the water near the shore
with Anana two seconds behind him. He had cut
the shrouds just in time to slip out of the harness.
The water closed over him, he sank, then his feet
touched bottom, and he tried to push upwards with
them.

They failed to obey him.

His head broke surface as he propelled himself
with his fatigue-soaked arms. Anana was already
swimming towards the shore, which was about
thirty feet away. Her legs were not moving.

They dragged themselves onto the grass like
merpeople, their legs trailing. After that was a long
period of intense pain as the circulation slowly
returned. When they were able, they rose and
tottered towards the high ground. Long four-
legged and finned creatures, their bodies covered
with slime, passed them. Some snapped at them
but did not try to bite. The heavier gravity, after
their many months of lightness on the moon,

pressed upon them. But they had to keep going. The hippopotamus-sized crocodiles were on land now.

They didn't think they could make it over the shoulder of a mountain. But they did, and then they lay down. After they'd quit panting, they closed their eyes and slept. It was too much of an effort to be concerned about crocodiles, lions, dogs, or anything that might be interested in eating them. For all they cared, the moon could fall on them.

CHAPTER TWENTY-TWO

KICKAHA AND ANANA ran at a pace that they could maintain for miles and yet not be worn out. They were as naked as the day they came into the world except for the belts holding their knives and the Horn and the device strapped to her wrist. They were sweating and breathing heavily, but they knew that this time they could catch the palace—if nothing interfered.

Another person was also in pursuit of the colossus. He was riding a moosoid. Though he was a half a mile away, his tallness and red-bronze hair identified him. He had to be Red Orc.

Kickaha used some of his valuable breath. "I don't know how he got here, and I don't know what he expects to do when he catches up with the palace. He doesn't know the codewords."

"No," Anana gasped. "But maybe that man we saw will open a door for him."

So far, Orc had not looked back. This was fortunate, because, ten minutes later, a window. French door rather, swung open for him. He grabbed its sill and was helped within by two arms. The moosoid immediately stopped galloping and headed for a grove of moving plants. The door shut.

Kickaha hoped that the unknown tenant would be as helpful to them. But if Orc saw them, he'd be sure to interfere with any efforts to help.

Slowly they neared the towering building. Their bare feet pounded on the grass. Their breaths hissed in and out. Sweat stung their eyes. Their legs were gradually losing their response to their wills. They felt as if they were full of poisons which were killing the muscles. Which, in fact, they were.

To make the situation worse, the palace was heading for a mountain a mile or two away. If it began skimming up its slope, it would proceed at an undiminished speed. But the two chasing it would have to climb.

Finally, the bottom right-hand corner was within reach. They slowed down sobbing. They could keep up a kilometer an hour, a walking pace, as long as they were on a flatland. But when the structure started up the mountain, they would have to draw on reserves they didn't have.

There was a tall window at the very corner, its glass or plastic curving to include both sides. However, it was set flush to the building itself. No handholds to draw themselves up.

They forced themselves to break from a walk to a trot. The windows they passed showed a lighted corridor. The walls were of various glowing colors. Many paintings hung on them, and at intervals statues painted flesh colors stood by the doors leading to other rooms within. Then they came to several windows which were part of a large room. Furniture was arranged within it, and a huge fireplace in which a fire burned was at the extreme end.

A robot, about four feet high, dome-shaped, wheeled, was removing dust from a large table. A multi-elbowed metal arm extended a fat disc which moved over the surface of the table. Another arm moved what seemed to be a vacuum cleaner attachment over the rug behind it.

Kickaha increased his pace. Anana kept up with

him. He wanted to get to the front before the palace began the ascent. The front would be only a foot from the slope, but, since the building would maintain a horizontal attitude, the rest would be too far from the ground for them to reach it.

Just as the forepart reached the bottom of the mountain, the two attained their objective. But now they had to climb.

None of the windows they had passed had revealed any living being within.

They ran around the corner, which was just like the rear one. And here they saw their first hope for getting a hold. Halfway along the front was a large balcony. No doubt Urthona had installed it so that he could step out into the fresh air and enjoy the view. But it would not be a means of access. Not unless the stranger within the palace had carelessly left it unlocked. That wasn't likely, but at least they could stop running.

Almost, they didn't make it. The upward movement of the building, combined with their running in front of it, resulted in an angled travel up the slope. But they kept up with it, though once Kickaha stumbled. He grabbed the edge of the bottom, clung, was dragged, then released his hold, rolled furiously, got ahead, and was seized by the wrist by Anana and yanked forward and upward. She fell backward, but somehow they got up and resumed their race without allowing the palace to pass over them.

Then they had grabbed the edge of the balcony and swung themselves up and over it. For a long time they lay on the cool metallic floor and gasped as if each breath of air was the last in the world. When they were breathing normally, they sat up and looked around. Two French doors gave entrance to an enormous room, though not for them. Kickaha pushed in on the knobless doors without success. There didn't seem to be any handles on the inside. Doubtless, they opened to a pushbutton or a codeword.

Hoping that there were no sensors to give alarm, Kickaha banged hard with the butt of his knife on the transparent material. The stuff did not crack or shatter. He hadn't expected it to.

"Well, at least we're riding," he said. He looked up at the balcony above theirs. It was at least twenty feet higher, thus, out of reach.

"We're stuck. How ironic. We finally make it, and all we can do is starve to death just outside the door."

They were exhausted and suffering from intense thirst. But they could not just leave the long-desired place. Yet, what else could they do?

He looked up again, this time at dark clouds forming.

"It should be raining soon. We can drink, anyway. What do you say we rest here tonight? Morning may bring an idea."

Anana agreed that that was the best thing to do. Two hours later, the downpour began, continuing uninterruptedly for several hours. Their thirst was quenched, but they felt like near-drowned puppies by the time it was over. They were cold, shivering, wet. By nightfall they'd dried off, however and they slept wrapped in each other's arms.

By noon the next day their bellies were growling like starving lions in a cage outside which was a pile of steaks. Kickaha said, "We'll have to go hunting, Anana, before we get too weak. We can always run this down again, though I hate to think

of it. If we could make a rope with a grapnel, we
might be able to get up to that balcony above us.
Perhaps the door there isn't locked. Why should it
be?''

"It will be locked because Urthona wouldn't
take any chances,'' she said. "Anyway, by the
time we could make a rope, the palace would be far
ahead of us. We might even lose track of it.''

"You're right,'' he said. He turned to the door
and beat on it with his fists. Inside was a huge room
with a large fountain in its center. A marble triton
blew water from the horn at its lips.

He stiffened, and said, "Oh, oh! Don't move,
Anana! Here comes someone!''

Anana froze. She was standing to one side, out
of view of anyone in the room.

"It's Red Orc! He's seen me! It's too late for me
to duck! Get over the side of the balcony! There're
ornamentations you can hang onto! I don't know
what he's going to do to me, but if he comes out
here, you might be able to catch him unaware. I'll
have to be the sacrificial goat!''

Out of the corner of his eye he watched her slide
over the railing and disappear. He stayed where he
was, looking steadily at her uncle. Orc was
dressed in a splendid outfit of some sparkling material, the calf-length pants very tight, the boots
scarlet and with upturned toes, the jacket double-
breasted and with flaring sleeves, the shirt ruffled
and encrusted with jewels on the broad wing-
tipped collar.

He was smiling, and he held a wicked-looking
beamer in one hand.

He stopped for a moment just inside the doors.
He moved to each side to get a full view of the

balcony. His hand moved to the wall, apparently pressing a button. The doors slid straight upward into the wall.

He held the weapon steady, aiming at Kickaha's chest.

"Where's Anana?"

"She's dead," Kickaha said.

Orc smiled and pulled the trigger. Kickaha was knocked back across the balcony, driven hard into the railing. He lay half-sitting, more than half-stunned. Vaguely, he was aware of Orc stepping out onto the balcony and looking over the railing. The red-haired man leaned over it and said, "Come on up, Anana. I'm on to your game. But throw your knife away."

A moment later she came slowly over the railing. Orc backed up into the doorway, the beamer directed at her. She looked at Kickaha and said, "Is he dead?"

"No, the beamer's set for low-grade stun. I saw you two last night after the alarm went off. Your *leblabbiy* stud was foolish enough to hammer on the door. The sensors are very sensitive."

Anana said, "So you just watched us. You wanted to know what we'd try?"

Orc smiled again. "Yes, I knew you could do nothing. But I enjoyed watching you trying to figure out something."

He looked at the Horn strapped around her shoulder.

"I've finally got it. I can get out of here now."

He pressed the trigger, and Anana fell back against the railing. Kickaha's senses were by then almost full recovered, though he felt weak. But if Orc got within reach of his hands . . .

The Lord wasn't going to do that. He stepped

back, said something, and two robots came through the doorway. At first glance they looked like living human beings. But the dead eyes and the movements, not as graceful as beings of animal origin, showed that metal or plastic lay beneath the seeming skin. One removed Kickaha's knife and threw it over the balcony railing. The other unstrapped the multiuse device from Anana's wrist. Both got hold of the ankles of the two and dragged them inside. To one side stood a large hemisphere of thick criss-crossed wires on a platform with six wheels. The robot picked up Anana and shoved her through a small doorway in the cage. The second did the same to Kickaha. The door was shut, and the two were captives inside what looked like a huge mousetrap.

Orc bent down and reached under the cage. When he straightened up, he said, "I've just turned on the voltage. Don't touch the wires. You won't be killed, but you'll be knocked out."

He told the humanoid robots and the cage to follow him. Carrying the Horn which he had removed from Anana's shoulder, he strode through the room toward a high-ceilinged wide corridor.

Kickaha crawled to Anana. "Are you okay?"

"I'll be in a minute," she said. "I don't have much strength just now. And I got a headache."

"Me, too," he said. "Well, at least we're inside."

"Never say die, eh? Sometimes your optimism . . . well, never mind. What do you suppose happened to the man who let Orc in?"

"If he's still alive, he's regretting his kind deed. He can't be a Lord. If he was, he'd not have let himself be taken."

Kickaha called out to Orc, asking him who the

stranger was. Orc didn't reply. He stopped at the end of the corridor, which branched off into two others. He said something in a low voice to the wall, a codeword, and a section of wall moved back a little and then slid inside a hollow. Revealed was a room about twenty feet by twenty feet, an elevator.

Orc pressed a button on a panel. The elevator shot swiftly upward. When it stopped, the lighted symbol showed that it was on the fortieth floor. Orc pressed two more buttons and took hold of a small lever. The elevator moved out into a very wide corridor and glided down it. Orc turned the lever, the elevator swiveled around a corner and went down another corridor for about two hundred feet. It stopped, its open front against a door.

Orc removed a little black book from a pocket, opened it, consulted a page, said something that sounded like gibberish, and the door opened. He replaced the book and stood to one side as the cage rolled into a large room. It stopped in the exact center.

Orc spoke some more gibberish. Mechanisms mounted on the walls at a height of ten feet from the floor extended metal arms. At the end of each was a beamer. There were two on each wall, and all pointed at the cage. Above the weapons were small round screens. Undoubtedly, video eyes.

Orc said, "I've heard you boast that there isn't a prison or a trap that can hold you, Kickaha. I don't think you'll ever make that boast again."

"Do you mind telling us what you intend to do with us?" Anana said in a bored voice.

"You're going to starve," he said. "You won't die of thirst since you'll be given enough water to

keep you going. At the end of a certain time—
which I won't tell you—whether you're still alive
or not, the beamers will blow you apart.

"Even if, inconceivably, you could get out of
the cage and dodge the beamers, you can't get out
of here. There's only one exit, the door you came
through. You can't open that unless you know the
codeword."

Anana opened her mouth, her expression making it obvious that she was going to appeal. It
closed; her expression faded. No matter how desperate the situation, she was not going to humiliate
herself if it would be for nothing. But she'd had a
moment of weakness.

Kickaha said, "At least you could satisfy our
curiosity. Who was the man who let you in? What
happened to him?"

Orc grimaced. "He got away from me. I got hold
of a beamer and was going to make him my prisoner. But he dived through a trapdoor I hadn't
known existed. I suppose by now he's gated to
another world. At least, the sensors don't indicate
his presence."

Kickaha grinned, and said, "Thank you. But
who was he?"

"He claimed to be an Earthman. He spoke English, but it was a quaint sort. It sounded to me like
eighteenth-century English. He never told me his
name. He began to ramble on and on, told me he'd
been trapped here for some time when he gated
from Vala's world to get away from her. It had
taken him some time to find out how to activate a
gate to another universe without being killed. He
was just about to do so when he saw me galloping
up. He decided to let me in because I didn't look
like a native of this world.

"I think he was half-crazy."

"He must have been completely insane to trust you, a Lord," Anana said. "Did he say anything about having seen Kickaha, McKay, and myself. He passed over us when we were on the moon."

Orc's eyebrows rose. "You were on the moon? And you survived its fall? No, he said nothing about you. That doesn't mean he wasn't interested or wouldn't have gotten around eventually to telling me about you."

He paused, smiled, and said, "Oh, I almost forgot! If you get hungry enough, one of you can eat the other."

Kickaha and Anana could not hide their shock. Orc broke into laughter then. When he stopped bellowing, he removed a knife from the sheath at his belt. It was about six inches long and looked as if it were made of gold. He shoved it through the wires, where it lay at Anana's feet.

"You'll need a cutting utensil, of course, to carve steaks and chops and so forth. That'll do the job, but don't think for one moment you can use it to short out the wires. It's nonconductive."

Kickaha said, fiercely, "If it wasn't for Anana I'd think all you Lords were totally unreformable, fit only to be killed on sight. But there's one thing I'm sure about. You haven't a spark of decency in you. You're absolutely unhuman."

"If you mean I in no way have the nature of a *leblabbiy* you're right."

Anana picked up the knife and fingered the side, which felt grainy, though its surface was steel-smooth.

"We don't have to starve to death," she said. "We can always kill ourselves first."

Orc shrugged. "That's up to you."

He said something to the humanoid robots, and they followed him through the doorway into the elevator. He turned and waved farewell as the door slid out from the wall recesses.

"Maybe that Englishman is still here," Kickaha said. "He might get us free. Meanwhile, give me the knife."

Anana had anticipated him, however. She was sawing away at a wire where it disappeared into the floor. After working away for ten minutes, she put the blade down.

"Not a scratch. The wire metal is much harder than the knife's."

"Naturally. But we had to try. Well, there's no use putting it off until we're too weak even to slice flesh. Which one of us shall it be?"

Shocked, she turned to look at him. He was grinning.

"Oh, you! Must you joke about even this?"

She saw a section of the cage floor beyond him move upward. He turned at her exclamation. A cube was protruding several inches. The top was rising on one side, though no hinges or bolts were in evidence. Within it was a pool of water.

They drank quickly, since they didn't know how long the cube would remain. Two minutes later, the top closed, and the box sank back flush with the floor.

It reappeared, filled with water, about every three hours. No cup was provided, so they had to get down on their hands and knees and suck it up with their mouths, like animals. Every four hours, the box came up empty. Evidently, they were to excrete in it then. When the box appeared the next time, it was evident that it had not been completely cleaned out.

"Orc must enjoy this little feature," Kickaha said.

There was no way to measure the passage of time since the light did not dim. Anana's sense of time told her, however, that they must have been caged for at least fifty-eight hours. Their bellies caved in, growled, and thundered. Their ribs grew gaunter before their eyes. Their cheeks hollowed; their legs and arms slimmed. And they felt steadily weaker. Anana's full breasts sagged.

"We can't live off our fat because we don't have any," he said. "We were honed down pretty slim from all the ordeals we've gone through."

There were long moments of silence, though both spoke whenever they could think of something worthwhile to say. Silence was too much like the quiet of the dead, which they soon would be.

They had tried to wedge the knife between the crack in the side of the waterbox. They did not know what good this would do, but they might think of something. However, the knife would not penetrate into the crack.

Anana now estimated that they'd been in the cage about seventy hours. Neither had said anything about Orc's suggestion that one of them feast on the other. They had an unspoken agreement that they would not consent to this horror. They also wondered if Orc was watching and listening through video.

Food crammed their dreams if not their bellies. Kickaha was drowsing fitfully, dreaming of eating roast pork, mashed potatoes and gravy, and rhubarb pie when a clicking sound awoke him. He lay on his back for a while, wondering why he would dream of such a sound. He was about to fall back into the orgy of eating again when a thought made him sit up as if someone had passed a hot pastrami by his nose.

Had Orc inserted a new element in the torture? It didn't seem possible, but . . .

He got onto his hands and knees and crawled to the little door. He pushed on it, and it swung outward.

The clicking had been the release of its lock.

CHAPTER TWENTY-THREE

WHILE THEY CLAMBERED down out of the cage, the beamers on the wall tracked them. Kickaha started across toward the door. All four weapons spat at once, vivid scarlet rays passing before and behind him. Ordinarily, the rays were invisible, but Orc had colored them so his captors could see how close they were. Beauty, and terror, were in the eye of the beholder.

Anana moaned. "Oh, no! He just let us loose to tantalize us!"

Kickaha unfroze.

"Yeah. But those beamers should be hitting us."

He took another step forward. Again the rays almost touched him.

"To hell with it! They're set now so they'll just miss us! Another one of his refinements!"

He walked steadily to the door while she followed. Two of the beamers swung to her, but their rays shot by millimeters away from her. Nevertheless, it was unnerving to see the scarlet rods shoot just before his eyes. As the two got closer to the door, the rays angled past their cheeks on one side and just behind the head.

They should have drilled through the walls and floor, but these were made of some material invulnerable even to their power.

When he was a few feet from the door, the beamers swung to spray the door just ahead of him. Their contact with the door made a slight hissing, like a poisonous snake about to strike.

The two stood while scarlet flashed and splashed over the door.

"We're not to touch," Kickaha said. "Or is this just a move in the game he's playing to torment us?"

He turned and walked back toward the nearest beamer. It tracked just ahead of him, forcing him to move slowly. But the ray was always just ahead of him.

When he stopped directly before the beamer, it was pointed at his chest. He moved around it until it could no longer follow him. Of course, he was in the line of sight of the other three. But they had stopped firing now.

The weapon was easily unsecured by pulling a thick pin out of a hinge on its rear. He lifted it and tore it loose from the wires connected to its underside. Anana, seeing this, did the same to hers. The other two beamers started shooting again, their rays again just missing them. But these too were soon made harmless.

"So far, we're just doing what Orc wants us to do," he said. "He's programmed this whole setup. Why?"

They went to the door and pushed on it. It swung open, revealing a corridor empty of life or robots. They walked to the branch and went around the corner. At the end of this hall was the open door of the elevator shaft. The cage was within it, as if Orc has sent it there to await them.

They hesitated to enter it. What if Orc had set a trap for them, and the cage stopped halfway between floors or just fell to the bottom of the shaft?

"In that case," Kickaha said, "he would figure that we'd take a stairway. So he'd trap those."

They got into the cage and punched a button for the first floor. Arriving safely, they wandered through some halls and rooms until they came to an enormous luxuriously furnished chamber. The two robots stood by a great table of polished onyx. Anana, in the language of the Lords, ordered a meal. This was brought in five minutes. They ate so much they vomited, but after resting they ate again, though lightly. Two hours later, they had another meal. She directed a robot to show them to an apartment. They bathed in hot water and then went to sleep on a bed that floated three feet above the floor while cool air and soft music flowed over them.

When they woke, the door to the room opened before they could get out of bed. A robot pushed in a table on which were trays filled with hot delicious food and glasses of orange or muskmelon juice. They ate, went to the bathroom, showered, and emerged. The robot was waiting with clothes that fitted them exactly.

Kickaha did not know how the measurements had been taken, but he wasn't curious about it. He had more important things to consider.

"This red carpet treatment worries me. Orc is setting us up just to knock us down again."

The robot knocked on the door. Anana told him to come in. He stopped before Kickaha and handed him a note. Opening it, Kickaha said, "It's in English. I don't know whose handwriting it is, but it has to be Orc."

He read aloud, "Look out a window."

Dreading what they would see, but too curious to put it off, they hastened through several rooms and down a long corridor. The window at its end held a scene that was mostly empty air. But moving slowly across it was a tiny globe. It was the lavalite world.

"That's the kicker!" he said. "Orc's taken the palace into space! And he's marooned us up here, of course, with no way of getting to the ground!"

"And he's also deactived all the gates, of course," Anana said.

A robot, which had followed them, made a sound exactly like a polite butler wishing to attract his master's attention. They turned, and the robot held out to Kickaha another note. He spoke in English. "Master told me to tell you, sir, that he hopes you enjoy this."

Kickaha read, "The palace is in a decaying orbit."

Kickaha spoke to the robot. "Do you have any other messages for us?"

"No, sir."

"Can you lead us to the central control chamber?"

"Yes, sir."

"Then lead on, MacDuff."

It said, "What does MacDuff mean, sir?"

"Cancel the word. What name are you called by? I mean, what is your designation?"

"One, sir."

"So you're one, too."

"No, sir. Not One-Two. One."

"For Ilmarwolkin's sake," Anana said, "quit your clowning."

They followed One into a large room where there was an open wheeled vehicle large enough for four. The robot got into the driver's seat. They stepped into the back seat, and the car moved away smoothly and silently. After driving through several corridors, the robot steered it into a large elevator. He got out and pressed some buttons, and the cage rose thirty floors. The robot got behind the wheel and drove the vehicle down a corridor almost for a quarter of a mile. The car stopped in front of a door.

"The entrance to the central control chamber, sir."

The robot got out and stood by the door. They followed him. The door had been welded, or sealed to the wall.

"Is this the only entrance?"

"Yes, sir."

It was evident that Orc had made sure that they could not get in. Doubtless, any devices, including beamers, that could remove the door had been jettisoned from the palace. Or was Orc just making it more difficult for them? Perhaps he had deliberately left some tools around, but when they got into the control room, they would find that the controls had been destroyed.

They found a window and looked out into red space. Kickaha said, "It should take some time before this falls onto the planet. Meanwhile, we can eat, drink, make love, sleep. Get our strength back. And look like mad for some way of getting out of this mess. If Orc thinks we're going to suffer while we're falling, he doesn't know us."

"Yes, but the walls and door must be made of the same stuff, *impervium*, as the room that held the cage," she said. "Beamers won't affect it. I don't know how he managed to weld the door to the walls, but he did. So getting in to the controls seems to be out."

First, they had to make a search of the entire building and that would take days even when traveling in the little car. They found the hangar which had once housed five fliers. Orc had not even bothered to close its door. He must have set them to fly out on automatic.

They also located the great power plant. This contained the gravitic machines which now maintained an artificial field within the palace. Otherwise, they would have been floating around in free fall.

"It's a wonder he didn't turn that off," Anana said. "It would have been one more way to torment us."

"Nobody's perfect," Kickaha said.

Their search uncovered no tools which could blast into the control chamber. They hadn't thought it would.

Kickaha conferred with Anana, who knew more about parachutes than he did. Then he gave a number of robots very detailed instruction on how to manufacture two chutes out of silken hangings.

"All we have to do is to jump off and then float down," he said. "But I don't relish the idea of spending the rest of my life on that miserable world. It's better than being dead, but not by much."

There were probably a thousand, maybe two thousand gates in the walls and on the floors and possibly on the ceilings. Without the codewords to activate them, they could neither locate nor use them.

They wondered where the wallpanel was which the Englishman had used to get away from Red Orc. To search for it would take more time than they had. Then Kickaha thought of asking the robots, One and Two, if they had witnessed his escape. To his delight, both had. They led the humans to it. Kickaha pushed in on the panel and saw a metal chute leading downward some distance, then curving.

"Here goes nothing," he said to Anana. He jumped into it sitting up and slid down and around and was shot into a narrow dimly lit hall. He yelled back up the chute to her and told her he was going on. But he was quickly stopped by a dead end.

After tapping and probing around, he went back to the chute and, bracing himself against the sides, climbed back up.

"Either there's another panel I couldn't locate or there's a gate in the end of the hall," he told her.

They sent the robots to the supply room to get a drill and hammers. Though the drills wouldn't work on the material enclosing the control room, they might work on the plastic composing the walls of the hidden hall. After the robots returned, Kickaha and Anana went down the chute with them and bored holes into the walls. After making a circle of many perforations, he knocked the circle through with a sledgehammer.

Light streamed out through it. He caustiously looked within. He gasped.

"Well, I'll be swoggled! Red Orc!"

CHAPTER TWENTY-FOUR

IN THE MIDDLE of a large bare room was a transparent cube about twelve feet long. A chair, a narrow bed, and a small red box on the floor by a wall shared the cube with its human occupant, Orc. Kickaha noted that a large pipe ran from the base of the wall of the room to the cube, penetrated the transparent material, and ended in the red box. Presumably, this furnished water and perhaps a semiliquid type of food. A smaller pipe within the large one must provide air.

Red Orc was sitting on the chair before the table, his profile to the watchers through the hole. Evidently, the cube was soundproof, since he had not heard the drilling or pounding. The Horn and a beamer lay on the table before him. From this Kickaha surmised that the cube was invulnerable to the beamer's rays.

Red Orc, once the secret Lord of the Two Earths, looked as dejected as a man could be. No wonder. He had stepped through a gate in the control room, expecting to enter another universe, possessing the Horn, the Lords' greatest treasure, and leaving behind him two of his worst enemies to die. But Urthona had prepared his trap well, and Red Orc had been gated to this prison instead of to freedom.

As far as he knew, no one was aware that he was locked in this room. He was doubtless contemplating how long it would be before the palace fell to

Urthona's world and he perished in the smash, caught in his own trap.

Kickaha and Anana cut a larger hole in the wall for entrance. During this procedure, Orc saw them. He rose up from his chair and stared from a pale-gray face. He could expect no mercy. The only change in his situation was that he would die sooner.

His niece and her lover were not so sure that anything had been changed. If he couldn't cut his way out of the cube, they couldn't cut their way in. Especially when they didn't have a beamer. But the pipe which was Orc's life supply was of copper. After the robots got some more tools, Kickaha slicked off the copper at the junction with the *impervium* which projected outside the cube.

This left an opening through which Orc could still get air and also could communicate. Kickaha and Anana did not place themselves directly before the hole, though. Orc might shoot them through it.

Kickaha said, "The rules of the game have been changed, Orc. You need us, and we need you. If you cooperate, I promise to let you go wherever you want to, alive and unharmed. If you don't, you'll die. We might die, too, but what good will that do you?"

"I can't trust you to keep your word," Orc said sullenly.

"If that's the way you want it, so be it. But Anana and I aren't going to be killed. We're having parachutes made. That means we'll be marooned here, but at least we'll be alive."

"Parachutes?" Orc said. It was evident from his expression that he had not thought of their making them.

"Yeah. There's an old American saying that there's more than one way to skin a cat. And I'm a cat-skinner par excellence. I—Anana and I—are going to figure a way out of this mess. But we need information from you. Now, do you want to give it to us and maybe live? Or do you want to sulk like a spoiled child and die?"

Orc gritted his teeth, then said, "Very well. What do you want?"

"A complete description of what happened when you gated from the control chamber to this trap. And anything that might be relevant."

Orc told how he had checked out the immense room and its hundreds of controls. His task had been considerably speeded up by questioning robots One and Two. Then he had found out how to open several gates. He had done so cautiously and before activating them himself he had ordered the robots to do so. Thus, if they were trapped, they would be the victims.

One gate apparently had access to the gates enclosed in various boulders scattered over the planet below. Urthona must have had some means of identifying these. He would have been hoping that, while roaming the planet with the others, he would recognize one. Then, with a simple codeword or two, he would have transported himself to the palace. But Urthona hadn't had any luck.

Orc identified three gates to other worlds. One was to Jadawin's, one to Earth I, and one to dead Urizen's. There were other gates, but Orc hadn't wanted to activate them. He didn't want to push his luck. So far, he hadn't set off any traps. Besides, the gate to Earth I was the one he wanted.

Having made sure that his escape routes were

open, Orc had then had the robots, One and Two, seal the control room.

"So you had our torments all fixed up ahead of time?" Anana said.

"Why not?" Orc said. "Wouldn't you have done the same to me?"

"At one time I would have. Actually, you did us a favor by letting us loose so we could savor the terrors of the fall. But you didn't mean to, I'm sure."

"He did himself a favor, too," Kickaha said.

Orc had then activated the gate to Earth I. He had stepped through the hole between the universes, fully expecting to emerge in a cave. He could see through its entrance a valley and a wooded mountain range beyond. He thought that it was possibly the same cave through which Kickaha and Anana had gone in southern California.*

But Urthona had set up a simulacrum to lull the unwary. To strengthen its impression, Urthona had also programmed the robots in case a crafty Lord wanted to use the gate. At least, Red Orc supposed he had done so. Orc had ordered the robot called Six to walk through first. Six had done so, had traveled through the cave, stepped outside, looked around, then had returned through the gate.

Satisfied, Orc had ordered the robots, One and Two, to seal up the control room door with *impervium* flux. Then he had stepped through.

"Apparently," Orc said, "that wily *shagg* (a sort of polecat) had counted on the robot being used as a sacrifice. So he had arranged it that the robot would not be affected."

*See *Behind the Walls Of Terra*, Philip José Farmer, Ace Books, 1977.

"Urthona always was a sneaky one," Anana said. "But he had depended on his technological defenses too long. Thrown on his own resources, he was not the man he should have been."

She paused, then added, "Just like you, uncle."

"I haven't done so badly," he said, his face red.

Kickaha and Anana burst out laughing.

"No," she said. "Of course not. Just look where you are."

Orc had been whisked away when he was only a few feet from leaving the cave or what he thought was a cave. The next second he was standing in the cube.

Kickaha drew Anana to a corner of the room to confer quietly. "Somehow, that mysterious Englishman discovered a gateway to another universe in the wall at the end of the corridor," he said. "Maybe he had found Urthona's codebook. Anyway, where one can go through, others can. And the Horn can get us through. But we can't get to the Horn.

"Now, what's to prevent us from getting Orc to blow the notes for us? Then we can make a recording of it and use it to open the gate."

Anana shook her head. "It doesn't work that way. It's been tried before, it's so obvious. But there's something in the machinery in the Horn that adds an element missing in recordings."

"I was afraid of that," he said. "But I had to ask. Look, Anana. Urthona must have planted gates all over this place. We've probably passed dozens without knowing it because they are inside the walls. Logically, many if not most of them will be quick emergency routes from one place in this building to another. So Urthona could outsmart anyone who was close on his heels.

"But there have to be a few which would gate him to another world. Only to be used in cases of direst emergency. One of them is the gate at the end of the corridor next door. I think . . ."

"Not necessarily," Anana said. "For all we know, it leads to the control room or some other place in the palace."

"No. In that case, the sensors would have shown Orc that the Englishman was in the palace."

"No. Urthona might have set up places without sensors where he could hide if an enemy had possession of the control room."

"I'm the A-Number One trickster, but sometimes I think you sneaky Lords put me to shame. Okay. Just a minute. Let me ask Orc a question."

He went to the cube. The Lord, looking very suspicious, said, "What are you two up to now?"

"Nothing that won't help you," Kickaha said, grinning. "We just don't want you to get a chance to get the drop on us. Tell me. Did the sensor displays in the control room indicate that there were hidden auxiliary sensor systems?"

"Why would you want to know?"

"Damn it!" Kickaha said. "You're wasting our time. Remember, I have to spring you if only to get the Horn."

Hesitantly, Orc said. "Yes, there are hidden auxiliary systems. It took me some time to find them. Actually, I wasn't looking for them. I discovered them while I was looking for something else. I checked them out and noted that they were in rooms not covered by the main system. But since nobody was using them, I assumed that no one was in them. It was inconceivable that anyone in a room where they were wouldn't be trying to find out where I was."

"I hope your memory's good. Where are they?"

"My memory is superb," Orc said stiffly. "I am not one of you sub-beings."

Kickaha grimaced. The Lords had the most sensitive and gangrenous egos he'd ever encountered. A good thing for him, though. He'd never have survived his conflicts with them if they hadn't always used part of their minds to feed their own egos. They were never really capable of one hundred percent mental concentration.

Well, he, Kickaha, had a big ego, too. But a healthy one.

The Lord remembered only a few of the locations of the auxiliary sensor systems. He couldn't be blamed for that since there were so many. But he was able to give Kickaha directions to three of them. He also gave him some instructions on how to operate them.

Just to make sure he hadn't been neglecting another source of information, Kickaha asked robots One and Two about the sensors. They were aware of only that in the control room. Urthona had not trusted them with any more data than he thought necessary for his comfort and protection.

Kickaha thought that if he had been master of this palace, he would have installed a safety measure in the robots. When asked certain questions, they would have refused to answer them. Or pretended that they didn't know.

Which, now that he thought about it, might be just what was happening. But they'd given him data that Urthona might not want his enemies to have. So possibly, they were not lying.

He took One with him, leaving Anana to keep an eye on her uncle. It wasn't likely that he'd be going any place or doing anything worth noticing. But you never knew.

The hidden system console was in a room behind a wall in a much larger room on the tenth floor. Lacking the codeword to gate through, he and One tore part of the wall down. He turned on the console and, with One's aid, checked out the entire building. It was done swiftly, the glowing diagrams of the rooms flashing by too swiftly on the screen for Kickaha to see anything but a blur. But a computer in One's body sorted them out.

When the operation was complete, One said, "There are one hundred and ten chambers which the sensors do not monitor."

Kickaha groaned and said. "You mean we'd have to get into all of them to make sure no living being is in one of them?"

"That is one method."

"What's the other?"

"This system can monitor the control chamber. It's controlled by that switch there." One pointed. "That also enables the operator to hook into the control-room sensories. These can be used to look into the one hundred and ten chambers. The man named Orc did not know that. The switch is not on the panel in the control room however. It is under the panel and labeled as an energy generator control. Only the master knew about it."

"Then how did you come to know about it?"

"I learned about it while I was scanning the displays here."

"Then why didn't you tell me?"

"You didn't ask me."

Kickaha repressed another groan. The robots were so smart yet so dumb.

"Connect this system with the control room's."

"Yes, master."

One strode ponderously to the control board and turned a switch marked, in Lord letters: HEAT. Heat for what? Obiously, it was so designated to make any unauthorized operator ignore it. Immediately, lights began pulsing here and there, a switch turned by itself, and one of the large video screens above the panel came to life.

Kickaha looked into the room from a unit apparently high on the wall and pointing downward. It was directed toward the central chair in a row of five or six before the wide panel. In this sat a man with his back to Kickaha.

For a second he thought that it must be the Englishman who had helped Orc. But this man was bigger than the one described by Orc, and his hair was not brown but yellow.

He was looking at a video screen just above him. It showed Kickaha and the robot behind him, looking at the man.

The operator rose with a howl of fury, spun out of his chair, and shook his fist at the unit receiving his image.

He was Urthona.

CHAPTER TWENTY-FIVE

THE LORD WAS clad only in a ragged skin bound around his waist. A longitudinal depression, the scan from the axe wound, ran down the center of his chest. His hair fell over his shoulders to his nipples. His skin was smeared with the oily dirt of his world, and a bump on his forehead indicated a hard contact with some harder object. Moreover, his nose had been broken.

Kickaha was shocked for a few seconds, then he went into action. He ran toward the switch to turn it off. Urthona's voice screamed through the video. "One! Kill him! Kill him!"

"Kill who, master?" One said calmly.

"You blithering metal idiot! That man! Kickaha!"

Kickaha turned the switch and whirled. The robot was advancing on him, its arms out, fingers half-clenched.

Kickaha drew his knife. Shockingly, Urthona's voice came out of the robot's unmoving lips. "I see you, you *leblabbiy*! I'm going to kill you!"

For a second Kickaha didn't know what was happening. Then illumination came. Urthona had switched on a transceiver inside the robot's body and was speaking through it. Probably, he was also watching his victim-to-be through One's eyes.

That had one advantage for Kickaha. As long as Urthona was watching the conflict from the control room, he wasn't gating here.

Kickaha leaped toward the robot, stopped,

jumped back, slashed with his knife with no purpose but to test the speed of One's reaction. The robot made no attempt to parry with his arm or grab the knife, however. He continued walking toward Kickaha.

Kickaha leaped past One and his blade flickered in and out. Score one. The point had broken the shield painted to look like a human eyeball. But had it destroyed the video sensor behind it?

No time to find out. He came in again, this time on the left side. The robot was still turning when the knife shattered the other eyeball.

By now Kickaha knew that One wasn't quick enough for him. It undoubtedly was far stronger, but here swiftness was the key to victory. He ran around behind One and stopped. The robot continued on its path. It had to be blinded, which meant that Urthona would know this and would at once take some other action.

He looked around quickly. There were stretches of bare wall which could conceal a gate. But wouldn't Urthona place the gate where he could step out hidden from the sight of anyone in the room? Such as, for instance, the space behind the control console. It wasn't against the wall.

He ran to it and stepped behind it. Seconds, a minute, passed. Was Urthona delaying because he wanted to get a weapon first? If so, he would have to go to a hidden cache, since Orc had jettisoned every weapon he could locate.

Or was the staying in the control room, where he was safe? From there he could order all the robots in the palace and there were several score or more, to converge on this room.

Or had he gated to a room nearby and now was creeping up on his enemy? If so, he would make sure he had a beamer in his hand.

There was a thump as the robot blindly blundered into the wall. At least, Kickaha supposed that was the noise. He didn't want to stick his head out to see.

His only warning was a shimmering, a circle of wavy light taller than a tall man, on the wall to his right. Abruptly, it became a round hole in the wall. Urthona stepped through it, but Kickaha was upon him, hurling him back, desperate to get both of them in the control room before the gate closed.

They fell out onto the floor, Kickaha on top of the Lord, fingers locked on the wrist of the hand that held a beamer. The other laid the edge of the knife against the jugular vein. Urthona's eyes were glazed, the back of his head having thumped against the floor.

Kickaha twisted the wrist; the beamer clattered on the tile floor. He rolled away, grabbed the weapon, and was up on his feet.

Snarling, shaking, Urthona started to get up. He sank down as Kickaha ordered him to stay put.

The robot, Number Six, started towards them. Kickaha quickly ordered Urthona to command Six to take no action. The Lord did so, and the robot retreated to a wall.

Grinning, Kickaha said, "I never thought the day'd come when I'd be glad to see you. But I am. You're the cat's paw that pulled the chestnuts out of the fire for me. Me and Anana."

Urthona looked as if he just couldn't believe that this was happening to him. No wonder. After all he'd endured and the good luck he'd had to find a boulder with a gate in it. For all he knew, his enemies were stranded on his world or more probably dead. He was king of the palace again.

It must have been a shock when he found the door to the control room welded shut. Somebody had gotten in after all. Possibly a Lord of another world who'd managed to gate in, though that wasn't likely. He must have figured that somehow Orc or Anana and Kickaha had gotten in. But they couldn't get into the control room, where the center of power was. The first thing he had probably done though, was to cancel the decaying orbit of his palace. After setting it in a safe path, he would have started checking the sensory system. The regular one, first. No doubt one of the flashing red lights on the central console indicated that someone was in a trap. He'd checked that and discovered that Orc was in the cube.

But he must also have seen Anana. Had he ordered the robot Two to kill her?

He asked Urthona. The Lord shook his head as if he was trying to throw his troubles out.

"No," he said slowly. "I saw her there, but she wasn't doing anything to endanger me for the moment. I started then to check out the auxiliary sensories just to make sure no one else was aboard. I hadn't gotten to the room in which you were yet. You connected with the control room . . . and . . . damn you! If only I'd gotten here a few minutes earlier."

"It's all in the timing," Kickaha said, smiling. "Now let us get on with it. You're probably thinking I'm going to kill you or perhaps stick you in that wheeled cage and let you starve to death. It's not a bad idea, but I prefer contemplating the theory to putting it into practice.

"I promised Orc I'd let him go if he cooperated. He hasn't done a thing to help, but I can't hold that against him. He hasn't had a chance.

"Now, if you cooperate, too, Urthona, I'll let you live and I won't torture you. I need to get Orc, your beloved brother, out of that trap so I can get my hands on the Horn. But first, let's check that your story is true. God help you if it isn't."

He stood behind the Lord just far enough away so that if he tried to turn and snatch at the beamer he'd be out of reach. The weapon was set on low-stun. Urthona worked the controls, and the concealed TV of the auxiliary system looked into the room with the cube. Orc was still in his prison; Anana and Two were standing by the hole in the wall.

Kickaha called her name. She looked up with a soft cry. He told her not to be frightened, and he outlined what had happened.

"So things are looking good again," he said. "Orc, your brother is going to gate you into the control room. First, though, put the beamer down on the table. Don't try anything. We'll be watching you. Keep hold of the Horn. That's it. Now go to the corner where you appeared in the cube when you were gated through. Okay. Stand still. Don't move or you'll lose a foot or something."

Urthona reached for a button. Kickaha said, "Hold it. I'm not through. Anana, you know where I went. Go up there and stand by the wall behind the control console there. Then step through the gate when it appears. Oh, you'll meet a blind robot, poor old One. I'll order it to stand still so it won't bother you."

Urthona walked stiffly to a console at one end of the enormous room. His hands were tightly clenched; his jaw was clamped; he was quivering.

"You should be jumping with joy," Kickaha said. "You're going to live. You'll get another chance at the three of us some day."

"You don't expect me to believe that?"

"Why not? Did I ever do anything you anticipated?"

He directed the Lord to show him the unmarked controls which would bring Orc back. Urthona stepped back to allow Kickaha to operate. The redhead, however, said, "You do it."

It was possible that the controls, moved in the manner shown, would send a high voltage through him.

Urthona shrugged. He flipped a toggle switch, pressed a button, and stepped away from the console. To the left, the bare wall shimmered for a few seconds. A hemisphere of swirling colors bulged out from it, and then it collapsed. Red Orc stood with his back almost touching the wall.

Kickaha said, "Put the Horn down and push it with your foot toward me."

The Lord obeyed. Kickaha, keeping an eye on both of them, bent down and picked up the Horn.

"Ha! Mine again!"

Five minutes later, Anana stepped out of the same gate through which Kickaha and Urthona had fallen.

Her uncles looked as if this was the end of the last act. They fully expected to be slain on the spot. At one time, Kickaha would have been angered because neither had the least notion that he deserved to be executed. There was no use getting upset, however. He had learned long ago not to be disturbed by the self-righteous and the psychopath, if there was any difference between the two.

"Before we part," he said. "I'd like to clear up a few things, if possible. Urthona, do you know anything about an Englishman, supposedly born in the eighteenth century? Red Orc found him living in this place when he entered."

Urthona looked surprised. "Someone else got into here?"

"That tells me how much you know. Well, maybe I'll run across him some other time. Urthona, your niece has explained something about the energy converter that powers this floating fairy castle. She told me that any converter can be set to overload, but an automatic regulator will cut it back to override that. Unless you remove the regulator. I want you to fix the overload to reach its peak in fifteen minutes. You'll cut the regulator out of the line."

Urthona paled. "Why? You . . . you mean to blow me up?"

"No. You'll be long gone from here when it blows. I intend to destroy your palace. You'll never be able to use it again."

Urthona didn't ask what would happen if he refused. Under the keen eye of Anana, he set the controls. A large red light began flashing on a console. A display flashed, in Lord letters, OVERLOAD. A whistle shrilled.

Even Anana looked uneasy. Kickaha smiled, though he was as nervous as anybody.

"Okay. Now open the gates to Earth I and to Jadawin's world."

He had carefully noted the control which could put the overload regulator back into the line if Urthona tried any tricks.

"I know you can't help being treacherous and sneaky, Urthona," Kickaha said. "But repress your natural viciousness. Refrain from pulling a fast one. My beamer's set on cutting. I'll slice you at the first false move."

Urthona did not reply.

On the towering blank wall two circular shimmerings appeared. They cleared away. One showed the inside to a cave, the same one through which Kickaha and Anana had entered southern California. The other revealed the slope of a wooded valley, a broad green river at the foot. And, far away, smoke rising from the chimneys of a tiny village and a stone castle on a rocky bluff above it. The sky was a bright green.

Kickaha looked pleased.

"That looks like Dracheland. The third level, Abharhploonta. Either of you ever been there?"

"I've made some forays into Jadawin's world," Urthona said. "I planned someday to . . . to . . ."

"Take over from Jadawin? Forget it. Now, Urthona, activate a gate that'll take you to the surface of your planet."

Urthona gasped and said, "But you said . . . ! Surely . . . ? You're not going to abandon me here?"

"Why not? You made this world. You can live in it the rest of your life. Which will probably be short and undoubtedly will be miserable. As the Terrestrials say, let the punishment fit the crime."

"That isn't right!" Urthona said. "You are letting Orc go back to Earth. It isn't what I'd call a first-rate world, but compared to this, it's a paradise."

"Look who's talking about *right*. You're not going to beg, are you? You, a lord among the Lords?"

Urthona straightened his shoulders. "No. But if

you think you've seen the last of me . . ."

"I know. I've got another think coming. I wouldn't be surprised. I'll bet you have a gate to some other world concealed in a boulder. But you aren't letting on. Think you'll catch me by surprise some day, heh? After you find the boulder—if you do. Good luck. I may be bored and need some stiff competition. Get going."

Urthona walked up to the wall. Anana spoke sharply. "Kickaha! Stop him!"

He yelled at the Lord, "Hold it, or I'll shoot!"

Urthona stopped but did not turn.

"What is it, Anana?"

She glanced at a huge chronometer on a wall.

"Don't you know there's still danger? How do you know what he's up to? What might happen when he gives the codeword? It'll be better to wait until the last minute. Then Orc can go through, and you can shut the gate behind him. After that, we'll go through ours. And then Urthona can gate. But he can do it with no one else around."

"Yeah, you're right," Kickaha said. "I was so eager to get back I rushed things."

He shouted, "Urthona! Turn around and walk back here!"

Kickaha didn't hear Urthona say anything. His voice must have been very soft. But the words were loud enough for whatever sensor was in the wall to detect them.

A loud hissing sounded from the floor and the ceilings and the walls. From thousands of tiny perforations in the inner wall, clouds of greenish gas shot through the room.

Kickaha breathed in just enough of the metallic odor to make him want to choke. He held his breath then, but his eyes watered so that he could not see Urthona making his break. Red Orc was suddenly out of sight, too. Anana, a dim figure in the green mists, stood looking at him. One hand was pinching her nose and the other was over her mouth. She was signalling to him not to breathe.

She would have been too late, however. If he had not acted immediately to shut off his breath, he would, he was sure, be dead by now. Unconscious, anyway.

The gas was not going to harm his skin. He was sure of that. Otherwise, Urthona would have been caught in the deadly trap.

Anana turned and disappeared in the green. She was heading toward the gate to the world of tiers. He began running too, his eyes burning and streaming water. He caught a glimpse of Red Orc plunging through the gate to Earth I.

And then he saw, dimly, Urthona's back as he sped through the gate to the world which Kickaha loved so much.

Kickaha felt as if he would have to cough. Nevertheless, he fought against the reflex, knowing that if he drew in one full breath, he would be done for.

Then he was through the entrance. He didn't know how high the gate was above the mountain slope, but he had no time for caution. He fell at once, landed on his buttocks, and slid painfully on a jumble of loose rocks. It went at a forty-five degree angle to the horizontal for about two hundred feet, then suddenly dropped off. He rolled over and clawed at the rocks. They cut and tore into the chest and his hands, but he dug in no matter how it hurt.

By then he was coughing. No matter. He was out of the green clouds which now poured out of the hole in the mountain face.

He stopped. Slowly, afraid that if he made a too vigorous movement he'd start the loose stones to sliding, he began crawling upward. A few rocks were dislodged. Then he saw Anana. She had gotten to the side of the gate and was clinging with one hand to a rocky ledge. The other held the Horn. Her eyes were huge, and her face was pale.

She shouted, "Get up here and away! As fast as you can! The converter is going to blow soon!"

He knew that. He yelled at her to get out of the area. He'd be up there in a minute. She looked as if she were thinking of coming down to help him, then she began working her way along the steep slope. He crawled at an angle toward the ledge she had grabbed. Several times he started sliding back, but he managed to stop his descent.

Finally, he got off the apron of stones. He rose to a crouch and, grabbing handsful of grass, pulled himself up to the ledge. Holding onto this with one hand, he worked his way as swiftly as he dared away from the hole.

Just as he got to a point above a slight projection of the mountain, a stony half-pout, the mountain shook and bellowed. He was hurled outward to land flat on his face on the miniledge.

The loose rocks slid down and over the edge, leaving the stone beneath it as bare as if a giant broom had swept it.

Silence except for the screams of some distant birds and a faint rumble as the stones slid to a halt far below.

Anana said, "It's over, Kickaha."

He turned slowly to see her looking around a spur of rock.

"The gate would have closed the moment its activator was destroyed. We got only a small part of the blast, thank God. Otherwise, the whole mountain would've been blown up."

He got up and looked alongside the slope. Something stuck out from the pile below. An arm?

"Did Urthona get away?"

She shook her head. "No, he went over the edge. He didn't have much of a drop, about twenty feet, before he hit the second slope. But the rocks caught him."

"We'll go down and make sure he's dead," he said. "That trick of his dissolves any promises we made to him."

All that was needed was to pile more rocks on Urthona to keep the birds and the beasts from him.

CHAPTER TWENTY-SIX

IT WAS A month later. They were still on the mountain, though on the other side and near its base. The valley was uninhabited by humans, though occasionally hunters ventured into it from the river-village they'd seen on coming from the gate. Kickaha and Anana avoided these.

They'd built a leanto at first. After they'd made bows and arrows from ash, tipped with worked flint, they shot deer, which were plentiful, and tanned the hides. Out of these they made a tepee, well-hidden in a grove of trees. A brook, two hundred yards down the slope, gave them clear cold water. It also provided fine fishing.

They dressed in buckskin hides and slept on bearskin blankets at night. They rested well but exercised often, hiking, berry- and nut-picking, hunting, and making love. They even became a little fat. After being half-starved so long, it was difficult not to stuff themselves. Part of their diet was bread and butter which they'd stolen one night from the village, two large bagsful.

Kickaha, eavesdropping on the villagers, had validated his assumption that they were in Dracheland. And from a reference overheard, he had learned that the village was in the barony of Ulrich von Neifen.

"His lord, theoretically, anyway, is the duke, or Herzog, Willehalm von Hartmot. I know, generally, where we are. If we go down that river, we'll come to the Pfawe river. We'll travel about three hundred miles, and we'll be in the barony of Siegfried von Listbat. He's a good friend. He should be. I gave him my castle, and he married my divorced wife. It wasn't that Isote and I didn't get along well, you understand. She just wouldn't put up with my absences."

"Which were how long?"

"Oh, they varied from a few months to a few years."

Anana laughed.

"From now on, when you go on trips, I'll be along."

"Sure. You can keep up with me, but Isote couldn't, and she wouldn't have even if she could."

They agreed that they would visit von Listbat for a month or so. Kickaha had wanted to descend to the next level, which he called Amerindia, and find a tribe that would adopt him. Of all the levels, he loved this the most. There were great forest-covered mountains and vast plains, brooks and rivers of purest water, giant buffalo, mammoth, antelope, bear, sabertooths, wild horses, beaver, game birds by the billions. The human population was savage but small, and though the second level covered more territory than North and Central America combined, there were few places where the name of Kickaha, the Trickster, was not known.

But they must get to the palace-fortress on the top of this world, which was shaped like a tower of babel. There they would gate through, though reluctantly, to Earth again. Reluctantly, because neither cared too much for Earth I. It was overpopulated, polluted, and might at any time perish in atomic-warfare.

"Maybe Wolff and Chryseis will be there by the time we get there. It's possible they're already there. Wouldn't that be great?"

They were on the mountain, above the rivervalley, when he said this. Halfway down the slope were the birches from which they would build a canoe. Smoke rose from the chimneys of the tiny village on the bend of the river. The air was pure, and the earth beneath them did not rise and fall. A great black eagle soared nearby, and two hawks slid along the wind, headed for the river and its plentitude of fish. A grizzly bear grunted in a berry patch nearby.

"Anana, this is a beautiful world. Jadawin may be its Lord, but this is really my world, Kickaha's world."

THE END